Ecstasy Supreme

"I'D LIKE TO KNOW WHAT INSPIRED YOUR ATTITUDE THIS MORNING," CARLA DEMANDED.

Jake pointed his finger in her face. "You took advantage of me last night. Is that how you get your jollies, by making love to half-drunk men who don't know what they're doing?"

Carla's eyes widened. "Let me tell you something. I don't sleep around, and if you hadn't been half looped last night, you would have been able to tell."

Jake stared at Carla's shattered face. "So why?" he asked bitterly. "If it wasn't for laughs, why?"

"Don't you remember? You begged me to, that's why. You said you needed me, that you were lonely. You needed another human being, and I was here. But before you start knocking my morals, you might think about a man who makes love to one woman but calls her by another woman's name. Last night you pretended I was Debbie. And that's about as low as you can get."

CANDLELIGHT ECSTASY SUPREMES

AUTUMN RAPTURE

Emily Elliott

A CANDLELIGHT ECSTASY SUPREME

Published by
Dell Publishing Co., Inc.
1 Dag Hammarskjold Plaza
New York, New York 10017

ISBN: 0-440-10349-5

Printed in the United States of America
First printing—December 1984

To Our Readers:

Candlelight Ecstasy is delighted to announce the start of a brand-new series—Ecstasy Supremes! Now you can enjoy a romance series unlike all the others—longer and more exciting, filled with more passion, adventure, and intrigue—the stories you've been waiting for.

In months to come we look forward to presenting books by many of your favorite authors and the very finest work from new authors of romantic fiction as well. As always, we are striving to present the unique, absorbing love stories that you enjoy most—the very best love has to offer.

Breathtaking and unforgettable, Ecstasy Supremes will follow in the great romantic tradition you've come to expect *only* from Candlelight Ecstasy.

Your suggestions and comments are always welcome. Please let us hear from you.

Sincerely,

The Editors
Candlelight Romances
1 Dag Hammarskjold Plaza
New York, New York 10017

CHAPTER ONE

Carla Jeffreys stared at the monitor in the small control room, a slight smile curving her lips as applause swelled from the live studio audience. "It was a good show today," she said as her director, Pete Garcia, cued the center back camera and it pulled away from the face of the young mystery writer whose first book had just hit the stands.

"Yeah, that little lady did a good job today," Pete agreed as the credits started to roll. Kevin Stanley, the host of *Winners All,* walked over and shook the author's hand as the last of the credits finished and Pete cut to a commercial. "With live TV, I always get a little nervous unless the guest is a pro."

The door to the studio burst open and Kevin ushered their guest into the control booth, while the audience started to make their way out of the studio by the front door. "Michelle, you were just great!" Carla said as she reached out to shake the young woman's hand. "Thank you so much for coming on the show for us today."

"Are you kidding? I appreciate the free publicity!" Michelle Stewart enthused. "I loved that closeup you did of the cover."

"You really handled the interview like a pro," Pete said as he added his thanks to Carla's.

"It was a lot easier than facing a classful of hostile sophomores," the teacher-turned-author admitted as everyone laughed. Carla and Kevin thanked her again, and Michelle made Carla and Pete promise to sit down some evening and help her with background for another mystery. Then Pete showed her out of the control room, followed by Kevin and Carla.

"So who are we having on the show tomorrow?" Kevin asked as he and Carla headed for the small but comfortable office they shared.

Carla pushed the door of the office open and consulted her wall calendar. "Alexander Haig," she said as she flopped down in her chair and kicked her shoes off. "I've written some dynamite questions for him."

Kevin sat down in his desk chair and whistled under his breath. "Good grief, Carla, how did you manage that?" he asked. "Last week it was Joe Namath and now Alexander Haig!"

"I hustle." Carla grinned. "But you have to admit that all my guests aren't big names." She wrinkled her nose. "And you know, sometimes I think the audience enjoys some of the unknowns just as much. They loved Michelle today!"

"Okay, be modest," Kevin scoffed. "Don't admit that in one short year you've made *Winners All* the most popular talk show in Corpus Christi. And done it with a live studio audience."

Carla smiled over at her young host, who at twenty-eight was exactly ten years her junior. In the last year she and Kevin had built a good working relationship and a solid friendship. Although as producer Carla was technically Kevin's boss, they worked well together as a team and Kevin was not above teasing Carla about anything and everything. He was also not above crying on her shoulder about his seemingly ill-fated love life, so she had spent a number of evenings listening to Kevin pour out his romantic woes. "Thank you, kind sir," she

10

said as she shoved her feet back into her shoes and winced a little when they pinched. "Have you seen Paul Simmons around?"

Kevin shook his head. "What do you want with Old Windbag tonight?" he asked. "It's five thirty . . . seven," he said as he consulted his watch. "Go on home. You're tired."

"No, I've got to see Wind—Paul before I leave," Carla said as Kevin snickered at her near slip. "I'm going to the CCC meeting tonight and want to check on a few things with him before I go." She stood and straightened the rumpled skirt of her striking designer dress. "See ya tomorrow," she said as she headed out the door, her short blond hair swinging around her ears. Her step still springy although it was late, she walked down the long corridor to the news director's office and knocked on the door. "Paul? It's Carla. Have you got a minute before you go?"

Paul, a telephone propped on his shoulder, motioned for Carla to come in and shut the door behind her. She did so and sat down in the chair across from him, waiting patiently for Paul to finish one of his long-winded telephone conversations. Fat, bald, and approaching fifty, Paul ran the news department with flair and imagination, and if he tended to talk too much, Carla assured herself that nobody was perfect. Besides, although Paul was really very fair with his employees, he enjoyed working with women in general and Carla in particular, and Carla's three years at the station had been a joy. Although *Winners All* was not under Paul's direction, a number of the news specials Carla had produced had been, and she had enjoyed working with him on those.

Paul finally wound down his lengthy diatribe and hung up the telephone. "Oh, the joys of being an affiliate," he exclaimed, then launched into a ten-minute rehash of his latest squabble with the parent company in New York. Carla nodded and laughed, amused by the tale in spite of its length. Finally Paul propped his feet on the desk and leaned back in the chair, resting his hands on his ample stomach. "Now what can I do for you?" he asked.

"I'm going to the Corpus Christi Coalition meeting tonight," Carla said. The Corpus Christi Coalition was the local antidrunken driving organization. "Just checking to see if you had called Jake Darrow for me like you promised you would."

Paul nodded. "I never got through to Jake but his secretary assured me that he had gotten the message and would be expecting you," he said.

Carla picked up a pen from Paul's desk and twirled it absently. "I could have called him myself, you know," she said.

"I know that, but Jake and I go back a long way and I thought he might be more receptive if I called him," Paul said. "He and I grew up across the street from one another in Pleasanton, you know. I used to take him to the baseball diamond on the edge of town to watch us older boys play baseball."

"Uh, about the special," Carla broke in, hoping to forestall one of Paul's lengthy tales about life in the old days. "I think I can have it ready for the end of September or the first of October with no problem, if you can schedule it for then. Public interest is running high these days on the problem of drunken drivers on the road, and I think a locally produced show discussing the situation here in Corpus will really hit the spot."

"Especially with the kind of attention Jake and the CCC have brought to it," Paul said. "It's a shame it had to take a tragedy like losing his wife, Debbie, to get someone like Jake involved. Since she died he's moved mountains to bring the problem to the public's attention."

"That's why I hope he'll agree to an interview," Carla said. "He must have quite a story to tell." Their conversation turning to technical matters, Paul talked to Carla for another hour, then she protested that she really had to go if she was going to be on time for the CCC meeting. She promised to let Paul know in the morning whether Jake agreed to an interview. Then she wished him good night and hurried to the parking lot, stopping for a moment in spite of her rush to breathe in the salty, tangy sea air that blew in from Corpus Christi Bay. The soft, warm May air tantalized her face, lifting the soft blond hair of her swinging wedge off her temples. I wish I could stand here all night, she thought as she unlocked the door to her Chevrolet Malibu and slid into the driver's seat.

Checking her watch, Carla decided that she had time for a soda but not dinner, so she pulled into a small Dairy Queen near the campus of Del Mar College and walked inside and ordered. The teenage counter girl handed her the soda and stared at Carla as she sat down alone in a booth, wondering what such a beautifully dressed and sophisticated-looking woman was doing in a fast-food restaurant.

Carla stared for a moment into the mirror that lined the wall and grinned inwardly at the girl's confusion. She often had that effect on people—her poise and sophistication often threw them until she put them at ease with her dazzling smile. That combination, along with a lot of talent and hard work, had taken her a long way in the television business, although she admitted to herself that "a long way" was really a far cry from independently wealthy. Her designer clothes were purchased at discount boutiques and at good sales, and her elegant

13

little apartment just a few blocks from the bay was decorated with more taste than money. She cocked her head and stared at the face in the mirror. She wasn't beautiful, but she had an elegant face to go with the elegant clothes and the elegant hair. Long, narrow, with finely etched features and vivid amber eyes, Carla's face had looked good at twenty and it still looked good at nearly forty; it would look good at sixty or seventy.

Carla turned her face away from the mirror and sipped her soda. Oh, I hope Jake Darrow agrees to that interview, she thought as she mulled over the special she had planned. Paul had made a few suggestions, of course, but the project had been Carla's idea and would be under her total control. She hoped to put together a show that would in some way shed light on both sides of the repeating tragedy. She wanted to tell the story of the drunken driver as well as that of his—or her—innocent victim, and in so doing maybe she and her viewers could gain some new insight as to the causes of the problem and possible solutions. As part of her interview with Jake Darrow, Carla was interested in featuring the Corpus Christi Coalition, a group of concerned citizens that had first come to her attention nearly a year ago when its members had called a press conference and publicly demanded an end to lenient sentences in the Corpus Christi courts.

Since then the organization had been drawn to the public's attention a number of times, calling for stiffer sentences and tougher laws. More than once she had sat in the control room and watched film clips of their dynamic president, Jake Darrow, his shock of iron-gray hair ruffled by the constant ocean breeze, as he faced the cameras explaining his group's latest efforts. Although outwardly calm and in command, Carla could sense the burning urgency that drove him and his group to devote

14

a large portion of their free time to fighting the slaughter on the streets and highways of Texas. Jake Darrow was a man with a cause, and it was up to her to get him to talk with her and the people of Corpus Christi about himself and that cause.

Glancing at her watch, Carla gulped down the rest of her soda and hurried out into the quiet twilight. She drove a couple of blocks and turned into the parking lot of a small Methodist church where the CCC met every month. Although she was a few minutes early, the parking lot was almost full.

She locked her car, walked up the steps, and entered the vestibule. There were groups of people standing around talking, and a young woman sat at a folding table right next to the sanctuary door. Carla looked around for a minute but did not spot Jake Darrow, so she approached the woman at the table. "Excuse me, is Jake Darrow here yet?" she asked.

"No, ma'am, he's not," the smiling woman said. "Are you a survivor or a victim?"

"Excuse me?" Carla asked, startled.

"Did you lose a family member to a drunken driver, or were you hit by one yourself?" the woman asked.

"Neither," Carla said. "At least not yet."

"Oh," the woman replied, "most of our visitors are either survivors or victims." She said no more but looked up at Carla in confusion.

"I'm a television producer," Carla explained. "I'm here to attend the meeting and talk to Mr. Darrow."

"Well, you're in luck, because that's him walking in the door," the woman said. "Right over there," she said, gesturing to a point behind Carla.

Carla turned around and stared across the room at the man who had been stopped at the door for a round of greetings. With the light at his back, Carla could not make out much more than the fact that he was of medium height and that he had on an expensive suit, but the commanding voice was even stronger than it had been on videotape. Even from across the room Carla could sense the aura of tremendous energy that the man radiated. He shook the outstretched hands and greeted everyone by name, his vibrant voice full of energy and vitality. No wonder CCC has been so successful, Carla thought as she watched Jake Darrow through eyes narrowed by the setting sun. If he threw that kind of energy into this organization, it was bound to be a success!

Suddenly Jake looked up from the people milling around him and stared across the room at Carla. He gazed at her for a moment, then eased his way out of the circle that surrounded him and made his way across the room to her. Carla wasn't sure, but she thought she detected a slight limp in his walk. "I'm Jake Darrow," he said as he extended his hand. Carla was surprised that, in her high heels, she and Jake Darrow were the same height.

"Carla Jeffreys," Carla said as she placed her hand into his and shook it. His palm was warm to the touch, and Carla found the sensation distinctly pleasant. "Paul Simmons was supposed to have left a message with your secretary about me. Did you get the message?"

Jake nodded and released her hand. "Yes, I found the message on my desk. I understand you're a television producer doing some kind of documentary?"

Carla nodded, her amber eyes locking into Jake's dark ones. He looks bigger on camera, she thought, surprised that Jake was a couple of inches under six feet. Then she realized that he was a broad-shouldered man and that the camera had picked up on that. The custom-tailored suit that he wore could not disguise the

16

strength in his hard-muscled arms and chest or the energy that radiated from his hard, fit body.

"Yes, I'm producing a documentary on the tragedy of the drunken driver in Corpus Christi," she said, dragging her thoughts away from Jake's physique and back to the business at hand. "I would very much like to feature you and the work of your organization in the program."

"That's what I gathered from Paul's message," Jake said. "Of course you realize that I can't say yes or no right now. But I would like to talk to you about it later if you would care to stay." Jake's manner was perfectly correct, but Carla could feel a reserve and wariness in him, as though he were not sure of her.

"Of course, I had planned to stay for the meeting in any event," Carla replied, noting with satisfaction Jake's look of surprise. He gestured toward the sanctuary and Carla followed the milling crowd in, sitting on the other aisle about halfway down the church.

At promptly seven thirty Jake turned on the PA system and called the meeting to order. Carla got out a pencil and a small notebook and flipped it open, not really intending to take extensive notes but ready to write if she saw or heard anything extraordinary. Jake greeted the assembled group and turned the meeting over to the recording secretary for the reading of the last month's minutes.

Carla listened to the minutes with half an ear, then her interest was rekindled when Jake took the floor again and asked for a treasurer's report. Yes, in a way he had been what she expected. The intense energy, the sense of purpose, had come through on the tapes she had viewed. But here, teasing the treasurer about her lack of funding, he seemed more warm somehow, more human than he had seemed on television. And the fact

17

that he was not overpoweringly tall made Carla feel more at ease and less intimidated than she would have been with a taller man. But he's no cupcake, she thought to herself as Jake called for the vice-president to come to the podium. If he decided that he did not want to be interviewed for her documentary, she suspected that heaven and earth could move and he would not change his mind.

As the treasurer sat down, Jake called for old business, and a couple of members gave follow-up reports on the status of a couple of bills in the Texas House of Representatives. Then a young woman whom Carla thought looked vaguely familiar came to the podium and gave an update on the number of DWI, or Driving While Intoxicated, convictions that each of the four Corpus Christi judges had handed down in the last month and the average amount of the fine and/or length of sentence. The judges who had handed down stiff sentences were enthusiastically cheered, and the ones who in the CCC's eyes were too lenient were roundly booed. The young woman, who Carla finally realized had been to the station a couple of times on behalf of the CCC, said that Jake would release this information to the media at a press conference scheduled for the day after tomorrow.

Carla watched and listened as a couple more members made short reports, then Jake introduced the speaker for the evening. Dr. John Barlow, a well-known Corpus Christi psychologist, had counseled numerous drunken-driving victims and the families of victims, and he had graciously agreed to share some of his valuable insight into the counseling of a grief-stricken family. Dr. Barlow took the podium and in a thoughtful, compassionate manner gave a mini-counseling course to CCC members.

Carla listened carefully to Dr. Barlow, but in spite of her interest in the speaker her eyes continually drifted to the man with the iron-gray hair who sat on the front pew. Would Jake grant her an interview, or would he feel that it would be an invasion of his privacy? In spite of the high profile he had taken in the last year, she knew nothing about him but what Paul had said—that he had formed the organization after his wife's death and that he owned two successful men's clothing stores in Corpus Christi. Jake himself had never divulged any information about his private life to the press, and Carla didn't even know if he had any children. From his reticence about himself Carla had gathered that he was a very private man, and she was afraid that he might not want that privacy invaded.

Dr. Barlow talked for over an hour, and although she enjoyed the presentation, Carla was grateful when he sat down and Jake returned to the podium. She shifted a little, pins and needles assaulting her bottom, as Jake reminded the members that they needed to sign up for an "available time" to counsel victims and their families. He adjourned the meeting and Carla stood up, grateful to be off the hard pew. Jake stopped long enough to thank Dr. Barlow and then made his way over to where Carla was standing.

"Did you enjoy the meeting?" he asked.

"Very much," Carla assured him. "It was very informative, and Dr. Barlow had some excellent advice for volunteer counselors. Is the CCC involved in that also?"

Jake nodded. "We're just getting it started this month. Someone in the organization will be on-call twenty-four hours a day to talk to victims and their families."

"That will be wonderful help to them, I'm sure,"

Carla replied. "Will you be available for the next few minutes? Maybe when the crowd thins out a little we can sit down and I can tell you a little more about what I have in mind for the special."

Jake glanced around the half-full church. "I have a better idea. There's a very nice restaurant just down the street. Why don't we discuss it over a cup of coffee?"

"Sounds lovely," Carla said. "I'll meet you there."

Jake said he would be along in just a moment. Carla left the church, sitting in her car for a moment to let the parking lot clear. Jake seems willing to talk about the program, Carla thought, but she could still sense a reluctance in him, a holding back on his part. Oh, she hoped he would agree to talk in front of the cameras!

But Carla was usually honest with herself and tonight was no exception. Her documentary was not the only reason she was interested in Jake Darrow. The energy and vitality that showed up on the television screen, the warmth and humanness that didn't—those two elements together made Jake Darrow the most appealing man she had met in a long time. He was interesting, stimulating, a little mysterious. And Carla certainly would not mind getting to know him a little better.

CHAPTER TWO

Carla drove the short half-block to the restaurant that Jake had suggested. She had just pulled into a parking place next to the building and gotten out of her car when a gray Lincoln pulled up. Jake Darrow got out of it, shutting the door behind him. As he walked toward her, Carla noticed that his limp had become worse, but he did not appear to be in any pain as he reached her and grasped her elbow gently yet firmly.

"Is this all right with you?" he asked.

"This is nice," Carla said as they walked together toward the entrance. As they passed through the door, Carla again noticed Jake's limp but tried politely to ignore it. Oh, well, he probably twisted his ankle over the weekend, Carla thought to herself as the hostess took Jake's name and assured him that their wait would not be long.

Carla sank down on the thick padded bench that was provided for customers waiting for a table. "Ahh, this feels better than that pew did," she murmured, sighing, as Jake sat down beside her. This close, Carla could catch a tantalizing whiff of a spicy aftershave that must have been left over from this morning, and the warmth of Jake's body reached hers from across the small space between them. Carla wondered briefly what it would feel like to run her hand down Jake's muscular forearm and touch the powerful muscles underneath the expensive suit coat, but she dutifully dragged her mind from his physical attributes and thought about what she could say to make him want to grant her an interview. As several minutes passed and Jake said nothing, Carla sneaked a glance in his direction and was surprised to see his head leaning back against the padded bench and his eyes closed. So you're not always a fireball of energy, she thought as she looked more fully into his tired face. You get weary just like the rest of us.

When the hostess called Jake's last name, he sat up instantly, chagrined at the smile Carla was trying to disguise. "Did I go to sleep on you?" he asked. "I'm so sorry!"

"Oh, don't apologize," Carla said, allowing her smile to come through. "I was sitting there wool-gathering and didn't even notice at first."

The embarrassment cleared from his face and together they followed the hostess to their table, Jake's hand warm and curiously pleasant in the small of Carla's back. They slid into the small booth and opened the menus their waitress handed them. Suddenly famished, Carla sneaked a peek at the food section of the menu and inwardly cursed Paul for keeping her so long she had to skip supper. That salad she had eaten at eleven this morning had definitely worn off!

The waitress returned in a moment and Carla dutifully ordered the cup of coffee that Jake had invited her for. He ordered the same, then looked longingly at the menu in his hands. "Carla, would you like to have something to eat? I don't know about you, but I missed both lunch and dinner today and I'm starved."

"You bet!" Carla replied, then blushed at the enthusiasm of her response. Jake grinned at her, then they sent the waitress for the coffee while they pored over the menu like two starving refugees. By the time the waitress had returned, Jake had selected a huge hamburger with fries and a salad and Carla had chosen a medium-sized steak.

"How did you guess that I was starving?" Carla asked as she sipped her steaming coffee.

"You had that just-gotten-out-of-a-meeting-with-Paul Simmons look on your face," Jake replied deadpan as Carla laughed out loud.

"You're right, Paul tied me up for over an hour right at suppertime," Carla agreed. "I guess Paul's been a talker from way back."

Jake nodded. "Don't you ever tell him, but I had Becky take those messages for me this week. As much as I love Paul, I just didn't have time for a day-long telephone conversation with the poor fellow."

Carla laughed again. "And all this time I thought it was just those of us down at the station!" She sipped her coffee and set the cup back in the saucer. "Did Becky's notes say much about what I wanted to talk to you about this evening?"

Jake shook his head. "Just that you would be at the meeting. So tell me, Carla Jeffreys, what you're doing and what part you want me to play in it."

"I'll start at the beginning if that's all right," Carla said. "I'm interested in doing a television special on the ongoing problem of drinking and driving here in Corpus. I think the public is very interested in and concerned with the problem right now, thanks to the work that you and the CCC have done in the last year. You've done a hell of a job, Jake." She looked Jake in the eye and he smiled faintly. "Anyway, this is what I have in mind. The documentary will run an hour, which comes to fifty-one minutes after commercials, and will be broken into three segments. The first segment will be short, mostly introduction, and will have interviews with a few

23

local officials such as the DA and so forth." Carla stopped and took another sip of her coffee.

"So far it sounds like every other special ever done on the problem," Jake said.

"So far it is," Carla said, not quite masking her irritation. "But an introduction is an introduction. Hopefully from there it will be unique. For the second segment I hope that you will be willing to grant us an in-depth profile of your life since you lost your wife and the work you have done organizing and heading up the CCC."

"How in-depth would the interview have to be?" Jake asked as the waitress brought their meals.

Carla composed her thoughts as the waitress placed her steak and baked potato in front of her and arranged Jake's hamburger basket in front of him. She sampled her salad as Jake took a huge bite out of his burger. "Remind me never to get between you and a meal," she teased.

Jake cocked an eyebrow at her. "From the looks of that steak I get the feeling that you don't have to diet to keep that slender figure of yours," he countered dryly.

Carla laughed. "You're so right," she agreed. "If any other woman my age ate the way I do she would roil out that door."

They both laughed, then Carla sobered. "Back to your question. The interview would be as in-depth as you care to make it. We would like to film you at your place of business, if that's possible, and of course we would like to show you with the CCC. Beyond that would be entirely at your discretion. If you would feel comfortable with it, I'd like you to sit down with Kevin and talk about the motivation behind the CCC, or what made you so determined to head up that kind of organization, but despite my years in the business I'm a little

24

hesitant about asking people to bare their souls on television unless they are very sure they want to do it."

Jake looked across the table skeptically. "And why should you hesitate to ask for a personal interview if that's what you want?" he asked. "Every other reporter in town does it."

Ouch, thought Carla. Somebody's done something to him to blot our good name. "But I'm not every other reporter in town," she said out loud. "First off, I'm a producer, not a reporter. Maybe I would be as pushy as they are if I were reporting the five-o'clock news, but I'm doing a documentary and if you prefer not to grant us that personal a look at your life, then that's your business. We'll fill the time in another way. But I think it would be dynamite if you did talk to us," she added. "Everyone in town knows about Jake Darrow, the driving force behind CCC, but nobody knows about Jake Darrow the man and why he's doing all this."

"Would my daughters have to be involved?" Jake asked.

"Daughters? I didn't realize that you had children," Carla replied.

In response Jake whipped out his wallet and showed her a wallet-sized family portrait. Carla took the wallet from his hand and stared at the all-American family. Jake, younger-looking and smiling, had his hand on the shoulder of a dark-haired, plump, and absolutely beautiful woman of about his own age. Beside Jake was standing a little girl of eight or nine, with curly blond hair and a sweet smile, and beside the woman sat a blossoming beauty of fifteen or sixteen. "What a lovely family," Carla breathed before she could stop herself. She stared at the portrait a moment longer, then handed the wallet back to Jake. "How old are the girls?" she asked.

25

Jake shut his wallet and put it back into his pocket. "Patty turns sixteen this month, and Sonia's nine," he said. "That picture was taken a month before we lost Debbie."

Carla's eyes flew up to meet Jake's, and for a moment the bitterness that she could see there frightened her a little. "It certainly left an empty place in your lives, didn't it?" she asked softly.

Jake nodded, the bitterness fading a little from his face and an overwhelming sadness replacing it. "Yes, the girls and I have had a hard time this last year," he admitted. "I guess the part that hurts the worst is the utterly senseless way she had to die. Such a stupid waste!"

Carla nodded, her sensitive nature going out to this grief-stricken man. "Yes, it was a stupid waste," she agreed for a lack of anything better to say, then paused a minute while Jake composed himself. "Anyway, if you will agree to any kind of interview or profile of yourself and your work with the CCC, that will be the second portion of the show." She hesitated and ate several bites of her steak.

"And the last part of the show?" Jake finally prompted, sensing her hesitation.

"The last part will be somewhat controversial. What I would like to do, the next time that we have a death due to a drunken driver here in Corpus, is to secure interviews with both the family of the victim and the drunken driver. If I can get both families to agree, I would like to follow both stories and show my viewers how the tragedy affected both the family of the victim and the drunken driver and his family."

Jake frowned and shook his head. "I'm not sure I like that," he admitted as he chewed absently on a French

26

fry. "Did you say that you intend to tell the drunken driver's side of it too?"

Carla nodded, afraid that her honesty was about to cost her an interview. "Yes, I do," she replied firmly. "The drunken driver has a story too. Maybe if some of them told us what is happening with them and *why* they insist on driving while they are intoxicated, it might make other potential drunken drivers out there stop and think before they do it themselves. Look, this is going to be a documentary, not an emotional sob story. We hope to show the pain of loss, but we also hope to shed a little light on why it is happening and what we can do to prevent it from happening so many times in the future. Like we did last year on *Just an Angry Moment,* the documentary covering the two teenagers involved in a shooting."

Jake's face cleared. "Was that show one of yours?" he asked.

Carla nodded. "I think it's the best documentary I ever put together," she admitted, remembering the program that had won her a statewide award. She had followed the lives of two boys involved in a shooting, one who would be confined to prison for a number of years, the other who would be confined to a wheelchair for life. "Until this one," she added.

"Well, if that's the kind of program you intend to produce, then I'd like to be a part of it," he said. "And I'll do the in-depth interview."

"That would be wonderful," Carla replied, smiling at him. "Do you want to include the girls?"

Jake shrugged. "I'll talk to them about it and see how they feel," he said.

"Will you be available for filming in a couple of weeks?" Carla asked as she polished off the last of her meal.

27

Jake nodded. "I don't see why not," he said as he ate the last of his hamburger and wiped his lips with his napkin. "Call my secretary tomorrow and she'll pick a date you and your crew can come to the store. If the girls want to be part of this we'll have to schedule a Saturday afternoon when they're free. Will that pose a problem?"

"None at all," Carla assured him as he signaled for the check. She started to get out her purse but Jake shook his head and motioned for her to put it away. "My treat," he said as they stood up. "It's been a long time since I had dinner with a pretty woman."

Carla smiled faintly and her face took on the faintest blush. "Thank you," she said as he took her arm and they walked toward the cash register. Jake's hand was warm on her arm and the attraction that she had put aside during dinner came back in full force, startling her with its intensity. She hadn't been this attracted to a man in a long time.

Jake paid the cashier and opened the door for Carla. Together they walked out into the warm night, a light breeze stirring Carla's hair and ruffling the gray lock of hair that insisted on falling across Jake's forehead. Carla had to fight a sudden urge to smooth that hair back with her fingers. They walked silently to her car, not speaking. Then Jake turned her to him, his fingers trembling. I want him to kiss me, Carla thought.

Carla stared, mesmerized, as Jake's dark eyes bored into her own. He ran his hands down her arms and leaned toward her, then drew back sharply and shook his head. Carla could understand his withdrawal—Jake was not the kind of man to kiss a woman whom he had just met and with whom he had a business relationship —but a part of her was disappointed that he had pulled

28

away from her. She would have loved to feel his lips on hers, if only for a moment.

"I'll call Becky in the morning," she said as she unlocked her car door and slipped inside. She smiled faintly up at Jake. "Thank you for agreeing to the interview."

"Good night," Jake said as he shut her car door.

He is as attracted to me as I am to him, Carla thought with surprise as she pulled out of the parking lot and headed home. She had felt an intense attraction to him, but she had honestly thought it was one-sided. But the near-embrace had shown her clearly that Jake felt that pull too. If he had been a different kind of man then he would have kissed her tonight. And what if he had? Did she have any business going past a pleasant working relationship with him? Did she have any business getting involved with Jake Darrow, a man who was still grieving the wife he loved and lost a year ago?

Jake drove slowly toward his Ocean Drive home and parked his car in the three-car garage next to Debbie's Buick. He got out of the car, but instead of going into the house, he sat down on the patio in one of Debbie's wrought-iron chairs and stared out at the moonlit bay, hoping that the sight and the sound of the beautiful little bay would calm him as it usually did. Tonight he had nearly kissed a woman other than his wife. Debbie, I'm sorry I was almost disloyal to you tonight, he thought, remembering the way the blood had pounded in his ears and the effort it had taken to pull away from Carla Jeffreys.

Jake stared out at the water and willed his heart to stop pounding. It wasn't that just any woman would have done. He hadn't felt particularly attracted to anyone else since Debbie died. And it wasn't that Carla reminded him in any way of Debbie, who had been dark

29

and plump and who had never worked outside her home. But he had been attracted to Carla, and if he had stood there just a minute longer he would have kissed her. Thoroughly confused, Jake gave up on the soothing influence of the pounding surf and went into the house.

Carla strode out of the kitchen carrying another plate of her delicious hors d'oeuvres. "Kurt, can I freshen your drink?" she asked as she set the tray down on the coffee table.

"Thanks, I don't mind if you do," Kurt replied as he handed his highball glass to Carla.

"How about you, Jeannie? Bradley? Are you ready for a refill?"

Jeannie Ryan stood up and smoothed her silk tunic over her harem pants. "Here, let me get mine and Bradley's," she said as her husband handed her his nearly empty glass. The two women left Kurt and Bradley moaning about the latest IRS ruling on tax shelters and crowded into the tiny kitchen. Carla mixed Kurt another highball and Jeannie poured herself and Bradley another glass of wine. "What have you fixed for us tonight?" she asked as she sniffed the air appreciatively. "It smells delicious."

Carla poured herself another glass of wine. "I found a recipe for chicken paprika last week in my new cookbook," she replied, putting the bottle back in the refrigerator. "I thought I'd try it out on you tonight."

"Ooh, I can hardly wait," Jeannie said as she took a sip of her wine. "This may sound horrible, but I look forward to dinner with you so much! It's nice to discuss something besides PTA and whose turn it is to clean the bathroom."

Carla laughed at her friend. Tonight Jeannie was the epitome of affluent sophistication, and to look at her one would never guess that she spent most of her time dressed in jeans organizing a busy family of three school-age children. Jeannie and Carla had been friends for years, and although they were both very busy, they made it a point to get together at least once a month with Bradley, Jeannie's husband, and whomever Carla was dating for dinner and maybe the symphony or theater. "That's quite all right, I get tired of talking about one-takes and which station is going to scoop the big scandal at City Hall," Carla assured Jeannie.

"Oh, is there a scandal at City Hall?" Jeannie asked eagerly.

"Jeannie, there's always a scandal at City Hall, or there's going to be." Carla laughed as they returned to the living room and handed the drinks to the men. Soon the four of them were enjoying a lively debate over the nuclear-arms proliferation.

In just a few minutes the timer on Carla's oven went off, and moments later she was placing a steaming platter of chicken paprika on the table, with rice and a spinach salad.

"Umm, Carla, this is delicious!" Bradley exclaimed after the first bite.

"This is definitely a success," Jeannie declared as Carla smiled modestly. "Fellows, you know that this is the first time Carla has even made this?"

"It wasn't all that hard," Carla protested. "I just followed the directions."

"Not hard, my foot," Kurt declared. "I swear, Carla, with talent like this I'm surprised some man never ran you to the altar. You'd make a wonderful wife!"

Jeannie looked at Carla, but Carla was only smiling blandly. "Oh, I don't know about that," she said lightly.

"Well, then, the least you could do would be to take

31

over the cooking in the hospital cafeteria. I have never tasted more horrible food in my life!"

They all laughed as Kurt expounded on the terrible food at the hospital where he was chief of obstetrics. Then Bradley started in on the horrible food at the school where he was principal, and Carla felt obligated to describe the cardboard offerings in the vending machine at the office. All four were laughing like kids at her description of the gluey sweetrolls when the telephone rang.

Kurt shook his head as Carla stood to answer the phone. "It's probably only a salesman," he protested. "Eat your dinner."

"No, it might be something important," Carla replied as she moved quickly into the kitchen, her silky caftan swinging around her legs. "Carla Jeffreys here," she answered.

"Carla, this is Fred down at the station. You said you wanted me to call you when we got the next DWI death. Well, we just picked up a call on the police monitor. There was an accident on the corner of Staples and Ayers streets. Two cars, one man believed to be dead. We're rushing a crew there now."

"Have them shoot extra footage," Carla commanded. "I'll meet them there. And thanks, Fred."

"Sure thing, Carla," he said as he hung up the phone.

"Well, Kurt, for once it isn't you getting called away," Carla said as she rushed past her dinner guests and into her bedroom. She shut the door and quickly stepped out of her caftan, peeling off her slip and pantyhose and putting on a pair of jeans and a knit shirt. As she put on her sandals, she felt her dangling rhinestone earrings and pulled them from her ears, then dashed back through the living room on her way to her guests.

"Carla, where on earth are you going?" Jeannie demanded when she saw what she was wearing. "Has there been an accident? Your stepmother?"

"Yes. I mean no! There's been a DWI accident and I need to use it in my special," Carla replied. "Y'all go ahead and finish your dinner—Jeannie, put my plate in the oven and I'll eat it when I get back. I'll meet you at the symphony if this doesn't take forever. See you." Carla banged out the front door leaving her own Saturday night dinner party in progress.

Carla swore softly as she approached the scene of the accident. She could see three patrol cars parked at strategic angles to discourage rubbernecking and to encourage the flow of traffic, but there was no way the cars could completely hide the mangled wreckage of the two vehicles involved in the crash. It was a wonder that anybody had survived the wreck if the car and the truck involved were anything to judge by.

Determined that her presence would not impede the rescue, Carla parked her car in the parking lot of a grocery store and walked across the street to the scene of the wreck. A policeman waved her back as she approached, but when she showed him her press card and pointed to the station's film crew, he motioned for her to pass. She picked her way through the shattered glass on the ground and stood beside Artie Newsome, the cameraman who stayed on call at the station to report to accidents such as this one. "They've been working to get that poor devil out for nearly thirty minutes," he volunteered as Carla watched the fireman wield his blowtorch on the crumpled car door.

"Is that the man they think is dead?" Carla asked.

Artie nodded. "They reached in and felt for a pulse a few minutes ago and came up zero, but they won't make it official until they have him out."

"Shoot more footage of them trying to free him," Carla suggested. "Do you have names and addresses yet?"

Artie shook his head and thumbed toward the van. "I think Jessica does, though."

Carla walked toward the van and stuck her head in the window. "Jessie, do you have names and addresses yet?"

"Just of the driver of the truck," Jessica said as she handed Carla her small notebook. "He was so drunk the officer had to get the information off his driver's license." Her small, delicate face twisted up in a grimace. "That's him over there sitting on the curb."

Carla took the notebook and squinted at it in the fading evening light. Don Tyson, an address in a nice but modest part of town, age twenty-one. She looked over at the man sitting on the curb gazing dumbly into space. Why, he's just a kid! Carla thought in amazement. She had always pictured the drunken driver as a dissolute middle-aged alcoholic. Not only was Don Tyson young, he was clean-cut and well groomed and if his glowing health was anything to go by, he was not a problem drinker. Unhurt except for a cut above his right eye, he sat quietly and watched dispassionately as the firemen worked to free the man in the mangled Toyota.

Carla walked back to Artie and pointed to Don Tyson. "Have you shot any film of him yet?" she asked.

Artie shook his head. "I usually wait until they bundle them into the police cars," he said.

"Well, go ahead and shoot some of him sitting there drunk like that, in case these families agree to do the special," she said. "Do you have plenty of footage of them trying to free the other man?"

Artie assured her that he did and proceeded to shoot

34

additional footage of Don Tyson, who was so inebriated that he didn't even try to shield himself from the camera. Then an ambulance drove up and Don Tyson was handcuffed and bundled onto a stretcher to be taken to the nearest hospital before going to the police station.

Carla, Jessica, and Artie waited for another thirty minutes before the firemen were able to free the man in the Toyota and lay him on the stretcher of a second ambulance. Although the paramedics felt for a pulse, it was obvious even to Carla's untrained eyes that the man was dead and had been for quite some time. Although Carla had seen quite a few dead bodies, both in her days as a street reporter like Jessica and on uncensored film clips at the station, she had never gotten used to the sight. She was feeling about as green as Jessica looked when they finally pulled a sheet over the man's battered face and put him into the waiting ambulance.

"Do you ever get used to it?" Jessica whispered to Carla.

"No, and you better hope you never do," Carla said as she slid her arm around the woman's shoulders and gave her a quick squeeze. Carla approached the policeman who appeared to be in charge and showed him her press card. "Could we please have the statistics on the deceased?"

The policeman flipped his notebook open and read off the facts. "Harvey Beadle. Fifty-one years old." The policeman gave Carla an address that was, ironically, only a few blocks from Don Tyson's.

"Can you tell me what happened?" Carla asked.

"Well, Tyson was too drunk to even talk to us," the officer drawled, his disgust evident in his voice. "The nearest we can figure is that Tyson ran a red light doing upward of fifty miles an hour and broadsided Beadle's car on the driver's side. Both vehicles slid half a block—" The policeman gestured to long dark skid marks that were barely visible in the fading twilight. "Anyway, Beadle never had a chance." The officer snapped shut his notebook and put it in his front pocket. "Tell me, ma'am, do you folks get as tired of reporting these things as I do of investigating them?"

"Yes, officer, we sure do," Carla said. "Thank you for the information." She walked back toward the van and sat on the passenger side, making a copy of both names and addresses before giving the notebook back to Jessica. "You two better get back to the station if you're going to get this on the ten-o'clock news. See you later."

"Do you want me to get some films at the hospital?" Artie asked. "You know, the grieving family?"

Carla bit her lip and shook her head. "I don't think so, Artie. That smacks of cheap emotionalism. We can do better than that. I'll talk to the families tomorrow, and if the Beadles agree we'll get some footage of the funeral."

"If you say so," Artie agreed. "Night, Carla."

Carla walked across the street to her car. As she unlocked the car door she noticed a young woman sitting on a bench, staring at the twisted, mangled wreckage in front of her. Carla was not sure from this distance, but she thought she could see the girl's shoulders shaking with sobs. She started to go back across the street, but stopped when a young policeman sat down beside the girl and appeared to be talking with her. Carla watched for a moment, then decided that her presence would not be needed.

Carla got into her car and drove slowly back toward her apartment. She unlocked the door and went inside, noting with gratitude that Jeannie and the men had cleared the table and put away the leftovers before leaving for the symphony. She checked her watch and started for the bedroom, then changed her mind and headed toward the kitchen instead. By the time she got dressed again and down to the auditorium, the symphony would be half over. Besides, she was not really in the mood to be entertained now. Although in her years in television she had seen plenty of live gore and grisly film, she had never been able to shrug off the loss of life as many of her colleagues did, and the sight of Harvey Beadle's lifeless body being pulled from the mangled car had upset her. She pulled the dinner that Jeannie had saved for her from the oven, but she could not make herself eat more than a bite or two.

Dumping the food down the disposal, Carla returned to the living room and lay down on the couch. I hope the families will agree to tell their stories, Carla thought as she gazed at the ceiling. It would be good journalism, and it just might help prevent this kind of tragedy from happening again. Carla blinked and sat up as a thought occurred to her. Had Jake Darrow been there when his wife died?

CHAPTER THREE

Carla checked the address in her notebook and put it back on the seat of her car as she read the street sign. Yes, this was where the Beadle family lived, so Carla turned right and read the numbers on the small houses as she slowly cruised down the street. That's it, she thought as she parked in front of a small brick house and turned off the motor. As she had expected, there were a number of cars parked along the curb and in the driveway. She noticed a gray Lincoln in the driveway just behind an old Chevrolet. I swear that looks like Jake Darrow's car, Carla thought as she walked up the sidewalk and stepped onto the front porch.

Carla pressed the doorbell and turned around to stare at the gray car. Why would Jake be here today? she asked herself as she waited for the door to open. The counseling program! she remembered suddenly. Jake was probably here counseling with the family.

The door was thrown open, and Carla instantly recognized the girl standing there as the same one who had been crying on the bus-stop bench the previous night. Carla got out her press card and showed it to her. "I'm Carla Jeffreys with station KGBD," she said as the girl stared at her press card. "Is Mrs. Beadle home?"

The young woman nodded and motioned for Carla to enter. "Mother's talking with Mr. Darrow right now, but if you'd like to come in I'm sure she will be able to talk to you in a few minutes."

Carla followed the girl into the small entry, amazed that she let her in so willingly. "I'm sorry about your father," she said as the girl shut the door behind her. Carla would have said more, but she saw no sense in mouthing platitudes that would mean nothing.

"I'm Susan Beadle," she said as she led Carla into the small, family room that was behind the living room. There were several people milling around a long table laden with food, and a couple of women were coming and going from the kitchen bringing fresh dishes of potato salad and fried chicken. At the other end of the room Jake was sitting next to a middle-aged woman who held a handkerchief in her hand that she was wringing as she talked. "It will be a few minutes before Mother will be able to talk to you," Susan said. "Have you had lunch?"

Carla shook her head. "Then why don't you get a plate of food and eat while you wait?" Susan invited as she gestured toward the table of food.

Carla shook her head. "No, I couldn't possibly," she objected.

"No, please have something," Susan protested. "We can't eat all of it."

Carla opened her mouth to object again, but Susan was ushering her to the table and Carla sensed that the family might be offended if she refused their hospitality. She glanced over at Jake. When she spotted a paper plate on his lap, she took one from the stack and served herself a small portion of potato salad and a piece of fried chicken. Since all of the chairs on the near end of the room were filled, she was forced to sit in a folding chair just a couple of feet from Jake. Loathe to interrupt, she munched on her chicken and listened unintentionally as Jake talked to Mrs. Beadle.

"But Mr. Darrow, it just don't seem right somehow," Mrs. Beadle protested. "Harvey never took a drink in his life! Our church taught it was wrong, you know, and we never even had it on Christmas. And now for a drunken driver to have killed him! Why, Mr. Darrow, why?"

"Mrs. Beadle, none of us know why a certain person is in the way of the drunken driver when he strikes. I've often wondered why it had to be my wife last year," Jake answered soothingly, oblivious to Carla and the others in the room.

"But what do you *do*, Mr. Darrow?"

"You get angry, Mrs. Beadle. And you stay angry for a long time. Don't be afraid of that anger and don't try to fight it. But don't turn it against yourself or your family."

Mrs. Beadle nodded as Jake continued. "You'll want to channel that anger in a positive direction. I know that in my case I started the CCC and I have put my anger to work in the fight to get drunken drivers properly punished and off the road."

"You think that I need to join the CCC? You think that will help?" Mrs. Beadle looked at him a little suspiciously and Carla listened with interest. Was Jake here just to recruit new members?

Jake placed his plate down on the floor at his feet. "Mrs. Beadle, that's up to you. I didn't come here today to sign up new members, but just to talk with you about coping with your loss and the grief and anger you're bound to feel. If joining CCC would help, then we would be more than glad to have you. But mostly we want to be sure that you have someone to talk to who knows how you feel right now."

"You're right, I *am* angry," Mrs. Beadle admitted. "I ought to be grieving and instead I'm angry. Harvey shouldn't have died like that! He of all people shouldn't have died like that! He just went to pick up our granddaughter's birthday present at the toy store, and he never came home. Oh, Mr. Darrow, it isn't fair, it just isn't fair!"

Mrs. Beadle started to sob quietly. Susan left her place at the table to go over and sit beside her, tears running down her cheeks as she held her crying mother in her arms. A young man who looked a lot like Susan sat down on the other side of Mrs. Beadle and held her hand, tears coursing down his cheeks. Carla wished every drunken driver could see this family as it was right now, devastated by grief. What about Don Tyson, the man who had done this to them? Without meaning to, Carla, shuddered in revulsion as she thought of the inebriated man sitting on the curb the night before. Was he still in jail? Had they already let him out on bond? Did he have any idea of the grief he had caused? Cautioning herself that her journalistic objectivity was about to go out the window, Carla forced her thoughts away from Tyson and listened as Mrs. Beadle's crying slowly tapered off to an occasional sob and Jake resumed talking to her.

As Jake talked with the shocked, grieving woman and her children, Carla had to admire the tact and compassion he showed. You're not alone, he told them over and over. Others have sustained this kind of loss and they will be available for you when you need them. You and your family will survive this. He talked a little more about coping with grief and not letting their anger eat them up inside, then promised that the CCC would help as much as possible with practical considerations, such as finding Mrs. Beadle a job and investing the life insurance money wisely.

Finally Susan whispered to her mother and gestured toward Carla. As Mrs. Beadle looked in Carla's direction, Jake's eyes followed the same path. When he recognized Carla, his eyes widened and his cheeks took on a faint color, but Carla was looking toward the Beadle family and she missed the interplay of emotion that crossed Jake's face for a moment before he could stop it.

"Mrs. Beadle, I know that today's a bad time for you so I won't stay long," Carla began. "I'm Carla Jeffreys of station KGBD. In the next few weeks our station would like to film a documentary on the problem of driving while intoxicated and its related tragedies here in Corpus. As part of the documentary, we would like to follow the story of the family of a victim of a drunken driver and also the drunken driver himself. If you would be willing to agree to be part of the documentary, in a few weeks we would like to tape you and your family while you talk about the effect this tragedy has had on your lives." Carla stopped and took a deep breath. "If the driver who hit Mr. Beadle last night also agrees to an interview, would you be willing to go before the cameras and tell your story?"

Mrs. Beadle looked from Jake to her children uncertainly. "Well, I don't know," she said hesitantly. "We're just ordinary folks. We're nothing fancy."

"I know that," Carla replied. "But that isn't what's important. What you would be doing is telling everyone what losing Mr. Beadle has done to your family. Then we would follow the case through the courts and later broadcast the eventual outcome of the trial."

Mrs. Beadle still looked uncertain. "What good will it do? Harvey's gone."

Carla looked the woman straight in the eye, her expression compassionate. "Mrs. Beadle, it won't do a thing for Harvey. But maybe, just maybe, if you are willing to tell your story before the cameras it might make another drunken driver think and it might save someone else's life."

"But won't it be an invasion of our privacy?" the young man asked. "What will we have to tell you?"

"You won't *have* to tell me anything that you don't want to tell me," Carla assured him, as she had assured Jake just a few nights earlier. "We'll let you know ahead of time what we intend to ask and you don't have to answer anything you don't want to."

"Do I have to let you know today?" Mrs. Beadle asked. "I just don't know what to do."

"I would be amazed if you did let me know today," Carla replied. "Think about it while I try to get in touch with the other driver and see if he's willing to be interviewed. You can let me know of your decision in a day or two." She reached in her wallet and handed Mrs. Beadle her business card. "May we shoot a little footage at the cemetery in case you do decide to do the interview?"

Mrs. Beadle hesitated then nodded. "Would you like some more chicken before you go? The neighbors and the church people all sent so much food that we'll never get it all eaten."

Carla shook her head. "No, but thank you. I'll be in touch later." She shook Mrs. Beadle's hand and smiled at Susan and her brother before turning her smile toward Jake.

Carla said that she would see herself out, then she found her way to the front door and closed it behind her. How awful for them to have to suffer such a tragedy, she thought as she fumbled around in her purse for her keys. I hope they're willing to let Kevin interview them.

Carla jumped as a firm hand closed around her upper arm. "Oh," she cried, dropping her purse so the contents of her bag spilled across the sidewalk. She whirled around and found herself staring straight into Jake's dark eyes. "Thank goodness it's you," she said as her fright faded. "I was afraid I was being accosted in broad daylight."

Jake laughed and released her arm, rubbing the place where his fingers had touched. "No, you're perfectly safe," he assured her as she knelt to retrieve her scattered possessions. Moving stiffly for a man of his age, Jake went down on one knee beside her and gathered up her lipstick and compact while Carla picked up her wallet and her keys. "Is that everything?" he asked.

"Just about," Carla replied as she located her brush on the edge of the sidewalk. "There. That does it." She stood up and offered her hand to Jake, who took it and held onto her arm as he stood up. "Did you want something?"

"I just wanted to thank you for not pushing the Beadles too hard this afternoon," Jake said as Carla unlocked her car. "They're going through a rough time right now and they don't need any additional pressure."

"Of course I didn't push the Beadles," Carla replied, a little irritated. "I know they're going through a rough time and I'm not about to add to their distress," she added tartly.

"Look, I didn't mean to insult you by thanking you," he replied as Carla, bristling with indignation, got into the car. "You were very kind and I just wanted you to know it."

Carla's momentary irritation disappeared and she favored Jake with one of her dazzling smiles. "But not half as kind as you," she said. "You were magnificent with them."

Jake shrugged. "I hope I helped a little," he said. "See you later."

"Good-bye," Carla replied, switching on her engine and heading down the street. He's even more appealing the second time around, she thought as she drove toward her apartment. His thoughtfulness and compassion for the grieving family had been beautiful to see, revealing him to be a fine human being as well as an exciting man. In the days since she had first met Jake, she had almost convinced herself that the attraction she had felt toward him was due to the moonlit night and the warm May breeze. But today it was hot and she had seen him in broad daylight; and he was still the most appealing man she had met in a long time.

Carla put on her long red evening dress. Stepping back, she smoothed the clingy fabric down her flat stomach and slender thighs and admired her reflection in the mirror. "Carla Jeffreys, you're gonna knock their eyes out," she told her image as she winked at herself in the mirror. Her image grinned back impudently. The shimmering red dress set off her blond hair and her light tan to perfection.

Sitting down at her makeup mirror in the bathroom, Carla proceeded to put on what she thought of as her "party face." Tonight she and Kurt were going to a gala affair honoring the mayor, and Carla, who had recently spent too many nights working late at the station, was looking forward to the lively party.

She flicked off the light in the bathroom and opened her closet to take out her evening sandals. She looked for them for a few minutes, then remembered that she hadn't put them away the previous night when she had changed in such haste. Sitting down on the bed, she pulled up the bedspread and peered underneath, pulling her shoes out one at a time. As she strapped on her shoes, she wondered for the hundredth time if the Beadles would talk on camera for her. They had seemed like such a nice family to Carla, showing a stranger hospitality even in their deep grief. And what about Don Tyson? Would he talk to her?

Shrugging, Carla promised herself that she would not think about the documentary any more that night. Crossing to the dresser, she flicked open the jewelry box and selected a Christian Dior rhinestone collar and a matching pair of ear clips. Carla owned a couple of real gold chains that she wore occasionally, but she preferred bold, striking accessories, and she could hardly afford those in real gold and diamonds!

Carla picked up her evening bag and headed out the door. She drove to Kurt's condominium to pick him up since his car was in the shop. In a few minutes the two of them were walking back to her car. "This ought to be a good party," Kurt observed as he opened Carla's door.

"Yes, I'm looking forward to it," Carla replied. As Kurt settled into his seat, she switched on the engine and put the car in gear. "Especially after missing the symphony last night."

"Where exactly did you run off to?" Kurt asked. "You took off in such a hurry that I never really did understand where you had gone."

"There was a DWI death last night," Carla said. "A kid in a pickup slammed into a Toyota. Killed the driver instantly. We shot extra footage and I'm hoping that the drunken driver and the family of the victim will agree to interviews for my next documentary."

"Haven't stories on drunken drivers been a little overdone lately?" Kurt asked.

Carla turned her head slightly and stuck her tongue out, drawing a comfortable laugh from him. "No, not the way I want to do it, it hasn't," she said, then she gave Kurt a thumbnail sketch of what she hoped to do with her special. "But I'll admit that it may take several accidents before I find two families who are willing to be interviewed." She braked for a red light.

"That is all well and good, but don't you think you might be stepping on a few toes?" Kurt asked. "I mean, there are a lot of basically decent people who drink and drive."

"And kill," Carla said. "Don Tyson looks like a decent man, and he killed someone last night."

"All right, all right, I surrender," Kurt said as he threw up his hands in defeat. "Speaking of drinks, I bet old Louie has a wide-open bar tonight."

"I know." Carla grinned. "But I'm much more interested in his buffet table. I had a little to eat at the Beadles' this afternoon, but I'm hungry!"

"Ah, the bottomless pit," Kurt teased as Carla drove through the wide gates that led to the home of Louis Sanderson, one of Corpus Christi's leading businessmen. Just a block off the ocean, the house had a magnificent view of the bay. Carla had to park about halfway down the winding driveway, since a solid wall of cars blocked her from any further progress.

She took Kurt's arm and let him escort her up the driveway to the elegant mansion. "By the way, who invited you to the party tonight?" Kurt asked as Carla rang the doorbell.

"The mayor," Carla replied. "He's invited me to nearly every one of the get-togethers honoring him since he came on the show last year."

47

"The perks that come with your job are sure nice," Kurt said as the door opened and a formally dressed butler escorted them into the crowded living room. They greeted Louis Sanderson and the mayor, who kissed Carla warmly on the cheek and volunteered to go back on *Winners All* again.

The formal greetings over, Kurt drifted toward the bar and Carla headed for the buffet table. Her mouth watering, she picked up a plate and started loading it with the delectable offerings of sliced smoked meats, raw vegetables with spicy dip, and the ever-popular guacamole. Carla had spotted a bowl of boiled shrimp and was about to spear a big one when the serving fork that she was using collided with the serving fork from across the table. Carla looked up, prepared to make the usual polite apology, and found herself looking straight into Jake Darrow's amused eyes. "S-sorry," Carla stammered as she stared into Jake's face. This was the first time she had seen him really smile, and the smile that he wore sent her blood pressure soaring.

"That's quite all right," Jake replied, eyeing her loaded plate with open amusement. "Tell me, do you go broke feeding yourself or do you just eat like this in public?"

Carla blushed at Jake's gentle teasing. "I told you I always eat like this," she reminded him.

"She sure has an appetite, doesn't she?" Kurt observed as he stood beside Carla with a drink in each hand. He handed Carla her drink and extended his hand to Jake. "I'm Kurt Shea," he said.

Jake took Kurt's hand and shook it. "Jake Darrow," he said. "Glad to meet you."

"I recognized you from your television appearances," Kurt said. "You and that organization have set this town on its ear."

"That's what we're trying to do," Jake replied.

"Well, I for one admire what you've accomplished," Kurt said as Carla juggled her loaded plate and her drink. "We're seeing fewer victims than we used to in the emergency room."

Jake smiled faintly. "That's good to hear."

"Come on, Carla, let's go find you a chair so you can eat in comfort," Kurt teased. "Good to meet you, Jake, and good luck."

Jake nodded and watched with narrowed eyes as Kurt led Carla to a low-slung couch and took her plate long enough for her to sit down. He's probably her lover, Jake thought, then wondered for a moment why the thought bothered him.

Carla ate while Kurt returned to the buffet table for a plate of his own. He had just returned to Carla when a familiar *beep* sounded accompanied by a garbled message. "I didn't realize you had the beeper with you," Carla said.

"The resident who was supposed to cover for us this weekend had to go out of town," Kurt explained. "Let me call in, it's probably nothing."

Kurt came back five minutes later with a rueful expression on his face. "I've got to go to the hospital," he said. "One of Jones's patients is having her seventh baby and she's already pretty far along. No, don't get up," he told Carla. "I'll get a cab."

"Nonsense," Carla replied. "Take your plate with you and you can eat while I drive." She set her half-empty plate on the end table, looking only a little longingly at the delicious delicacies she had to leave behind. "No, I mean it, Kurt, take the plate," she said when Kurt went to set it aside. "You won't get to eat for hours."

Looking only a little sheepish, Kurt carried his plate

with him toward the front door. "Going so soon?" Louis asked as they passed the receiving line.

"I just got buzzed," Kurt explained. "I have a delivery tonight."

"Carla, are you going with him?" the mayor asked.

"Yes," Carla explained, "but I'll be back in a few minutes." They hurried out to Carla's car and got inside, Kurt carefully balancing his plate of food on his knee while Carla drove toward the hospital.

"Darrow's got his eye on you," Kurt observed as he speared his boiled shrimp with a fork.

"What makes you say that?" Carla asked, startled by the observation.

"He just does, that's all," Kurt said.

"You're not getting away with that and you know it," Carla chided him. "What makes you think Jake has his eye on me?"

"The look he gave me when I took your arm," Kurt said. "He looked like he wanted to strangle me."

Carla shrugged. "He probably thinks you're my lover."

"Half of Corpus thinks I'm your lover," Kurt said as he munched on a piece of raw carrot. "But none of them looks at me the way he did tonight."

A tiny hope flared in Carla, a hope that she immediately quenched. "It doesn't much matter if he has his eye on me or not," she replied. "The man's still in love with his dead wife. It's written all over him. He's not going to be really interested in me or any other woman until he gets over her."

Kurt shrugged. "Broken hearts do have a way of healing," he said as Carla pulled up in front of the hospital. "Thanks, love," he said as he got out and shut the door. "I'll walk home. Go on back to the party and have a good time for me."

"Will do, Kurt," Carla replied as she wheeled her car around and headed back toward the Sanderson mansion. *So Kurt thinks that Jake has his eye on me. I wish!* Carla thought.

The winding driveway was still full so that Carla had to park at the foot of the drive. She made the long walk up to the mansion and nodded to Louis and the mayor on her way back into the living room. Although she was sorry that Kurt had to miss such a good party, it didn't bother her in the least that she was now without an escort. She often went to parties by herself even before she met Kurt and when he was busy. Still hungry, she headed back to the buffet table for another plate of food.

As Carla put a last shrimp on her fresh plate, she noticed Jake standing at the end of the table, open amusement in his eyes. "What, didn't you get enough before?" he teased as Carla blushed.

"I didn't get to eat much of it," she explained as Jake laughed at her embarrassment. "I had to take Kurt over to the hospital to deliver a baby."

"Well, I hope you get to enjoy this plate," Jake said solemnly as Carla grinned. Jake watched her as she made her way toward the bar, wondering why she didn't seem to mind that Kurt had been called away. Maybe they weren't really all that close. Then again, maybe they were very close, so close that she would see him no matter how late it was. Shrugging, Jake looked at his watch and headed for the bar. He planned on being at the party for at least another two hours, so it would be all right for him to drink a Scotch and soda.

Carla made her way through both the food and her tequila sunrise in record time. Looking around the room, she spotted a number of people she knew, so she got another drink and started around the room, greeting friends and sipping her drink. Being both well-liked and interesting, she was warmly greeted. Lonny Kimbrell, a former New Orleans Saint who had been on her show in the past year, entertained her for a half-hour with the hilarious tale of his round with his agent over a possible movie cameo. Lonny's wife, Maggie, then proceeded to tell Carla about her squabble with their son's first-grade teacher while Lonnie freshened all their drinks.

Then Carla drifted off toward Julio Martinez, who lived in Nashville but who was in town visiting relatives. Julio, one of the hottest up-and-coming country singers of the year, was leaving Corpus the next day but promised Carla he would appear on her show when he came back to town in a couple of months. He introduced Carla to his brand-new wife, and Carla spent a few minutes talking to the young woman while Julio got them all fresh drinks at the bar.

Her face flushed, Carla next visited with a couple of businessmen whom she had met through Paul Simmons and then with the new DA, who complimented Carla's documentary *Just an Angry Moment* and who was delighted to hear that she was doing one on the drunken driving problem. Carla smiled and thanked the DA. Just as she had promised Kurt, she was enjoying the party. She was in her element. She enjoyed talking to people and getting to know them, and she loved to do it at a party. Tonight had been just what she needed.

Finally Carla looked at her watch and gasped. It was almost midnight, and if she didn't get home and to bed she was not going to be able to get up in the morning! She found her evening purse mashed down between two sofa cushions. Thanking Louis and the mayor, she headed out the front door and was almost down the steps when a hand closed gently around her arm. Terrified, she gasped and whirled around to find herself looking into Jake Darrow's face. "Good grief, Jake, do you intend to make a career of scaring me to death?" she demanded.

"Sorry," Jake said as he released her arm. "I didn't mean to frighten you again."

"Then what did you want?" Carla asked a little abruptly. This close, she could smell Jake's tangy aftershave and the smell of cigarettes that clung to his clothing, and she had the ridiculous desire to lean close to him, to put him to the test. Did he really have his eye on her, as Kurt had said?

"I'd like to drive you home tonight," Jake said as he slid his hand down her arm.

"Thanks, but I have my car here," Carla replied. "I'll see you." She started to move away but Jake did not release his grip on her arm.

"I know you have your car here," Jake replied. "That's not why I want to drive you." He looked over at Carla's bewildered expression. "You've been drinking."

Carla stepped back as though he had slapped her. "I beg your pardon," she said coldly. "I'm not drunk."

"I didn't say that," Jake replied smoothly. "I said you've been drinking."

"So have you," Carla replied.

"I've had nothing but club soda for the last hour and a half," Jake said. "How much have you had?"

Carla counted the drinks she had consumed on her fingers. "And how many in the last hour?" Jake asked.

"All right, all right." Carla sighed, exasperated. "I'll go with you. I've had two in the last hour. But what about some of the others? A lot of them have had a whole lot more than I have!"

"I know that," Jake replied grimly. "But I'm leaving now. Besides, I can't drive them all home."

"But what about my car?" Carla protested as another

53

thought struck her. "I have to get to work in the morning."

"Call a cab to run you over here," Jake suggested. "Look, you can drive if you want to—you're not legally drunk—but you would be better off riding with me. It's up to you."

"I guess you're right," Carla replied as Jake took her arm. She didn't think she was all that far gone, but she sure didn't want to risk Jake's changing his mind about doing her show, and he would think her the worst kind of hypocrite if she drove tonight. Jake escorted her to his car and opened the door. "Nice," Carla breathed as she smelled the leather upholstery and ran her hand down it. "This is even nicer than Kurt's Mercedes."

"Don't you let the Mercedes people hear you say that," Jake teased as he got in and switched on the engine. Jake asked Carla her address as he worked his way out of his parking slot.

"Well, both cars are quite a switch from my Chevy," Carla volunteered. "Kurt's car scared me to death the first time he let me drive it, but I've gotten used to it now."

"And how long ago was that?" Jake asked.

"Nearly a year ago," Carla said. "My car was in the shop and he lent the Mercedes to me for a day."

"You've known him a long time," Jake said as casually as he could manage. "Are you close?"

"You mean are we sleeping together?" Carla asked as she stared boldly across the seat, her tongue loosened by the drinks she had consumed.

"I—I didn't mean that," Jake stammered.

"Yes, you did," Carla said, a grin playing around her mouth.

"Well, are you?" Jake replied.

Carla shook her head. "No, we're not," she admitted.

"Although everybody in Corpus probably thinks we are after all this time."

Jake's face contorted in a frown of puzzlement. "I'll admit that I don't understand," he said. "You're obviously very fond of one another."

"We are," Carla replied. "But the spark just isn't there for either one of us. We enjoy each other's company, we help each other out when we need it, but I'm afraid that's as far as it goes. We even talked about becoming lovers once, but the physical pull is missing. I know he dates other women and I imagine that he sleeps with some of them."

"What about you?" Jake asked as he put on the blinker and turned the corner. "Do you date other people?"

Carla shrugged. "When I get the opportunity," she said. "Unfortunately, my job is quite demanding and takes a lot of evenings. And then, the swinging singles' scene simply does not appeal."

"Yeah, I know what you mean," Jake said. He pulled into the parking lot of her complex and turned off the engine. "So you're lonely sometimes."

Carla shot a startled look in Jake's direction. "I'm lonely a lot of the time," she admitted. "But what made you say that?"

"Because the singles' scene does not appeal to me either, and I'm lonely a lot of the time too," he said.

Carla stared across the seat at Jake, understanding in her eyes. Yes, she could understand his being lonely, because in spite of her job and Kurt she was often lonely. It wasn't just a surface loneliness—she had friends who could do something about that—but it was a loneliness deep within her, the kind of loneliness that even a good party couldn't banish entirely. And Jake

55

felt that kind of loneliness too, she was sure of it, now that his wife was gone.

Jake got out of the car and opened Carla's door for her, taking her arm as he escorted her to the front door she pointed out to him. "Thank you for driving me home," she murmured as she fumbled around in her small bag for her key.

"Thank you for letting me," Jake said, placing his hand on her nape and turning her around to face him. This close, the scent of his spicy aftershave assaulted her and the brightness of his eyes ensnared her. She stared at him, her lips parted slightly, her breathing rapid. The electricity sparkled between them, the tension built, until Carla thought she would scream.

Slowly, as though he were fighting himself, Jake drew Carla to him and let his lips come down on hers. At first his lips were cool and soft, but as Carla opened her mouth to him, Jake deepened the kiss, opening his mouth and thrusting his tongue inside her parted lips. Her senses reeling, Carla gave no thought to what she should or should not do, whether she should let Jake kiss her and hold her like this. This was good, this was right, and she wanted Jake to hold her and touch her like this, she wanted his intimate embrace. It would drive away the loneliness for a little while, at least.

Without really realizing what she was doing, Carla reached up and wound her fingers into the crisp iron-gray hair at his nape, her long fingernails scratching his scalp in a sharp pleasure-pain that caused Jake to gasp a little. Jake's hand was cupping Carla's neck, holding her to him so that she could not have pulled away if she had wanted to. Carla moaned and arched her body closer to Jake's until they were hip to hip, shoulder to shoulder. I like kissing a man who's my height, Carla thought as she slid her hands across Jake's broad shoulders and down his arms, feeling the tension in the taut muscles of his forearm and wrist.

Carla slid her hands around his sinewy waist and locked them at the base of his spine, unashamedly pressing the evidence of his masculinity even closer to her. Moaning, Jake could feel her hard, firm breasts against the wall of his chest, and it was all he could do to keep from reaching out and touching them. Her breasts felt hot and sweet against him. She felt good in his arms, she felt like she belonged there.

But she didn't belong there; Debbie did. Thinking that, Jake hesitated, then started to move away from Carla. As his fingers trailed away, Carla moaned and made a motion to press him closer to her.

Carla blinked when Jake abruptly broke off the kiss and thrust her away from him, then her cheeks burned when she realized that her body had practically begged the man to make love to her. "T-thanks for the ride home," Carla stammered. "See you later."

"Good night," Jake muttered gruffly as Carla let herself inside and turned off the porch light. Jake waited until the door was shut, then he walked slowly down the stairs and got into his car, his mind and emotions in a turmoil. He had wanted Carla Jeffreys tonight. He, Jake Darrow, the man who had hardly looked at another woman besides Debbie Nelson Darrow since he was sixteen years old, had wanted to make love to Carla so badly that he could taste it.

Jake shook his head from side to side, as though he could shake his desire for Carla away. Why was he so surprised? He had expected to feel physical desire for a woman sooner or later. He was only forty-one, and he had always been virile. But this was something more than physical desire, and that confused him. He had been relieved, no, delighted when Carla had said that she and Kurt were not lovers. And then, when she had admitted that she was lonely, he had wanted to take her into his arms and ease her loneliness; and he had done so. What was going on with him?

Jake drove through the deserted streets, wondering what was happening to him. He couldn't understand it. He knew that he was still in love with Debbie, that he hadn't gotten over her, not by a long shot. So why did he desire Carla so much?

Carla sat down on the edge of her bed and started taking off her shoes, an embarrassed blush coloring her cheeks. She had certainly had more to drink than she thought she had! It was a good thing she *hadn't* tried to drive. But had it been any better to have Jake drive her home? First she told him all about her platonic relationship with Kurt, which was none of his business, and then she had kissed him like a love-starved schoolmarm. Oh, Carla, you blew it tonight, she thought as she put her head into her hands. So much for the poised, sophisticated television producer! My dear, you really should have counted your drinks.

Carla shed her clothes and threw them into the chair beside the bed, promising herself that leaving a mess this once wouldn't matter. Not bothering with her nightgown, she climbed between the cool sheets and laid her whirling head on the pillow. She cringed again when she remembered how she had responded to Jake. It was the alcohol, she assured herself. She wouldn't have acted like that sober.

But what had made Jake respond to her as he had? she wondered as sleep overtook her. She could blame her uninhibited response on the alcohol, but Jake had not been drinking. So why had he kissed her like that?

CHAPTER FOUR

Carla parked her car in front of the Tysons' small house and licked her lips reflectively. Objectivity, Carla, she reminded herself as she picked up her notebook and got out of the car. She had to be objective about Don Tyson. Pushing away the image of the drunken young man sitting on the curb staring dumbly at the man he had just killed, she forced herself to pretend she had never seen Don Tyson before, that she had not spoken to him on the phone to arrange this meeting, that this was the first time she had encountered the young man. Hitching her purse strap back up on her shoulder, Carla walked up the sidewalk and rang the doorbell of the small, freshly painted house.

In a moment Carla heard footsteps on the other side of the door, then it was thrown open by a very young woman with circles under her eyes and a baby on her hip. Why, she's little more than a child herself! Carla thought. She's no older than Susan Beadle. "I'm Carla Jeffreys," Carla said as the young woman reached out and unlatched the screen door.

"I'm Cindy Tyson," she said as she pushed open the screen door. "Don's in the bedroom. I'll call him." Carla stepped into the small living room and stared at the profusion of photographs lining the walls. The Tysons' wedding picture was displayed prominently over the sofa, and several large photographs of the baby and a little boy of about two lined the other wall. What darling children, Carla thought as her face softened.

The door from the back of the house opened, and Carla recognized the man who stepped through it as the same one who had been sitting on the curb the other night. Don Tyson seemed even younger now, a boy almost, although his face showed the strain of the past two days. He had a bandage on the cut on his forehead and his temple was badly bruised, but otherwise he had suffered no outward effects from the wreck. Dressed in a pair of jeans and a work shirt, his eyes clear and his face sober, today it was hard to realize that this man had taken another man's life Saturday night. "I'm Don Tyson," he said as he extended a large, roughened hand to Carla.

"Carla Jeffreys, KGBD," she said. "Thank you for letting me come today."

Don motioned her toward one of the chairs, then he sat down on the couch. Cindy came back in and sat down beside him, taking his hand lightly in hers. "I put the baby to sleep," she said softly. "We can leave Donnie at Mother's until suppertime."

"Do you mind if my wife stays?" Don asked as he clasped her hand tightly in his.

"No, of course not," Carla assured him. "In fact, what I am about to ask you to do will involve her as much as it will you."

The Tysons looked at each other. "I'm one of the program producers over at the station," Carla explained. "Right now I'm working on a documentary on the problem of drunken driving"—she paused as Don flinched—"and in one of the segments we would like to follow a specific case where a person has died as a result of someone driving while intoxicated." Carla stopped and bit her lip, carefully phrasing the next question in her mind. "If the Beadle family agrees to an interview, would you be willing to go on television and tell your side of the story?"

Don stared across the room at Carla. "My side of the story? You mean, why did a jerk like me get drunk as a skunk in the local dive and kill a decent, law-abiding grandfather on his way to buy his grandkid a birthday present?"

"Don, stop it!" Cindy pleaded. "Don't do this to yourself!"

"Well, I can read the papers too, hon," Don said as he turned stricken eyes back to Carla. "I killed a perfectly innocent man the other night. Hell, he wasn't even guilty of a traffic violation!"

"No, he wasn't," Carla agreed slowly as she mentally revised her picture of Don Tyson. He was not the thoughtless, callous monster the CCC and other groups like it portrayed the drunken driver to be. This man was very conscious of what he had done. "Don, just how do you feel about what happened the other night?" she asked softly.

An anguished groan escaped the man. "God, I feel terrible," he said. "I can't eat, I haven't slept since I sobered up, the boss sent me home at noon after I tried to fit a door to the wrong cabinet for the third time this morning. All I can see, all I can hear is that damned crash Saturday night." He broke off and buried his head in his hands for a minute, then raised tear-filled eyes to Carla. "I wouldn't wish the guilt I'm feeling on anyone."

"Oh, but Don, it was my fault too!" Cindy cried as she touched Don's arm. She turned haunted eyes on Carla. "I'd been giving Don a rough time about things," she admitted. "You know, about there never being enough money to buy new furniture or to move out of

61

this little house. We had a fight that afternoon," she continued as her eyes filled with tears. "Don just couldn't stand the nagging any more, so he slammed out of the house and drove off." Cindy stopped and swallowed a lump in her throat. "Four hours later they called me from the police station. Honestly, it wasn't all Don's fault, it wasn't!"

Carla nodded, her objectivity disappearing as she watched the tortured young couple fighting not to break down and cry in front of her. A part of her wanted to comfort them, to tell them that everything was going to be all right. In spite of her earlier preconceived notions, she sincerely liked the Tysons and felt for them in their plight.

Yet at the same time the professional reporter in her sensed a wonderful story. The Tysons were young, they were decent, they were attractive, and yet Don Tyson had killed a man with his vehicle because he had been drinking too much. He had become a statistic. But Don Tyson wasn't just a statistic, he was a husband, a father, an employee, a nice guy. And he would make people think. If it had happened to Don Tyson, it could happen to them too.

Carla gave the Tysons a moment to compose themselves, then she cleared her throat. "I know you feel terrible about this, and it wouldn't be the easiest thing in the world to let us interview you in front of the camera," she said softly. "But if you were willing to talk to us, it might make other people out there, people just like you, realize that it could happen to them too. They could end up doing the same thing you did Saturday night, without meaning to." Carla started to add more but fell silent.

"You think, if I did go on television, it might help someone else?" Don asked.

"It might," Carla said, nodding. "It might make someone else think before they drink and then drive."

"What do you think, hon?" Don asked, turning to his wife. "Would Cindy be involved?" he asked Carla.

"If she's willing," Carla said. "What I'm trying to do is to show the effect of the tragedy on both families, not just the family of the victim. This has affected you both deeply, every bit as deeply as it has the other family. I'd like the viewers to see that."

Cindy took a deep breath. "We ought to, Don," she said. "If it really could keep something like this from happening again. But what will your attorney say?"

"I guess I better check with him," Don said as he got up off the couch. "I'll call him."

Well, there it goes, Carla thought, watching the door close. Don's attorneys would never agree to letting him tell his story in public. She should have thought of that before planning the program. Preparing herself for the inevitable refusal, she asked Cindy about her children and was listening to an account of the older one's latest antics when Don poked his head through the door. "My attorney would like to talk to you for a minute," he said.

Carla followed Don back to a small, cheerful kitchen. He handed her the telephone and the gravelly voice on the other end of the line asked her a few questions about the program. Carla told him just what she had told the Tysons, stressing that she wanted to tell what happened from Don's point of view and that a character assassination of Don and Cindy was the furthest thing from her mind. She then handed the telephone back to Don and walked back into the living room, carefully avoiding a Cookie Monster puppet in the middle of the floor.

Don followed her out to the living room a moment later. "He thinks it might be a good idea," he told Carla and Cindy. "With the public so down on drunken drivers right now, he thinks it might help if they could see us as people just like them. Carla, I'll do it, if the other family agrees."

Carla smiled inwardly but was careful to keep her face composed. "I appreciate it very much," she said as she rose and shook both Don's and Cindy's hand. "If the Beadles agree, we'll be taping in a couple of weeks. Can I give you a call a little closer to taping? We'll set a time and a place then."

The Tysons nodded. Don opened the front door for her, and she strode over to her car and got in. Turning on the air conditioner full blast, she sat a moment staring at the Tysons' small house. She felt sorry for them and that surprised her a little. She had come today expecting to loathe the young man who had caused the suffering she had witnessed at the Beadles', but instead she had come away feeling almost as much compassion for them as she did for the victim's family. Yes, Don Tyson was guilty—he had admitted as much himself. And he was tortured by that guilt.

And their problems are only beginning, Carla thought as she put her car in gear and started slowly down the street. Right now they were both too consumed with guilt to see beyond that. But there would be a hearing and a trial in the future, and if Carla had actually recognized the voice she had heard on the telephone, Don had hired one of Corpus's leading criminal lawyers, a lawyer who wouldn't come cheap. Even if Don did get off without a prison sentence, the young carpenter would be in debt for years. And, of course, he might very well have to go to prison for several years. Don didn't realize a whole lot of what was coming, Carla thought. But he would before very long.

Carla glanced down at her watch as she turned the

corner. Had the Beadles come to a decision yet? The funeral had been this morning, but perhaps they had discussed it yesterday after she and Jake had left them. She started to drive by their street, thinking that maybe she was intruding, but on remembering the warmth with which she had been greeted the day before, she didn't think they would mind if she stopped by for a minute.

Susan Beadle again greeted her at the door. There were fewer people in the little house today, just the immediate family. A woman who introduced herself as Mrs. Beadle's sister offered Carla a plate of food from dishes lining the kitchen counter. Lenore Beadle insisted, saying that they couldn't possibly eat it all. Mrs. Beadle sat down across from Carla at the table and her sister thrust a glass of iced tea in front of each of them.

"Have you had a chance to think about the interview, Mrs. Beadle?" Carla asked as she nibbled on a piece of fried chicken.

Mrs. Beadle nodded. "Please call me Lenore. Susan and I talked about it last night," she said as she sipped her iced tea. "She says we ought to do it if the other folks will. She says maybe it'll help somebody else."

"Maybe it will," Carla agreed. She sipped her iced tea and pushed a glob of potato salad around on her plate. "The Tysons did agree to the interview this afternoon."

Mrs. Beadle turned lackluster eyes on Carla. "Then we'll do it," she said, wrinkling her brow. "I wonder what made him agree to talk to you?"

"The same reason you are," Carla replied. "He wants to keep it from happening again."

"Then why didn't he keep it from happening the other day?" Mrs. Beadle flared suddenly.

"That I don't know," Carla admitted, knowing that

the fight with Cindy did not fully explain why Don had turned to alcohol on Saturday night.

Mrs. Beadle's face resumed its wooden expression. "Mr. Darrow said we should do the show," she volunteered. "We're joining the CCC, you know."

"That's good," Carla said, wondering privately why Jake had encouraged the Beadles to do the program and very grateful that he had done so. She set a date with the Beadles to do their taping and wrote it in her notebook, then wiped her fingers on a napkin and thanked the family for the meal before leaving.

She drove quickly back to her office in the midafternoon traffic. *Winners All* was not due on the air for another hour, but she had a telephone call to make and she wanted to have plenty of time for it. She walked into her office, stepped over Kevin's long legs, and pulled the phone book out of the desk drawer. Flipping to the *D*'s, she ran her manicured finger down the listings until she came to two listings, one for Darrow's Menswear and the other one for Darrow's Duds.

A little smile playing around her mouth, Carla dialed the number for Darrow's Menswear first. A sedate middle-aged voice answered the telephone and against a serene backdrop of Musak told Carla that Mr. Darrow was at the other store. Carla dialed the other number, and a young-sounding voice straining to be heard over Michael Jackson's "Thriller" agreed to find Mr. Darrow. In just a moment Jake's voice sounded on the other end of the line. "Jake Darrow here," he said loudly.

Carla gulped as she remembered the fiery abandon with which she had kissed him last night. "This is Carla Jeffreys," she said softly.

"Huh? Sorry, you're going to have to speak up," Jake yelled into the receiver.

"This is Carla," Carla repeated loudly.

"Oh—just a minute," Jake replied. There was the sound of being put on hold, then Jake spoke to her again, this time with only the faintest sound of the music behind him. "And what can I do for you today, Carla?" he asked smoothly.

You can kiss me again, she thought as her face turned red and she turned away from Kevin's knowing glance. "I—I just wanted to thank you for encouraging the Beadles to do the show," she said. "They've agreed to the taping."

"That's good," Jake said. "What about the other bastard? Is he going to do it too?"

Carla swallowed back a sympathetic comment about Don Tyson. "Yes, the Tysons have agreed to the taping," she said. "Speaking of taping, we're going to need some footage of you at work, at a CCC meeting, maybe speaking before a group, that sort of thing. Would Friday be all right with you?"

"Sounds great. Do you need any of me swimming or in the shower?" he teased.

A tiny laugh escaped before Carla could stop it. "The shower no, we're not on cable, but if you're not kidding about the swimming we could use a little footage of that."

"Great, I'll see you at six a.m. on Friday then," Jake replied.

"Six?" Carla squealed.

"That's when I work out. I have to for my bad back," Jake explained. "I have to speak to a men's breakfast that morning at seven thirty."

"Six it is," Carla replied, making a face at the telephone and groaned, "I'll have a cameraman with me."

"I'll even make y'all coffee," he volunteered. "See you Friday."

"See you," Carla said as she hung up the telephone and made a note to set her alarm for five Thursday night.

How does Jake do it? Carla asked herself as she yawned into the mirror and checked her makeup. Had she forgotten something essential? No, she appeared to be fully made up and her hair fell into its usual sleek wedge. I guess I just feel like I forgot something, she thought as she put blusher and an eyelining pencil in her purse along with her usual lipstick and compact. On a long day like today, she was likely to need more than her usual noon lipstick and powder refresher.

Carla drove through the dark, deserted streets to the station, she and Artie the cameraman drove the station's van to the fashionable address on Ocean Drive that Jake had given them. As they parked in front of the house, the front door opened and Jake emerged, wearing jogging shorts, a sleeveless T-shirt, and expensive running shoes. Carla wondered just how serious Jake's back injury was, since the fit state of his body indicated that he got plenty of exercise. She swallowed as her eyes traveled the length of Jake's hard body, taking in the broad, powerfully muscled chest, the trim waist and flat stomach, and the hard, rippling muscles of the legs that extended from his slim hips. Does he lift weights? she asked herself as her eyes devoured the bulging muscles in his chest and arms.

"Yes, I do, three times a week," Jake replied, and Carla realized that she must have voiced her question out loud. She looked at his face and the amusement there made her turn bright red. She instantly lowered her eyes, but upon encountering that same broad chest and shoulders, she looked away and gave instructions to

68

Artie. "I'd like to get footage of Jake while he works out."

They followed his car to the health club near Jake's house, and in just a few moments Artie was busy filming Jake as he worked out on the various machines at the club. Carla noticed that Jake could lift a considerable amount of weight with his arms and his chest, but that he was careful to avoid any leg workouts or do anything that would aggravate a bad back. How did a man his age come to have such a problem with his back? she wondered as she told Artie to get a closeup or two of Jake working on an arm curl.

Jake worked out on weights for about a half an hour, then he disappeared into the back for a minute and emerged clad in a swimsuit. He slipped into the pool and Artie shot some footage of his swimming. Jake was a good swimmer, shooting through the water like an arrow, and Carla could not stop staring at the graceful symmetry of his hips and legs. When she figured they had filmed enough, she motioned to Artie to stop taping. "We'll drive back and wait for him at his house," she said.

Jake drove up about thirty minutes later and motioned for them to come inside. By the time they had reached the front door, he had disappeared into the back, but on the kitchen counter in a coffee maker was the coffee he had promised. As they each poured themselves a cup of coffee, Carla glanced around at the large, beautifully decorated yet comfortable home, with its wide picture windows that opened onto the bay.

Jake reappeared just a few moments later, dressed in a three-piece suit that was tailored to fit his broad muscular body to perfection. His face was freshly shaved and his hair was still damp from the shower. Carla was hard put to decide whether she liked him better like this, the picture of urbane sophistication, or sweaty and disheveled in his workout clothes. "I called and told the program chairman for the Rotary Club I'd be bringing two guests for breakfast," he volunteered as he sipped his coffee. When Carla and Artie murmured their thanks, Jake grinned. "Well, considering the hour at which I got you folks out of bed this morning, it was the least I could do!"

Artie shot a little footage of Jake as he drove away from the house, and then they followed him through the early-morning traffic to one of the downtown hotels that lined the bay. After entering one of the meeting rooms, Jake introduced Carla to the president of the club and explained what she and Artie would be doing.

After checking the room's lighting, Carla and Artie watched as many of Corpus Christi's prominent businessmen seated themselves at the tables scattered throughout the room. They were served a substantial breakfast, and Carla made quick work of the eggs and sausage. She then pushed her plate aside and got out her notebook and pen, ready to take down anything she might be able to use later when she wrote Kevin's voice-over.

As the dishes were cleared, the president of the club opened the meeting with a few announcements, then introduced Jake, who was greeted with an enthusiastic round of applause. He stepped up to the podium and, with the force and energy that so characterized the public Jake Darrow, he held forth for the next forty minutes on the problem of drunken drivers and what needed to be done about them.

Very briefly he mentioned his own loss, then he explained that drunken driving was a widespread problem, about the existing legislation, and about how much more needed to be done. Much of what Jake was saying

70

Carla already knew; in preparing for her program she had become almost as well versed on the problem as he. But she admired the way he captured the imagination of the businessmen in front of him, how he wove facts and figures together from heartwrenching stories of Corpus Christi tragedies. The businessmen gave Jake their full attention, seeming not to notice the television lights. A few appeared to disagree with Jake's position, but most faces reflected admiration for the man who stood in front of them and a hearty endorsement of his cause.

Promptly at nine thirty, Jake ended his speech and was given an enthusiastic round of applause. The meeting was adjourned just a few moments later, and Jake approached Carla as Artie unstrapped his minicam and put it in its case. "I'm going to the downtown store first today," he said. "I'll spend the morning there and then I'll be at the mall store this afternoon."

"Which one is first—middle-aged menswear or the Michael Jackson look-alike shop?" Carla teased.

Jake laughed out loud. "Oh, please, middle-aged menswear first!" he pleaded. "I can't stand that music until after lunch!"

Actually, Darrow's Menswear was a delightful store catering to the businessmen of the community, and Carla thoroughly approved of the various lines of better suits and accessories. She made a mental note to send Kurt this way the next time he was in the market for a suit.

They filmed Jake in his office. He had the same energy and drive in his business dealings that he had in his fight against drunken driving, and by noon Carla, an energetic person herself, was exhausted from just watching him. How does he keep up this pace all day and then head up an organization like CCC in his spare time? she wondered. Either task would be a full-time job for most people.

Then the production team followed Jake as he drove to his other store, located in one of the malls in the south part of town near the Padre Island Causeway. Darrow's Duds catered to the younger, more casually dressed man.

Business was as brisk as it had been in the downtown store, and Jake never quit moving all day. Carla jotted down a few questions about his business that she could ask him later, but mostly she waited and she watched, and as she watched she became more impressed with Jake Darrow. He was an astute and dynamic business-man, but he was as unfailingly polite to his employees as he was to his customers, treating them with respect even when he found fault with the job done. He did not rely on tricky gimmicks to bring in his customers, but let his superior merchandise be its own best advertise-ment. During one of the rare lulls in Jake's day, he told Carla how he had started the first store seventeen years ago with several thousand dollars he had borrowed from his father. At first he said he had done all the buying as well as running the business end of it, but now all he had time for was the final say about whether a particular garment ended up on his rack.

Carla wondered at first if it was just her imagination, but by the end of the day she was sure that Jake's limp had become more pronounced, and a couple of times she thought she saw a grimace of pain on his face when he thought no one was looking. No one else seemed to notice the limp or the pain, or if they did notice they were ignoring it. Jake and his employees closed the store promptly at six. The day's shooting ended when the employees left, just as soon as the cash register had been cleared and the money sorted for deposit at a local bank. Artie switched off the TV light. "Where to next, sir?" the tired cameraman asked.

"Oh, unless you want to film me reading the paper and brushing my teeth, this is all I have planned for today," Jake replied, his own face just a little tired. "If you had come yesterday, you could have come to a PTA meeting with me that went on until ten."

"I'm just as glad we missed that one." Artie sighed as he unhooked his minicam and packed it away.

"No, I wish we had filmed that," Carla demurred as Artie walked out of the office. "That would have been great—the concerned community."

"I gave the same speech I did this morning," Jake said as he stood up from his desk chair. He flinched halfway up and his face contorted with pain. "Oh, damn," he muttered under his breath as he forced his body upward.

"Jake, are you all right?" Carla asked, extending her hand.

"Yes, I'm fine," he said through gritted teeth as he pushed himself upright. He stood for just a moment, then he stepped away from the desk.

"Are you sure? You've been limping a little," Carla ventured.

"Damn it, I'm *all right,*" Jake ground out under his breath.

"S-sorry," Carla stammered, backing away from him at his angry response. "I just thought—"

"Well, don't worry about it," Jake said dismissively as he tried to stifle another wince. He was obviously in pain, but from his response Carla was sure that he did not want to talk about his bad back. Carla watched him as he packed his briefcase, and gradually, as his face cleared, she could see the pain was fading. She was glad

73

that he felt better, of course, but it hurt that he hadn't wanted to talk to her about his problem.

"Hey, Carla, I'm ready to go," Artie called through the open door. "My old lady's waitin'," he added.

"Yes, mustn't be late for that old lady of yours." Carla laughed. "His old lady's twenty-three years old and was runner-up for Miss Corpus Christi last year," she told Jake.

Jake eyes widened and he glanced out at the skinny, balding cameraman. "You have to be kidding!" he whispered.

Carla shook her head, her eyes dancing.

"Come *on*, Carla," Artie nagged.

Suddenly Jake took Carla's arm and walked with her out of the office. "Sorry, fella, Carla and I are going out to dinner. We have a few things we need to touch base on about the filming today," he said smoothly. "You can go back to the station alone and I'll get Carla home later. Wouldn't want to keep you from your old lady, Artie."

Artie's face split into a huge grin. "Thanks, Jake," he said as Carla handed the keys to the van to him. Artie graced her with a winking leer as he loped out of the store, his camera case bouncing against his side.

Jake looked into Carla's astonished face. "You could have asked," she sputtered.

Jake frowned. "Sorry. I thought I did," he said, then his face broke into a smile. "No, really, I thought it would be better to cut through the hemming and hawing and the polite 'No, I can wait' we would have gotten from him, and if that little notebook is as full of questions as I think it is, you do need to ask me a few things."

"Yes, I do," Carla admitted. "Can I have a minute to freshen up?"

Jake pointed her toward a small employee washroom, and in just a few minutes her makeup was repaired and she was sitting beside Jake in his car. "Want to eat somewhere on the bay?" he asked.

Carla nodded, and Jake selected a well-known seafood restaurant that overlooked the water. The warm sea breeze ruffled Carla's hair as they walked from the car to the restaurant, and once they were in the lobby Carla passed her fingers through her hair in an attempt to repair the wind's work. She was hoping that her hair looked all right when Jake reached out and flicked his fingers through it and smoothed her bangs.

"There," he said. "You look just fine."

"Thank you," Carla said. She could feel the imprint of his fingers where his hand had touched her forehead, and his casual act had seemed perfectly natural yet at the same time intimate. She stared into the dark eyes that were level with hers and a shudder of excitement coursed down her spine.

The headwaiter came to seat them then and the spell was broken. They were shown to a table near the window overlooking the bay. Carla sat down and stared out at the water, sparkling in the rays of the late-afternoon sun, and rested her chin in her hand. "Looking out that window, you would think there wasn't a problem in the world," she murmured.

"No, you wouldn't," Jake agreed as he stared out the window with her. "And watching you sitting there looking out the window, I'd have to say that you've never had a problem in the world," he said. "You haven't had many, have you?"

Carla's eyes clouded. "Then you would have to be wrong," she murmured just loud enough for Jake to hear. "I've had my share." Her face cleared immediately, though, and she turned away from the window and picked up her menu.

After the waiter had taken their order, Carla pulled out her notebook. "Do you mind?" she asked as she hunted around in her purse for a pen.

"Of course not," Jake replied. "That was the purpose of this dinner. Besides the pleasure of your company," he added sincerely.

Carla smiled and read the first question she had jotted down about his work. Jake elaborated a little on the history of his businesses and told her about the new store he was planning to open in San Antonio late in the fall. She went through most of her minor questions before they were through with their salads and decided to save her really big question for later.

Their waiter brought them huge platters of seafood, and Carla's face reddened when she realized that she had ordered more food than Jake had. He glanced over at her platter and laughed out loud. "Don't you ever stop eating?" he asked.

Carla shook her head and waded into the fried shrimp, putting a dent into her meal before she spoke again. Their conversation was limited for the next few minutes while they both assuaged their appetites. Finally, her hunger sated, Carla picked up her notebook. "I've got just one more question, and it's kind of a biggie," she said. "I'd like you to elaborate on it if you can." Jake took a sip of his coffee and nodded. "How do you do it all?" she asked. "I mean, how do you run two stores, raise two children alone, and still find time to put in the countless hours you put in for the CCC?"

"On the record or off?" Jake asked.

"Whichever you prefer," Carla replied.

"On the record, I'll say that I have a lot of energy, that I delegate the managing of my businesses when I have to, that I feel the CCC is more than worth my time because of what we've accomplished in the short time we've been active, that my children believe in what I'm doing and are understanding about my absences." He paused.

"And off the record?" Carla prompted.

"Oh, it's all true," Jake replied. "I do have a lot of energy, at least I have enough, and I do have good managers and believe in the CCC. And the girls are just great. But I sure do get tired sometimes. Four or five eighteen-hour days in a row every week would wear anyone out. And I miss my girls."

"Where were they this morning?"

"Are you kidding? I could no more pry them out of bed before seven than I could fly to the moon!" Jake laughed.

Carla laughed with him, then her face sobered. "So what keeps you going?" she asked. "Why do you keep driving yourself the way you do?"

"Debbie," Jake replied, his voice steady. "And all the ones like her. I'm going to be at this until there aren't any more Debbies or Harvey Beadles."

Carla paused, her mind racing. This was the real Jake Darrow, not the public man that Corpus Christi was familiar with. This man got tired, got lonely for his children, yet kept up his crusade because he believed in it. This was the man she wanted to interview. "Would you be willing to say that in an interview?" Carla asked. "All of it, even about getting so tired and missing your girls? I think people could understand that."

Jake thought a minute. "Why?" he asked. "Doesn't the work I've done in CCC speak for itself?"

"Of course it does," Carla replied. "But I think that if you said to them what you've just said to me, it would make people identify with you and what you're doing just that much more. You would seem more human and less like Superman."

"Is that how I come across?" Jake laughed, then he sobered. "Sure, I'll say it all on record."

"Thanks," Carla said quietly.

"So how about yourself?" Jake asked. "All we've done is talk about me tonight. Tell me a little bit about yourself, Carla."

"Oh, there isn't much to tell," she said as she glanced down at her watch and shook her head. "If you're going to get home before your girls have to go to bed, we better get going. It's getting late." She looked out over the bay, the water almost purple in the deepening twilight.

Jake nodded and signaled for the check, wondering for a moment why she had not wanted to tell him anything about herself. He felt a little odd. She knew all about him, and he didn't even know where she was from or if she had ever been married. They left the restaurant a few moments later and drove in silence toward Carla's apartment. The sky was almost dark and the light from a nearly full moon turned the water of the bay into shimmering velvet. Carla could feel the blood start to pound in her veins at Jake's nearness. The last time they had been alone together, he had kissed her and she had welcomed the embrace. She had been drinking that night, of course, but she wanted to kiss him just as badly now, and tonight she was stone-cold sober. She glanced over at Jake and saw that he was gripping the wheel tightly.

Jake parked in front of her apartment and got out to open her door. He slid his arm around Carla's shoulders and pressed her close to him, then walked with her up the stairs and waited patiently while she found her key. "Thank you for taking pity on a lonely man and having dinner with him," he said as Carla pushed open her door.

"It was my pleasure," she replied, her voice thick and deeper than usual from the tumult of emotion that was running through her.

Jake followed her inside and pulled the door shut behind him. "I can't stay, but if I don't kiss you just once tonight I'm going to go out of my mind," he said as he drew Carla to him, sliding both arms around her shoulders and pressing her close to his body. "I need to touch you, Carla," he whispered as his broad hands outlined the bones in her slender shoulders.

"I need to touch you too," Carla whispered, her eager fingers threading their way through his hair. Slowly, slowly their mouths drew closer, then Jake groaned and met Carla's lips with his own, his mouth opening to hers and his teeth meeting her lips. Carla opened her mouth to his and her tongue met his in an erotic duel. Shivers of delight coursed down her back and into her legs as Jake caressed the fine bones of her neck and shoulders, and ran a finger down her spine. He pressed her to the length of his virile body, making her aware of every bone and muscle of his chest and hips. Carla felt the evidence of his desire grow against her, but instead of feeling embarrassed the sensation gave her a feeling of sweetness, of power. Jake Darrow wanted her tonight. His body was proof enough of that.

Jake deepened the kiss until Carla thought she would faint with pleasure, then he withdrew his mouth from hers and kissed her cheeks, her temple, her jawline, her eyelids, every inch of her elegant face. "You're a tall woman," he whispered when he reached up to kiss her forehead.

Carla kicked off her shoes and stared up a couple of inches into Jake's eyes. "Not all that tall," she protested as she reached up and pushed the iron-gray lock off Jake's forehead.

"Yes, you're almost as tall as I am," he said as he bathed her forehead in light sweet kisses. "Tall and slender and beautiful," he whispered, then captured her mouth for another tender kiss. Their mouths met and mingled, the tenderness of the embrace sending a melting warmth through Carla's body as she let her hands slide down around his waist. Jake's hand crept upward and brushed first against the side of Carla's breast, then when she did not pull away, his hand became bolder, seeking out her nipple and caressing it until it was a hard bud in his hand. He touched her other breast too, bringing it to the same point of sensual awareness. Her breasts rising and falling in rhythm with her breathing, Carla realized that at this moment she could deny Jake nothing. If he moved to make her his lover, she could not and would not stop him.

Slowly, as though waking from a dream, Jake and Carla moved away from each other, first their lips separating, then their bodies, then the hands that somehow hated to break contact. "I really do have to go," Jake said as he ran his hand down the side of her face. "Thank you for a wonderful evening," he whispered as he opened the front door and closed it behind him.

"Good night, Jake," Carla whispered into the empty room. She picked up her shoes and carried them into the bedroom, then stripped off her clothes and stepped into a hot shower, glancing at her hard, tight nipples in the mirror as she passed. Oh, but she was attracted to Jake Darrow!

Carla squirted shampoo into her hair and soaped it absently. Yes, she wanted Jake Darrow. She hadn't desired a man this badly in a long time, but her desire for Jake was more than physical. And how did he feel about her? She was sure he was still in love with his dead wife. Yet he had wanted her tonight. His body had told her that much. And she didn't think Jake was the kind of man to be attracted to just any willing woman. A tiny hope flared inside Carla. Maybe, she thought as she rinsed her hair and got out of the tub, just maybe Jake Darrow wants me as much as I want him. Oh, I hope so, Carla thought as she toweled herself dry and pulled on a sleep teddy. I certainly hope so.

CHAPTER FIVE

"Are you fellas ready?" Carla asked as she drove up to Jake's home and turned off the engine on the van. Although Carla and Artie had done the tapes of Jake at work, this was the first actual interview they would be taping for the drunken driving special, and Carla and Kevin were both a little nervous. Although it really shouldn't matter, it seemed like the first interview was always crucial to the outcome of a program. If the first interview went well, it was a good omen and the rest of the special would go well too, but if not, the special was off to a bad start. Belatedly Carla wished she had taped the district attorney first, since he was very much at ease before the camera and she was assured of a good interview with him. Although she knew that Jake did well before cameras, his daughters were an unknown quantity. If they froze up, the interview would be downhill from there.

Kevin nodded and popped open the door of the van. "Hey, Artie, I'll carry the sound equipment," he volunteered as Artie struggled to carry a huge case full of lighting equipment. Carla picked up the minicam case and the three of them carried their burdens to the front door and rang the bell. In a minute the door opened and a lovely teenage girl, the girl in Jake's family portrait, motioned for them to come inside. "I'm Patty Darrow," she said sullenly as Carla and Artie trooped past her

into the entry. "And you must be Miss Jeffreys. Hello."
The girl brightened considerably when good-looking
Kevin followed them in and shut the door behind him.
"Uh, hi!" Patty said, a girlish smile lighting her face.
"I'm Patty Darrow."

"Kevin Stanley," Kevin replied as he smiled and
shook Patty's hand with his free one. "And how are you
today?"

Patty batted her eyelashes at Kevin, and Carla and
Artie struggled not to laugh out loud. "Patty, do you
know where your dad wants us to shoot this?" Carla
asked.

Patty tore her eyes away from Kevin and looked at
Carla warily. I wonder if she knows I've been out with
Jake, she thought, then dismissed the thought. Both
dinner engagements had been about the special, even if
he had kissed her until she was reeling, and Patty had
no cause for jealousy. "Patty?" she repeated when the
girl did not answer.

"Uh, he said to leave it up to you," Patty replied as
she looked from Carla to Kevin.

"Artie? Where do you think?"

Artie wandered into the spacious family room and
looked around. "This will be fine, as long as no direct
light comes in these windows," he said as he got out a
light meter and started setting up his lights. "Maybe a
few shots at the kitchen table—you know, for variety."

At that moment Jake appeared from the back of the
house accompanied by a little blond girl of about nine
or so. Jake introduced her to Carla and Kevin, and
Sonia Darrow shook Carla's hand and smiled a sweet
smile that had Carla melting on the inside. "I'm glad to
meet you," the little girl said as Carla resisted the urge
to take her in her arms and hug her. She smiled down
wistfully at the darling little girl, trying to cover up the

sadness she felt whenever she was around a child like Sonia.

"Patty, have you met Miss Jeffreys yet?" Jake asked.

Patty nodded, her dark hair bouncing around her shoulders. "Sure did, Dad."

"Okay, folks, if we could get this moving, we'll be finished before you know it," Carla said as Artie switched on the bright television lights and gestured to a sofa and chair that was sitting in front of the huge picture window.

"Mr. Darrow, I understand that Carla has already discussed with you the order in which we would like to film this, so if you're ready, would you sit down on the couch and forget the camera if you can?" Kevin said.

Jake sat down alone on the sofa and Kevin sat down in the chair across from him.

Kevin muffed his first question and had to start over, but Jake answered quietly and with self-confidence. The first few questions were impersonal, covering the organization of the CCC after Debbie Darrow's death and some of the CCC's local victories in the last year. Jake answered confidently, his dark eyes blazing as he described a few CCC victories. When those questions were completed, Carla asked Jake to get up and motioned for the girls, who sat down side by side in the space left by their father. Artie adjusted the lights and Kevin asked them a few warmup questions about their ages and school. They learned that Patty was sixteen and a junior at King High School and that Sonia was nine and in a private elementary school. He asked them a few more questions primarily to put them at ease, questions that would be edited out of the interview later.

Then Kevin moved on to the first important question. "Patty, what was it like for you when your mother died? How did you feel?"

The girl hesitated for a moment and Carla was afraid she was going to freeze up, then her voice rang out strong and steady. "I couldn't believe it," she said. "I couldn't believe that Mother was gone. I would wake up in the morning and think I had heard her call me to get up—she always did that, she would call us to get moving—only it was just my alarm clock. I'd forget she wasn't going to be there when I got home from school. Things like that."

"How do you feel about the way your mother died?" Kevin asked.

Patty thought a minute. "Angry," she said. "Angry and bitter. There was no reason for my mother to die."

Carla glanced over at Jake and saw him look at his daughter with pain in his eyes. Her first impulse was to cross the room and take him by the hand, but of course she could not do that, so she turned her attention back to Kevin and the girls.

"And how about you, Sonia?" Kevin asked. "How was it for you?"

The little girl shook her head back and forth, her long blond curls bouncing. "I didn't believe it, not really, not for the longest time," she admitted. "I thought Mom would be back."

"And now?" Kevin asked.

"I know she won't be," Sonia admitted baldly.

Kevin turned to Patty with the next question. "And how do you feel now about your mother's death?" he asked.

Patty's lips compressed into a thin line. "I miss her," the girl said bitterly. "I liked my mom—you know, not just loved her, but I liked her. I could talk to her about anything—boys, sex, college—and she listened, she really did. Now all that's gone."

Kevin seemed momentarily taken aback by the bitter-

85

ness in the girl's voice. "Can't you talk to your dad?" he asked.

"Of course, but it's not the same," the girl declared.

"Sonia, how is it for you now?" Kevin asked.

"Well, I miss the way my mom used to make fried chicken on Friday nights. You know, with lots of gravy. Mrs. Lopez, our housekeeper, can't make good chicken at all. And I miss Mom at night. She and Daddy used to come in and kiss me together. Now he comes alone."

Carla reached up and brushed a tear out of her eye.

Kevin sat back and Artie switched off the hot lights for a minute. "Jake, would you mind sitting down between the girls? Kevin has some questions for the three of you," Carla asked.

Jake obligingly moved over and slid his arm around Sonia's shoulder. The taping resumed as Kevin asked the next question. "Mr. Darrow, since your wife's death, you've organized the Corpus Christi Coalition and have made real progress here in dealing with the problem. But what about the effect on your home life? Does it take up a lot of your spare time?"

"Well, losing Debbie certainly had an effect on our home life, and yes, the CCC does take up a lot of time," Jake answered slowly. "But remember, my days are flexible and often I can either do the CCC work during my office hours or slip away for a few hours with the girls in the middle of the day. That's the advantage of being the boss, you know." He smiled faintly.

"How about you, Patty? Do you resent the time your father spends away from you?" Kevin asked.

"No. Absolutely not," Patty answered firmly.

"Why not?" Kevin asked.

"Because his work might spare some other kids from losing their mother," Patty said bitterly.

"And don't forget Daddy," Sonia piped up. "His

86

back was hurt real bad and he didn't even get to go to Mom's funeral. And he still limps, you know."

Jake glanced down at his daughter in disapproving surprise and Artie shut off the camera, then Jake looked over at Carla. "Does that have to stay in?" he asked tersely. "I would prefer that it not be public knowledge. I don't want people thinking I'm just bitter about my own injuries."

"Of course not," Carla replied as she made a note to edit out Sonia's spontaneous comment. But she couldn't help wondering why he was so touchy about his back and so unwilling to discuss it with her or anyone else. Was the memory of the accident so very painful that he just couldn't bear to face it?

"I just have one more question for Sonia, and then the girls will be finished," Kevin said. Artie started taping again and Kevin turned to the little girl. "How do you feel about your daddy's work in the CCC?" he asked. "Do you like it, or do you wish he were home more?"

Sonia looked up at her father wistfully. "I know his work is important if it can save other kids' mothers," she said. "But I do miss him when he's gone."

I bet she does, Carla thought as her heart went out to the little girl. She glanced over at Patty and her heart went out to the older one too, hiding her hurt and her loneliness for her mother behind a wall of bitterness. Carla looked away from Jake and his daughters and over at the mantel where the formal family portrait of the Darrow family held a place of prominence. In the larger version of the photograph, Patty's resemblance to her mother was striking, and Carla wondered if it ever hurt Jake to look at the girl.

Sonia and Patty got up from the couch, and Patty reminded her father that she was to spend the rest of the afternoon and evening out on Padre Island with her best friend's family. She disappeared into the back of the house, but Sonia came and stood beside Carla. "Did I do all right?" she asked.

"Hon, you did just fine," Carla assured her.

The lights were adjusted once more and the camera started rolling again, Artie's suggestion to move to the kitchen table forgotten. This interview was turning into dynamite and none of them—Carla, Kevin, or Artie—wanted to do anything to disrupt the flow of gut-wrenching honesty coming from this family. Kevin checked his cue sheet. "Mr. Darrow, I think nearly everyone in Corpus Christi is familiar with the ruckus your organization has raised, and many of our viewers are probably wondering why you're doing this. What motivates you to keep at it like you have?"

"You heard my daughters just a few minutes ago talking about how badly they miss their mother," Jake replied, his dark eyes burning. "Well, I miss her just as much as they do." Then he hesitated, and Carla was afraid he was having second thoughts about this part of the interview, but when he spoke his voice was clear and strong. "It was like losing my right arm—no, it was like losing a part of myself. Debbie and I were married for nearly twenty years and had gone together for four years before that. She was my lifeline, my anchor, my sanity in an insane world. She was the other half of me, and that half's gone now." Jake cleared his throat and his voice became husky. "It's like there's a big hole in the middle of this family." He reached up and wiped a tear from his eye, then continued, his voice stronger.

"My wife should not have died the way she did. The man who hit our car had two DWI convictions in the last two years, but he was out on the streets, with a perfectly legal driver's license and a point one-two percent alcohol content in his bloodstream. The courts had slapped his wrists with only a fifty-dollar fine on both of his previous convictions. And the sad part is that Debbie's death was not unique. I won't quote statistics, but it happens a lot."

"But the legislature has toughened the laws a lot," Kevin said. "Do you consider this progress?"

"Of course," Jake replied. "But the laws should be even tougher than they are now, and uniformly enforced."

"Mr. Darrow, a lot of people have accused you of being out for revenge for your wife's death. Can you answer that?"

"Yes, I can," Jake said. "If revenge were my only motive, I would have stopped my crusade when Debbie's killer was convicted and sentenced, which was some time ago. But the slaughter goes on, and countless other families will have to suffer the same pain of loss that we have unless somebody tries to do something about it."

"Don't you get tired of the grueling schedule?" Kevin asked.

"Of course," Jake replied. "But someone has to do something about it."

Kevin asked Jake a few more questions, but Carla hardly heard them. Her heart ached for the heartbroken man and his bruised children, yet at the same time she felt tentacles of discouragement wrapping around her. The passionate caresses she and Jake had shared last week had meant nothing. He might have felt a physical attraction to her but he was still very much in love with his dead wife. Debbie must have been something, Carla thought as she glanced at the family portrait, to inspire the kind of love Jake and the girls felt for her, and Carla didn't think she could compete with that. As Jake answered the last remaining question, Carla wished with all her heart that she could inspire that kind of love and devotion in a man, and not just the physical attraction that she and Jake had shared.

Finally Kevin finished with Jake's questions and Jake got up off the couch and walked over to where Carla and Sonia stood side by side. "Is that it?" he asked, apparently recovered from the emotional interview.

"Not quite," Carla explained as Artie adjusted the lights to fall on Kevin. Kevin then read off, one at a time, the questions he had asked Jake and the girls while Jake and Sonia watched, puzzlement in their eyes. "We'll splice the questions in later," Carla explained. "It would get boring to see nothing but your faces."

"Thanks!" Jake teased.

Artie shot some footage of the family portrait on the mantel, then he declared their afternoon's work finished and started packing up the equipment. Carla and Kevin both thanked Jake and Sonia and assured them the interview had been wonderful. Carla started to move away and realized that, without her being aware of it, Sonia had slipped her hand into hers and was holding it tightly. Her hand feels so good there, Carla thought wistfully. She squeezed the little girl's hand gently and Sonia released hers. "Would you like to see the camera before we pack it up?" Carla asked.

"Sure I would," Sonia said as Carla picked up the minicam and held it up for the girl to look through. She showed Sonia where the controls were and then she let the girl look through the viewfinder herself. Clara held onto the camera but let Sonia move it around the room and showed her how to focus it so that her father's image was clear. "This is neat!" Sonia gurgled as she looked out over the bay. "Do you ever get to work the camera?"

"No, but I used to work in front of one," Carla said as Sonia handed her back the camera.

"Naw, Carla's too pretty to hide behind one of these things," Artie said as he took the camera from Carla and placed it in its case. "I think she ought to be in front of it more often, myself."

"So do I," Sonia said shyly. "You're sure pretty."

"Why, thank you, Sonia," Carla replied, touched by the child's sincere compliment. She reached out and touched the thick curling hair that fell to the middle of Sonia's back. "You have the prettiest hair I've seen in a long time."

Sonia turned up her nose. "It gets hot," she complained.

"Go get me a barrette, punkin, and I'll get it up off your neck," Jake offered. Sonia scampered away to get a barrette and Carla bent to help Kevin with a stubborn tripod.

She snapped the tripod closed and stood up. "You have beautiful girls, Jake," she said.

"Yes, and they handled that interview like a couple of pros," Kevin said as he snapped another tripod shut. "I was afraid they would break down or something, but they had more composure than a lot of grownups I've interviewed."

"They've had to grow up a lot in the last year," Jake said as he reached around and started to rub his back.

Instantly Artie stepped up to Jake and placed his hands around the small of Jake's back. "Let me," he said as he dug his fingers into the muscles that Jake had been rubbing.

Jake looked startled but Carla and Kevin nodded encouragingly. "Let him," Carla urged, thinking of the relief Artie had brought her more than once. "He's wonderful."

Carla finished packing the equipment while Artie's magic fingers eased the pain in Jake's back. "What happened, Jake?" he asked.

"Crushed discs and a couple of broken lumbars," he said tersely.

"Should you be working out?" Carla asked.

"For crying out loud, I'm not an invalid!" he snapped. "Artie, that feels wonderful."

Carla shrugged, pretending to herself that his rejection of her concern had not hurt. Artie released Jake's back and picked up his camera case. "See you soon, Jake," he said as he walked out the door.

"Now I can understand why Miss Corpus stays," Jake muttered as Carla and Kevin laughed. Sonia bounced back into the room and handed Jake a brush and a barrette. Deftly Jake picked up the thick hair and with a few strokes of the brush and flicks of the wrist, he had Sonia's hair up in a neat ponytail. She thanked him and kissed his cheek.

"Well, punkin, it looks like it's just you and me for supper tonight," he said. "Where would you like to go?"

"For hamburgers!" Sonia said. She looked across the room at Carla. "Could Miss Jeffreys come too, Daddy?" she asked.

Jake looked a little embarrassed. "Sonia, Miss Jeffreys might have other plans tonight. A pretty lady like her doesn't sit home on Saturday night."

A lot you know, Carla thought.

Sonia whirled around. "Do you have something planned, or could you come with us?" she asked.

"Well—uh, no, but I'm sure your daddy would like to spend the evening with you," Carla stammered, not noticing the way Jake's face brightened.

92

"Yes, I would like to spend the evening with Sonia, but we'd love for you to come, Carla," Jake said.

Carla started to shake her head, but two pairs of eyes pleaded with her not to say no. "Then I'd love to come," Carla said. "Kevin, can you and Artie remember to put the tape in my desk drawer?"

Kevin nodded and thanked Jake and Sonia again. He caught Carla's eye and winked knowingly as he headed out the door. He had seen the look on Jake's face that Carla had missed.

"Thanks, Miss Jeffreys," Sonia bubbled. "And you too, Daddy. Can we go for a picnic on the beach?"

Jake looked over at Carla's dry-clean-only dress and shook his head. "Miss Jeffreys is too pretty to get all sandy on the beach, now isn't she? Better stick to a restaurant."

Carla looked down at her elegant dress. "I could go home and change," she offered.

Jake checked his watch and shook his head. "It's almost six now," he said. "It's too late for a picnic anyway. Tell you what, Sonia. We'll let you pick where you want to go."

"How 'bout the Burger Works?" Sonia asked.

Jake started to shake his head again but Carla caught his eye. "That's fine with me," she said.

"Have you ever been there?" Jake asked.

"No, but I'm sure it's fine," Carla declared firmly.

"Please, Daddy, they have the best games in town!" Sonia wheedled.

Jake shrugged his shoulders. "Burger Works it is," he declared as he picked up a set of car keys off the mantel. The three of them climbed into the front seat of the car, and Sonia chattered nonstop all the way to the restaurant. As Carla opened the car door she could hear the sound of a player piano coming out of the door. Sonia got out and scampered toward the noisy restaurant. Jake stood in the parking lot beside Carla. "I tried to tell you," he teased as Carla stared at the purple-striped awning sheltering the front door.

"Whatsmatta, 'fraid I can beat you at Pac-Man?" Carla challenged him, then they both laughed. "No, this isn't my usual sort of place, but if it pleases that darling child, it's fine with me."

Jake took Carla's hand and they walked into the noisy hamburger bar. They located Sonia in the video arcade just off the dining room, and upon extracting a promise from Jake that she could play a few games after supper, the girl accompanied them to the window where Jake placed their order. They took a number and Carla found them a table in the back of the dining room, away from the worst of the noise.

Jake and Sonia sat down across from one another, with Carla between them. "Miss Jeffreys, did your friend mean it when he said you used to work in front of the camera?" Sonia asked.

"Would you like to call me Carla like your daddy does?" Carla asked. Sonia nodded and Carla continued. "When I was younger, I used to be a television reporter. I would go around and get news stories. And then for a while I did the weather."

"Why aren't you doing that any more?" Sonia asked. "Are you getting too old?"

Jake choked on a sip of water. *"Sonia!"*

"No, Daddy, I heard my teacher telling the teacher next door that somebody wasn't on television any more because she was too old. Is that what happened to you, Carla?"

Carla burst out laughing at the look on Jake's face. "No, Sonia, I'm hardly too old to be on television," she laughed. "You have to be *really* old before you're too

94

old for television. And before you ask and embarrass your daddy," she continued as Sonia's mouth started to open, "I'm thirty-eight."

"Gosh, you sure don't look that old," Sonia said.

"You sure don't," Jake agreed as Carla blushed a little.

"So why aren't you still on television?" the little girl persisted.

"Because I like what I'm doing now a whole lot better," Carla said. Their number came over the loudspeaker and Jake got up to get their tray. "I get to meet a whole lot of interesting people now that I didn't before."

"Like who?"

"Like Alexander Haig." Sonia looked blank. "And Senator John Tower." Nothing. "And last week I met John Schneider—"

"John Schneider! Beau Duke on the *Dukes of Hazzard?* You met *John Schneider?* Tell me about him!"

Carla was busy answering Sonia's questions about the popular television star when Jake came back. They helped themselves to their burgers, Sonia never breaking off her stream of questions, then Jake slipped in a few questions about some of the other celebrities who had been on *Winners All.* Carla talked about the show for a few moments, then without Jake or Sonia quite realizing it she changed the subject and plied the little girl with questions about school and her friends. Sonia chattered happily about her teacher and her friend Babs and went on to tell Carla some of the pranks she had pulled on Mrs. Lopez, the housekeeper. But from what Sonia said, and from what she didn't say, Carla could tell that the little girl was lonely and that she hadn't gotten over losing her mother any more than her father had. Carla stared across as Sonia tried in vain not to drip the juicy burger all over the table. She's darling, Carla thought as she wiped her lips and stuffed back into her own juicy burger a slice of tomato that had fallen out. That old forgotten longing surfaced in Carla, the one that she had suppressed for a long time, and she spent a few wistful minutes wishing she had a little girl like Sonia.

They finished eating and Jake made good on his promise of a few video games. Sonia immediately challenged Carla to a game of Pac-Man. Carla, who had never played a video game in her life, held her own in a hotly contested race to eat all the dots and not get zapped by the ghosts. Jake did a marvelous job on one of the rockets-in-space games, confessing that he was a frustrated spaceship pilot who had been born two hundred years too soon. They played the machines until Jake and Carla were both out of quarters, then Jake put his arm around a sleepy Sonia and headed her out the door. "Come on, punkin, I'm taking you home," he said. Jake was pleasantly surprised at how well Sonia and Carla had taken to each other, and he wondered why a woman like Carla, who was so good with his child, had none of her own. Had she gotten too caught up in her career to make time for them, or had she just never found the right man to have a family with?

Carla expected Jake to take her home first and was surprised when Jake pulled up in front of his home instead. "Come on, child," he said as Sonia started to protest. "Mrs. Lopez will be back by now."

Sonia cut off her protest and looked from Jake to Carla. Smiling shyly, she wished Carla good night and walked with Jake up to the front door. He stuck his head inside for a minute, then he returned to the car and climbed in behind the wheel. "Mrs. Lopez will see that Sonia gets to bed," he said. "The girls pick at her, but she really does a pretty good job."

"I just love Sonia," Carla said warmly. "Jake, she's precious!"

"Yes, we were lucky to have her," Jake said as he pulled back out on the street. "Debbie and I had an Rh problem after Patty was born. We lost a son in between the girls. Sonia was born by the grace of God."

"I'm sure that makes her just that much more special," Carla said quietly. "Patty's beautiful too," she added.

"Yes, she is," Jake said as they turned off Ocean Drive and onto a side street. "Spitting image of her mother. But she's had a really hard time with Debbie's death. You heard her today."

"She probably needs time, Jake," Carla said. "You know it had to have thrown her."

"Yes, and she and Debbie were always close," he said. "Sonia's done better because she was a daddy's girl." He paused and sighed. "I worry about them both."

And who worries about you? Carla started to ask, but she left the question unvoiced. No one worried about Jake Darrow. She knew by now that there were no women in his life, and if there were relatives, they were not evident. I wish I could take care of him, Carla thought before she could stop herself.

Jake pulled up in front of her apartment. "I'll walk you to your door," he volunteered as he opened first his door, then hers. He slipped his hand around her waist and followed her into her apartment. "Thank you for coming tonight," he said. "I realize that Burger Works isn't your usual Saturday night entertainment."

"Oh, Jake, I had fun," Carla asssured him.

"And you made a lonely little girl very happy," he

said as he slipped his arm around her shoulders. "You made two lonely people happy."

"Three," Carla admitted. "There were three lonely people there tonight," she said as she reached across and kissed Jake lightly on the lips. "You, me, and Sonia."

"You know the real reason I took Sonia home first?" he asked. "I wanted to kiss you, and I didn't want Sonia to watch."

Carla curved her arms around Jake's neck. "In that case, I'm glad you took her home first," she murmured as she reached out and kissed Jake lightly for the second time.

"Damn, someone's got to teach you how to kiss a man," Jake said as he leaned forward and took her lips lightly with his. His kiss started out as gentle as hers had been, but he quickly deepened it, opening his lips to her and demanding that she do the same. Carla moaned and pressed herself closer to him, her fingers finding the hard ridges of the muscles in his back and digging into them. Jake's hands slid down her back, pressing her against him so that she could feel the evidence of his desire for her.

Jake slowly lifted his lips from Carla's and, without breaking most of the body contact between them, managed to guide her to the couch. "I'd sweep you up off your feet, but I can't with this damn back," he explained as he pushed her into the cushions of the couch and followed her there. She opened her mouth to speak but he covered it in a deep, sweet kiss as he bore Carla down into the soft cushions. Half sitting, half reclining, Carla kicked off her shoes and welcomed the hard warm heaviness of Jake's body as it moved against hers. She strained against him to deepen their embrace, making no protest when he started undoing the front buttons to her dress. Slowly, one button at a time, he unfastened her bodice until he had almost reached her waist, then his lips left hers and started down her chin to her neck, planting moist sweet kisses down her neck and onto her shoulders. Shivers of pleasure coursed through Carla as his invading lips worked their magic on her.

Carla's fingers unsnagged Jake's top button. "Is turnabout fair play?" she asked as she unhooked button after button, until Jake too was bare nearly to the waist. Eagerly she plunged her hands into the opened shirt and touched the wealth of dark curly hair that covered his chest. Her fingers greedy, she touched the curling hairs and found one small male nipple nestled there. Her fingertips tormented it until it was a hard ball in her hand.

"What are you doing?" Jake rasped against her throat.

"Touching you," Carla whispered. "Getting to know your body."

"As I want to get to know yours," Jake said, reaching up and unhooking the front closure of Carla's bra. Gently he laid the cups open, baring Carla's small high breasts to his eager gaze. "Beautiful, just beautiful," he said as he dipped his head and sampled one of the small tips. He teased and tormented it until it became hard in his mouth, then he trailed a row of kisses across her chest until he found the other crest. He teased that one too, until it was swollen with passion. Carla moaned and pressed herself closer to him. Madness, beautiful, beautiful madness, she thought as spasms of pleasure tore through her. Make love to me, Jake, she thought as his marauding lips teased and tormented her breasts to even greater heights of pleasure. Make me yours, she thought as his hand slid around her waist and pressed her closer to him, her own hands ruffling the iron-gray hair on the top of his head.

She's beautiful, Jake thought as his lips caressed her breasts into hard knots of pleasure. She's small and high and firm and her skin's like cream, he thought as his lips trailed from her breasts to her neck to her lips. He captured her lips in a passionate caress, pressing his chest against her breasts and feeling the hard twin knots of desire thrusting into his chest. I want her. I want to make love to her like I've never wanted—

Shaken by his thoughts, Jake abruptly broke off the kiss and moved stiffly into a sitting position, burying his head in his hands. Carla blinked and stared up at him, too bemused by passion to even sit up for a minute. She started to pull Jake back down to her, but she took one look at the misery on his face and sat up herself instead. She reached out her hand touched his arm, wincing when he flinched away. "What's wrong, Jake?" she asked as she reached up to button her dress.

"Carla, I'm sorry," Jake moaned. "I feel like a jerk."

"Why?" she asked softly. "It was beautiful."

Jake nodded. "Yes, it was, and a part of me wants to carry you off into that bedroom and make love to you."

Carla nodded. "And the other part?"

"I feel disloyal to Debbie," he murmured.

Carla swallowed the hurt that cut into her and laid her hand on Jake's arm. "I can understand that," she said quietly.

Jake sighed and patted her hand. "Thank you," he said as he buttoned up his shirt. "Not too many women would have."

"That's all right," Carla said. "And I hope that you can get over those feelings before too much longer."

She felt Jake stiffen beside her. "Why should I get

100

over feeling disloyal to Debbie?" he asked stiffly. "This *is* being disloyal to Debbie."

"No, it isn't," Carla pointed out quietly. "Debbie's gone, Jake. She isn't here to be disloyal to any more."

Jake bolted from the couch and whirled around, his face contorted with fury. "Damn it, Debbie may be gone but I still have feelings for her. And as long as I do, I'm going to feel disloyal!"

Carla stood slowly, her bare feet making her have to look up at Jake just a little. "I'm sorry you feel that way, Jake," she said calmly, masking her hurt and her anger at his words. "I really doubt that Debbie would have wanted you to turn away from caring and affection for the rest of your life, just because she's gone."

"You don't know anything about me and Debbie!" Jake snapped. "And you don't know anything about the way I feel about her, or the way she felt about me! So don't try to tell me what she did or didn't think!" Jake jerked open her front door and slammed it behind him.

Carla slid down into the rumpled cushions, still warm from Jake's hard body, and let the mask of composure slip from her face. An expression of angry pain replaced it. She stared at the front door and listened as Jake started his engine and roared away into the night. Yes, he had hurt her badly tonight, and although a part of her tried to understand his point of view, another part of her was angry, blazingly angry. What about her, Carla? Didn't she have feelings too? Didn't her needs count? She had needed Jake tonight, and he had let her down.

Carla rubbed her temples and tried to understand how Jake felt, but she couldn't quite understand his intense loyalty to a woman who had been gone for a year. He couldn't even touch another woman without feeling guilty. Carla tried to swallow her anger over his

101

rejection and made herself think of him. Would he ever be able to love another woman? Carla rubbed her temples harder as an unexpected thought crossed her mind. Would Jake ever be able to love her?

CHAPTER SIX

"Carla, what am I doing wrong?" Kevin wailed as he hung up the telephone. "This is the third time in a month Cecily has refused a date."

"Maybe she's already busy," Carla suggested as she snapped shut the minicam case.

"On *Monday?*" Kevin asked. "I think I'm getting the brushoff."

"Maybe so," Carla said, preoccupation making her distant. Today Kevin was going to interview the Tysons, and tomorrow they were scheduled to talk to the Beadles. Carla doubted the wisdom of scheduling the two interviews so closely together, but Artie was tied up all weekend with an important conference downtown and since he was Carla's favorite cameraman, she scheduled the interviews so she could use him.

"Do you think I'm getting the brushoff?" Kevin asked.

"How many times did you take her out?" Carla asked.

"That's just it," Kevin said. "I met her at a singles' bar about a month ago and have asked her out every weekend since, but she's always been busy or something."

Carla looked at her watch and then over at Kevin. "Did you just call her at home?" she asked. Kevin nodded. "At ten in the morning?" Kevin nodded again.

"And what would an ordinary working girl be doing at home at ten in the morning?"

"I dunno," Kevin admitted.

"Kevin, a working girl wouldn't be home at ten in the morning. Wake up, man! She's *married*," Carla said. "She was in that bar on a lark or something."

"Then why did she give me her number?" Kevin asked, bewildered.

"I don't know," Carla said as she handed Kevin a tripod. "Maybe she'd been drinking too much and didn't realize what she was doing. Or maybe she had argued with her husband. Here, we better get going if we're going to make it to the Tysons' by ten thirty." She looked over at Kevin's forlorn face. "Sorry, pal," she said. "Better luck this weekend."

"Yeah," Kevin replied, then his face brightened. "Anyway, I guess this is better than meeting a two-hundred-pound irate husband!" He picked up the mini-cam case and Carla shut the door of their office behind them. They met Artie at the van and Carla drove across town to the Tysons' small home. From the outside the house looked as bright and cheerful as it had before, but as Cindy showed Carla and the men inside, Carla could feel the tension and the depression that had moved into the house to stay. They crowded into the living room and Artie began setting up his lights while Kevin moved a rocking chair closer to the couch where Don and Cindy would be sitting. When Don wandered in a few moments later, Carla was shocked by the difference in his appearance. Underneath the inexpensive shirt and slacks he appeared to have lost at least fifteen pounds, and although the cut above his eye had healed, his eyes were tired and his cheeks were sunken. He's aged years in the last two weeks, Carla thought as her heart went out to the young carpenter.

Cindy returned a moment later in a different dress and with the baby in her arms. Behind her trailed a boy of about two, sucking his thumb and clutching a ragged blanket. "Donnie, get your thumb out of your mouth," Cindy admonished the little boy sharply.

"Let him alone, hon," Don said tiredly.

"But they'll take a picture of him with his thumb in his mouth," Cindy protested.

"Cindy, it won't matter," Carla said as the child clutched his mother's skirt and peered around her. Carla got down on one knee and made a funny face at the child, who laughed out loud at the silly lady.

"Come here, son," Don said as he picked up the little boy and sat down with him on the couch. Artie motioned for Cindy to sit down beside her husband with the baby, and adjusted the lights as quickly as he could, before the children got hot and tired.

"We'll get a few questions with the children on your laps," Kevin said as he settled into the rocking chair next to the couch. "Then we'll want just the two of you."

"My next-door neighbor can take the children when you're through with them," Cindy volunteered. Kevin asked them a few background questions, like how long they had been married and what Don did for a living, then Carla asked them to put the children down on the floor.

Cindy and Don both looked puzzled. "We're going to shoot a little footage of the children playing," Carla explained. "Then later we'll splice it in between your questions. That way it will look like the children are playing here in the room."

Artie and Kevin rearranged the lights and Cindy brought a few of their toys, then Artie filmed a good ten minutes of nothing but Donnie playing with his Big

Bird and Cookie Monster puppets and the baby crawling around the room and chewing on her teething ring. Carla watched with soft eyes as the children did what children do, then she looked up and caught an expression of intense pain on Don Tyson's face as he watched his children on the floor. It's beginning to sink in, she thought as she looked at his anguished face. He's beginning to realize that he might really be taken away from them.

Finally Artie turned off the camera, declaring he had enough, and Cindy scooped the children up and took them to her neighbor's while Kevin and Artie readjusted the lights. Cindy returned to the living room and sat down beside Don and slipped her hand in his, just as she had the first day Carla had talked to them. She's very dependent on him, Carla thought as she saw Don squeeze his wife's hand reassuringly. What would it be like for Cindy if Don had to go to prison?

Don and Cindy both clipped their mikes back on and Kevin sat down in the rocking chair. When Artie signaled, Kevin came on with his first question. "Don, according to your attorneys, you are planning to enter a guilty plea on your DWI charge." Don nodded faintly. "Could you tell us what prompted you to drink that much and then drive your truck?"

"I hadn't set out that afternoon to drink that much, honestly I hadn't," Don said. "I—well, I left the house about four. I just had to get away for a little while, and I thought a few beers would calm me down. So I ended up at the Last Watering Hole and started drinking. I lost track of how many beers I poured down."

Kevin glanced down at the next question but decided to put it on hold. "Why did you feel you had to get away for a little while?"

Don hesitated and Cindy spoke up. "We had been

106

arguing for most of the afternoon," she admitted in a quavering voice. "I'd been hassling Don about wanting a bigger house and a new car, and he said we couldn't afford it. I said some ugly things to him that afternoon, and I guess he just had to get away." Her eyes dropped into her lap. "I would give my eye teeth to go back and do that afternoon differently," she murmured.

Kevin turned back to Don. "But why alcohol?" he persisted. "Why not go down to the beach or something?"

"Why not alcohol?" Don countered. "It makes you forget it all for a little while." He sighed and shifted on the couch. "That's what my dad used to do when things were going bad for him. He'd go down to the local beer joint and have a few, and he would feel better."

"And how do you feel about using alcohol that way now?" Kevin asked.

"I wish to God I'd never heard of the stuff," Don said.

Kevin's next question was addressed to both the Tysons. "How do you folks feel about what happened that night?" he asked.

They looked at him as though he were crazy. "Terrible, absolutely terrible," Don admitted. "A dozen times a day I see that little car in front of me."

"He dreams about it nearly every night," Cindy said softly. She lifted her head and stared into the camera. "I feel terrible too, you know," she said. "If I hadn't been giving Don a hard time, this never would have happened."

"Don't torture yourself, Cindy," Don pleaded.

"Do you think you deserve to go to prison?" Kevin asked.

Don's eyes widened at the question and Cindy seemed to shrink into the couch. "Probably—probably

I do," he said haltingly. "But if they sentence me to prison, what's going to happen to my family?" He turned anguished eyes in Cindy's direction. "Cindy quit high school to marry me. She's never held a job in her life. What's going to happen to her and the babies? They need me."

Kevin ended the interview on that note and then Artie taped him asking his questions again. Somberly Carla and the men packed their equipment. She thanked the Tysons for their cooperation and promised them that she would do a follow-up interview after the trial, if the trial was scheduled before the show aired. Carla trudged to the van and stowed the minicam case in the back, then climbed dispiritedly behind the wheel. Artie and Kevin got in and pulled the doors shut behind them. "Fantastic interview, wasn't it?" Kevin asked.

"Yeah, if you don't mind watching people bare their private hell to the camera," Carla said.

"Hey, that's what you wanted, remember?" Kevin admonished her. "This special isn't supposed to be a piece of cake, Carla. You wanted to catalogue a little of the human suffering involved, and you did that today."

"But didn't it bother you, just a little, to talk to them, and the Darrows too, for that matter?" Carla asked.

"Of course it bothered me," Kevin replied, then he reached over and patted Carla on the arm. "We're a couple of softies who landed in the wrong business," he said as Carla nodded her head in agreement.

Carla parked the van in front of the Beadles' home and rubbed the space between her eyes. She had spent most of the previous afternoon with a technician who helped her edit the Tyson tape, and she had worked until nearly eleven writing the voice-over. She guessed she ought to be proud of the interview Kevin had obtained, but instead the haunted face of Don Tyson had kept her awake for hours once she had climbed into bed. Were the laws correct in sending him to prison? Yes, they were, she assured herself over and over. He had taken an innocent man's life, and he had to pay for that. But what about Cindy and her children? What would happen to them if Don had to go away?

Carla and the two men carried their equipment to the front door, and as they waited for someone to answer Carla noticed a gray Lincoln turning the corner and coming up the street. Was that Jake's car? As the car drew closer, Carla spotted the familiar head of iron-gray hair and her heart started to pound. They had not seen one another since the night they had taken Sonia out and he had left her apartment in anger, and Carla was unsure of how Jake was feeling about her right now.

Jake pulled his car up behind the station's van. He had been delighted when the Beadles had called him and asked him to be present at their interview. It would give him a chance to see Carla again. He had done a lot of thinking in the dark hours of the night since he had seen her last, and he was willing to concede that she might have a point. He was not old and he was certainly virile. He missed the warmth and the caring that a woman could bring to his life, even if he just wasn't ready emotionally to let another woman take Debbie's place, not even in the physical sense. But he had to admit that Carla was right. It had to come sooner or later.

But he had insulted Carla that night, and he never had quite built up the nerve to call her and tell her he was sorry. Today would be a good chance to test the waters and see if he had muddied them beyond repair, or if Carla just might forgive him. He got out of the car and walked up the sidewalk just as Susan Beadle opened the front door. "Hello, everybody," she said cordially as the four of them trooped into the small house. "Where do you want us to set up?"

Carla looked around at the small living room and family room, conscious of Jake's eyes boring into her back. "How about over here?" she asked, gesturing to the couch in the family room. "That way we can utilize some of the natural light coming in through these windows."

Artie and Kevin started setting up lights and Carla knelt down in front of the minicam case. "How are you, Carla?" Jake asked, his eyes on her neck where her hair just cleared.

"Fine, just fine," she said as she picked up the camera and straightened. She met Jake's eyes and read the sheepishness, the uncertainty there. Her eyes softened at the message they were sending to her. *I'm sorry,* his eyes seemed to say.

It's all right, hers said back to him. "Did the Beadles ask you to come today?" Carla asked.

Jake nodded. "Moral support," he said. Carla nodded and handed Artie the camera. Lenore Beadle came in and greeted everyone warmly, her natural charm evident now that some of the shock of her grief had worn off. Lenore sat down in the middle of the couch and her son, Gary, sat beside her. Susan sat in one of the lounge chairs to one side of the couch and Kevin in a rocking chair on the other.

Kevin asked them a few preliminary questions, some of which would be edited out later, then he moved on to the questions that would be the heart of the interview. "Mrs. Beadle, how has losing your husband the way you did affected your family?"

Carla stood quietly beside Jake as Lenore Beadle described the pain and anguish of waking up without her husband of twenty-five years. She described exactly the same kind of hurt and loss that Jake had portrayed for the camera so vividly just a couple of weeks earlier, only Lenore's grief was fresh since she hadn't had time to come to terms with her loss. She was overcome by tears once, and Artie shut off the camera to give her a few minutes to compose herself. Carla's heart went out to this grieving woman just as it had to the Tysons.

Finally Lenore composed herself and Kevin went on with the interview. "Mrs. Beadle, how do you feel about the way your husband died?" he asked.

Lenore's eyes hardened with anger. "Harvey was murdered, same as if that young man had shot him with a gun," she said.

"That's right," Susan said bitterly.

"But the young man who hit your husband had no intention of killing anyone that night," Kevin said.

"Maybe he didn't intend to, but he did," Lenore said baldly. "Harvey didn't intend to die that night, either."

"So what about you and your children?" Kevin asked. "How are you coping with what has happened?"

"We're going on, just like Dad would have wanted us to," Gary said proudly. "Susan and I both got jobs at night to help out with the groceries, and Mom's working at a new job."

"We miss Daddy real badly, but we're going to make it," Susan said.

"My children have been wonderful," Lenore volunteered. "I don't think I could have made it without them." She paused and looked across the room at Jake. "We've joined the CCC," she said. "We want to do what we can to see that this kind of thing is brought to a stop."

Carla stood beside Jake, her mind in a whirl. She

111

wholeheartedly believed in what Lenore, Jake, and the CCC were doing, yet was it possible, just by tougher laws and longer sentences, to stop the carnage on the streets and highways? Wouldn't there always be a Don Tyson who was drinking for a foolish reason, who didn't know when to stop, who didn't realize when he was simply too inebriated to drive a car? Were laws and courts the solution to the problem?

Artie filmed Kevin asking his questions, then Carla thanked the Beadle family for a good interview. The doorbell rang and Susan went to answer it, returning with a tall young man in jeans and sneakers. The young man seemed vaguely familiar to Carla, but she could not place him. He greeted Lenore and Gary and promised that he would not keep Susan out too late. The girl picked up a packed beach bag and kissed her mother on the cheek before she left with the young man.

Lenore smiled as the door shut behind the young couple. "He's such a nice young man," she said approvingly. "He's been wonderful to Susan."

"He seems familiar, somehow," Carla said. "I feel like I've seen him before."

"He's one of the officers who answered the call the night of the accident," Jake said quietly.

"Of course," Carla replied. "Susan was sitting on the bench crying and he was trying to talk to her."

Artie and Kevin made quick work of the equipment, since *Winners All* aired in just an hour. Carla told Lenore how glad she was to see the Beadles putting their lives back together, and Lenore shot a grateful look over toward Jake. "Mr. Darrow's a lot of the reason we're doing this well," she said. "He's talked to us several times, and he gave me a job in his downtown store."

"I'm sure that does help," Carla said.

112

"How is the show coming along?" Jake asked. "Do you have much more to do on it?"

"It's coming along nicely," Carla said. "We've done most of the taping, and now I have to sit down and write the voice-overs. We're well within schedule."

"How have the interviews gone?" Jake asked.

"Terrific," Carla replied. "Say, would you like to see some of the tapes sometime? They've all been great."

"Sure," Jake replied. "I'm free tonight. Would that be a good time for you?"

"Tonight will be fine," Carla said. "The show is over at five. Why don't you come about then?"

"Why don't I come at five thirty and bring you some supper?" Jake suggested. "Wouldn't want you to dry up and blow away." He winked and left.

A few moments later Carla followed Kevin and Artie to the van. Had she done the right thing in offering to show Jake the tapes? Normally she let no one but Paul Simmons and the technicians at the station see a work in progress, but Jake had helped her so much, letting him see the tapes seemed only right. Besides, she was proud of them. She had captured on film the anguish of the grief-stricken Beadles, the guilt and pain of the Tysons, the burning urgency that drove Jake Darrow. She was proud of what she had done, and she could hardly wait to show him, to hear his reaction.

Jake walked through the door of Carla's office promptly at five thirty, carrying a purple-striped sack that smelled tantalizing. Carla looked at the bag and laughed out loud. "Burger Works?" she asked.

Jake looked down at the bag and laughed ruefully. "I know, I know, but they do make about the best hamburgers in town," he said as he put the bag down on Carla's desk and pulled up Kevin's chair. Carla cleared away the papers that littered her desk and stuffed them into a desk drawer as Jake opened the bag and spread their feast before them. Carla stuck a straw down the hole in the plastic cover and sipped her soda gratefully. "This is welcome about now," she said, unwrapping the hamburger.

"I missed lunch," Jake admitted as he bit into his hamburger. "I was talking to the family that lost their teenage daughter last week."

"There's been another death?" Carla asked as she picked up a French fry and bit it in half.

"Yes, out on the causeway," Jake said. "It happened about ten in the evening."

Paul Simmons stuck his head around the door. "Jake, I thought I saw you come in," he said, walking into Carla's office and pulling up a chair. Jake set his hamburger down and extended his hand to Paul. "So how have things been going for you and the girls?"

Carla listened while Jake told Paul all about Patty's science fair project and Sonia's progress in math, then Paul launched into a tale about the science fair project his son had done five years ago. Jake and Carla sneaked each other amused looks as Paul rambled on about how great a project it had been and how the judges had thought so too, then he launched into a diatribe on the problems in public school education. Carla and Jake smiled and nodded and umm-hummed in all the right places as they finished their burgers and fries. Carla wadded up the papers and threw them into the wastepaper basket as Paul rambled on. Finally Jake sneaked a look at his watch and stood up. "Uh, Paul, it's been great talking to you, but I need to be getting home to the girls as soon as I've seen the tapes Carla said she was going to show me."

"Oh, is Carla going to show you the tapes on the

114

special?" Paul asked. "I've only seen the ones she made of you and the girls, but if the rest are anywhere that good she's got a fantastic program in the works. It's going to be every bit as good as the one she did last year on those two boys. She won an award for that one, did you know?"

Somehow Paul managed to ramble on for ten more minutes cataloguing Carla's producing accomplishments, which embarrassed Carla a little, then he left them after extracting a promise from Jake that he and the girls would join the Simmons family next week for dinner. After Paul left, Carla and Jake looked at each other and started to laugh. "That guy does love to talk," Jake said.

"His nickname around here is Old Windbag," Carla admitted as she entered the control room. The evening news was long over and the set was deserted. A lone technician sat staring at the network sitcom, ready to cut to a local commercial when he received the cue. Carla opened a cabinet and pulled out a videotape canister, then she motioned for Jake to follow her out of the room. "I hate to disturb Jerry by playing it in there. We can use another player in the back."

Jake followed her through the building to another control room that looked out on another empty set. *"Winners All?"* Jake asked as he peered into the empty studio.

Carla nodded. "We had a good show today," she said idly as she put the tape into the machine. "A plastic surgeon talked about nose jobs." She switched on a monitor and watched the flickering images. "Are you interested in seeing our sage and illustrious DA?" Carla asked.

Jake shook his head. "I could quote him." He assumed a pinched expression. " 'We're prosecuting all drunken driving cases to the extent of the law,' " he said ponderously as he looked down his nose.

Carla laughed out loud. "Have you ever thought of replacing Rich Little?" she asked, punching a button on the console in front of her. The image of the district attorney flashed by as she sped past it, then she released the button and backed up a little when she spotted the Darrows' family room. She turned up the volume and moved aside so that Jake could see himself on the tape. "I've written the voice-over for this section of the tape, but Kevin hasn't taped it," she said as Jake stared at the miniature version of himself on the monitor.

"I look fat," he said suddenly.

Carla laughed. "The camera does put on pounds," she said. "Now look at Kevin, and compare his image there to the way he really looks."

Jake nodded his head. "I see what you mean," he agreed. He stared at himself as he told Kevin about organizing the CCC, and then he watched his daughters as they told Kevin how badly they missed their mother and what losing her had done to them.

"They came across well," Carla murmured as Jake nodded. They watched in silence as the tape cut back to Jake by himself. Jake stared at his image, his face a study in conflicting emotions as he watched himself describe the pain of losing his wife and his determination to see that the slaughter be stopped. He stared down with burning eyes at the small screen.

As the tape flickered off, he turned to Carla, bemusement across his face. "I had no idea I came across like that," he said as Carla unloaded the tape from the player and inserted another one.

"Why do you think you've been able to accomplish so much in so short a time?" Carla asked, switching on the tape. "I haven't had time to edit this tape of the Beadles," she said. "What you see is what we filmed."

Nevertheless, Jake could see the potential in the Beadle tape as the family members poured out their grief and anguish at the loss of their husband and father. With the proper editing, this portion of the show would be a powerful message as to what drinking and driving could do. He watched the tape with interest, and he felt deep admiration growing in him for the woman who was putting this together. She was doing a public service and didn't even realize it.

"That tape was fantastic," Jake said as the images flickered off the monitor.

"It will be once we've edited it," Carla agreed. "The Beadles responded like pros." She removed the Beadle tape and inserted the one she had made of the Tysons. "I stayed here half the night to edit this one," she said as she switched the tape on. "In a way I'm proudest of this."

Jake watched the screen with interest as a nice-looking, clean-cut young man and his pretty wife came onto the screen, each holding a young child. Jake watched as Kevin asked the man what had happened the day of the wreck, and as he watched the tape his interest slowly turned to anger. My God, Carla couldn't show this to the world! Why, she made this couple seem human! Jake nearly gagged as he watched the way she had spliced in the children crawling around on the floor. Good grief, this man was a killer, not a Boy Scout! He didn't deserve this kind of sympathetic treatment from the media.

Unaware of Jake's mounting anger, Carla switched off the tape player and the monitor and took out the Tyson tape. "You know, I feel as sorry for them as I do

117

the Beadles," she said, putting their tape back in its holder.

"Good God, how can you say a thing like that!" Jake demanded as he swung her around and stared angrily into her face. "That man's a killer, and you have him there on the screen looking like Mr. Wonderful. Do you have any idea how that will affect our chances of a conviction?"

Baffled, Carla stared into Jake's face. "What's with you?" she asked. "I taped what I found. And I found a rather nice young man who went out and drank too much and killed a man and who is now going to have to pay the price. What did you think I was going to find, some kind of monster?"

"Damn it, Carla, what's the matter with you?" Jake yelled. "You ask me and the Beadles to appear on your precious production and we agree, thinking maybe if we do that we can help prevent the kind of pain and suffering we've known, and then you have the gall to make that kind of tape of the killer and put it on the same show that we're on. No way, Carla. You're not using that tape of Tyson."

"The hell I'm not!" Carla snapped, also angry and not bothering to hide it. "That tape of the Tysons is going to do more good than a thousand tapes of you and the Beadles, and let me tell you why. Because drunken drivers are not monsters, not derelicts. They're people just like you and me. And if the public can see somebody just like them who's killed someone and is now in trouble, it might make them think the next time they're about to drink and drive."

"That's a stack of baloney," Jake thundered. "I mean it, I'm not appearing on the same program as that murderer. I'll sue if you use Tyson's tape with mine."

"Fine," Carla said calmly. "I'll pull your tape and

118

then say that the CCC refused to appear on the program because we had included an interview with a drunken driver."

"And make us look like a bunch of fanatics!" Jake shouted.

"Well, aren't you?" Carla asked nastily. "You're so wrapped up in your own feelings of hate and bitterness that you refuse to admit that maybe, just maybe, a drunken driver is a person too. Look, you knew what I was going to do before you ever agreed to do the interview. I laid it all out for you that first night, and if the knowledge that Don Tyson is a human being just like you and the Beadles doesn't please you, then that's just too damn bad, because he goes on the program. With you or without you."

"All right, use my tape! Do your damned show!" Jake thundered, his voice filled with bitterness. "Whitewash that damned killer into a normal human being if you so desire. Ruin our chances of a conviction if that's what you want!" He stopped and swallowed, then spoke again, his voice barely above a whisper. "Maybe someday you'll feel a little of the grief you're so damned skilled at filming in others. And then you may change your tune," he said as he slammed out of the room.

Carla stared at the closed door, then turned the machine back on and ran the Tyson tape again. No, she had not portrayed Don as a Boy Scout, she had not slanted the interview to make him appear in a favorable light. She had been honest and objective in her reporting, and the bias had been in Jake's eyes only. She switched off the machine, took the tapes back to the main control room, and left the building. I had no idea, Carla thought as she drove home through the purple dusk. I had no idea he was so bitter. And that bitterness is such a waste, she thought angrily, no matter how justified it is. She couldn't help but feel that he was carrying it too far.

On entering her apartment, Carla poured herself a glass of wine and sat down in her lone folding chair on the balcony, staring at her very distant view of the bay. She had known that Jake was hurt and grieving, of course, but tonight was the first time she had seen the depths of his bitterness and hatred. He really hates drunken drivers, she thought with a shiver. He simply can't see them as fellow human beings who have done something wrong.

Carla sipped her wine and let the warm sea breeze blow in her face. Would Jake ever be able to get over that kind of soul-corroding bitterness? Carla wondered as she took a deep breath of the tangy salt air. Would he ever be able to feel any compassion for drunken drivers or their families? Would he ever be able to get over his feelings of betrayal every time he touched another woman?

You better watch it, Carla, she told herself as she watched the waves whitecap in the bay. You're starting to fall for that man in a very big way. Carla shook her head at her stupidity. She was starting to fall in love with a man who was not only still in love with his dead wife, but who was filled with hate and bitterness. And she didn't need that in her life. She had already been through the wringer once, a long time ago, and she didn't need to go through it a second time with Jake. And she had needs too, physical and otherwise, that Jake in his grief was not able to meet. Yet there was something about him that made it impossible for her to turn away. Oh, Jake, I could love you so easily, she thought. And you're probably the last man I ought to be falling for.

CHAPTER SEVEN

Kevin bit his lip to keep from laughing as he walked into his and Carla's office. "Carla, where did you find that one?" he asked as Carla buried her head in her hands and shook it back and forth. "It was like pulling teeth to get him to answer a simple question."

Carla groaned as she lifted her head. "And he was so cute and funny at the party last month!" she wailed. The young accountant had been entertaining and witty last month when he had told Carla all about tax shelters, but today on the show he had stiffened up and had answered Kevin in monosyllables, then tripped on the edge of the platform as he left the set. "Paul's going to have something to say about this one," she predicted.

"Oh, not more than two hours' worth," Kevin predicted cheerfully as the telephone rang. He picked it up and identified himself, listened a moment, then handed the receiver over to Carla. "Jake Darrow," he mouthed. "For you."

Carla stared at the receiver as though it were a snake in her hand. She had not heard from Jake since they had exchanged such bitter words last week, and since she didn't need to tape him any more she had thought that their dealings were over. She was still angered and appalled by the hatred and bitterness she knew he felt toward drunken drivers, and she was afraid that bitterness now spilled over onto her. Hesitantly she reached out and took the receiver from Kevin, wondering if Jake had decided to pull his tape after all. "Hello, this is Carla," she said softly.

"I'll be in Austin tomorrow to lobby for that new bill on DWI penalties," Jake said briskly, no warmth in his voice. "If you think you could use some footage in your special, you and your crew are welcome to come."

Carla thought for a moment and nodded. "We can make it. *Winners All*'s being preempted by a telethon."

"Fine. I'm staying at the Driskill. I'll meet you in the lobby at eight A.M." With that, Jake hung up brusquely. Well, he's still angry, Carla thought as she put the telephone back in the cradle. Tough. But if Jake was still angry with her, why had he asked her and the crew to film him in Austin? Well, she realized after a moment's reflection, if she was going to be there by eight in the morning, she didn't have time to sit around and analyze Jake's motives.

Carla told Kevin the news and Kevin went in search of Artie, who was willing to make the trip if he could take his girl friend along. Much to Carla's amazement, Paul offered to put them up in the Driskill at the station's expense if they would take their own vehicles, since the van was already booked for the next day. Nobody objected to a night in the luxurious old hotel, so Carla called and reserved three rooms. She then headed home and showered, packed, and was on the road in less than an hour.

Carla had a lot of time to think during the five-hour drive to Austin, but she was no closer to guessing Jake's motives when she pulled up in front of the hotel than she had been when she had left her apartment. She had no idea what had prompted Jake's invitation, especially since his tone of voice had made it clear that he was still angry with her. Who knows? she thought as a uni-

122

formed bellhop carried her bag and makeup case from her car to the desk. Maybe he thought he could impress her with how hard he and his organization were working. Maybe he thought he could convince her not to use the Tyson tapes. Whatever the reason, Carla was committed to spending another day in his company, a fact that did very little for her peace of mind as she undressed and wrapped herself in her lacy robe. Since she had skipped supper, she ordered a sandwich and a glass of wine from room service. That plus the exhaustion of driving over two hundred miles after putting in a full day's work put her to sleep the minute her head touched the pillow.

As they had arranged before leaving the station, Carla met Kevin and Artie in the hotel's coffee shop at seven thirty. They had eaten and were ready when Jake stepped off the elevator promptly at eight. Jake greeted them all politely but with no warmth, and Kevin and Artie, who knew about Jake's anger and were proud of their part in the tapes, responded in kind. Carla nodded her head at Jake's greeting and got out her notebook. "Who are you scheduled to meet with today?"

"I thought you might be able to use some tapes of actual lobbying in your special. Senators Williams and Cantu have agreed to meet with me on camera, as has Representative Richardson. I'll be talking privately with a couple of others later in the day." He looked down at his watch. "I'll meet you at the capitol in a half hour." He turned on his heel and walked out the door.

Artie whistled under his breath. "It may be the first week of June but I can feel the icicles," he said.

"That's all right, I think he felt a few of ours too," Carla said dryly.

"Carla, did you explain to him just what you were planning when he agreed to the filming?" Artie asked.

123

"Of course she did," Kevin defended her hotly. "Darrow just thought we would be doing an hour-long show praising him and his organization. When he found out there was a little bit of real journalism going on, he got mad."

Carla shook her head slowly as Artie and Kevin each picked up a camera case. "No, I don't think he expected it to be the Jake Darrow Hour," she said. "I just don't think he knew what to expect."

They piled into Artie's ancient station wagon and drove up the street a few blocks toward the capitol. Artie spent another ten minutes looking for a parking place, but they were waiting on the steps when Jake strode up the lawn of the building. Artie shot some footage of Jake coming up the steps, then Jake motioned for them to follow him into the stately capitol building. In just a few minutes they were setting up lights in Senator Williams's office. The senator, an arch-conservative from West Texas, greeted them all warmly and answered a few questions on tape for Kevin. Then he and Jake settled in facing one another across the senator's wide desk.

Jake talked to the senator for the better part of an hour. Artie filmed the first twenty minutes of it, then at Carla's signal he turned off the camera and lights. Senator Williams was openly sympathetic to Jake's cause, and most of the meeting was a strategy session in which the two men planned the upcoming fight in the legislature for an even tougher law for first-time DWI offenders. Although she was still angry with Jake, Carla had to admire the way he and the senator planned to promote the bill.

They left the senator's office around ten thirty. "Has Senator Williams always been that supportive of tough drunken-driving legislation?" Carla asked as Jake pulled the door to the outer office shut behind him.

Jake nodded. "Of course, considering that he does represent the Bible Belt, it would be political suicide not to."

Carla shrugged. "Who cares, as long as he supports the bill?" she asked.

Jake nodded and grinned ever so slightly. "I guess you're right," he conceded. "Now, I've dealt with Senator Cantú before. This fellow's a whole different ball game."

Senator Cantú greeted them with the typical politician's smoothness, and Carla remembered reading something about his lackluster record after two terms in the legislature and also remembered, as Kevin asked him a few questions, that his district was well within the Corpus Christi viewing range. All he wants is free publicity, she thought halfway into the discussion. He interrupted Jake continually, hogging the spotlight until Carla longed to snap off his balding head. He proclaimed that he was certainly aware of the problem and told of how he had worked so hard to get the last law passed. He promised Jake that he would do what he could to see that the new law was firm and fair, just so long as it did not infringe on the personal rights of his constituents. Carla racked her brain but could not remember what his part in the last bill had been.

Finally he and Jake concluded their discussion and the smiling senator showed them out the door. "Is it my imagination, or does that guy reek of insincerity?" Carla asked. "What was his position on the last bill?"

"He's the bastard who watered it down at the last minute," Jake said derisively. "Said it wouldn't have passed otherwise."

"And would it have?" Artie asked as they trudged down the hall.

Jake paused as they waited for an elevator. "I think so," he said as he checked his watch. "My next appointment's not until one," he said. "Want to grab a bite to eat somewhere?"

Carla and her crew nodded. Looks like the icicles are thawing a little, she thought as Jake pointed to a legislative watering hole across the street. Artie and Kevin locked their equipment in the back of the station wagon and soon they all were seated in the crowded restaurant. Over steaks and salads Jake was cordial and they responded in kind, and by the end of the meal Carla thought they were back on the same easy footing they had been on before she had shown him Don Tyson's tape. Carla couldn't help but be glad that they were on friendly terms again. Their argument had upset her badly, and although she had in no way changed her position on Don Tyson or on using the tape she had made of him, she did not want continued hostility between her and Jake.

"So what's Representative Richardson like?" Carla asked as they walked back up the steps and entered the capitol. "Is she a sincere backer or just another publicity hound?"

"I don't know," Jake admitted. "She's new and I haven't had occasion to talk with her yet."

"Oh, sure, she's the widow of that representative who died last year," Carla mused. "She was appointed to his seat and then went out and won it on her own."

"Yes, and I don't know whether she has ideas of her own or if she's just the ghost of her late husband," Jake said. "He was very ambivalent on the issue."

They were greeted by Fayrene Richardson herself, a tall, statuesque redhead in an expensive designer suit and a ring on her finger that cost more than Carla's yearly salary. But her smile and her interest were both genuine, Carla had to admit as she listened to Jake and her talk about the legislation that would come before the House soon. Representative Richardson's questions were sharp and Jake's answers concise yet persuasive, and by the end of the hour, when the representative pledged her vote to the bill, Carla had decided not only was Fayrene Richardson not a ghost of her late husband, but she would in time prove herself to be twice the representative he had ever thought of being. It had been a pleasure to watch her and Jake as they exchanged ideas.

Carla thanked the representative for letting them tape the sequence, then they left her office and walked down to the end of the corridor. "I'm using some of her and Senator Williams in the special," Carla said. "We'll cut a little of the day-in-the-life footage."

"What? Nothing of that marvelous Senator Cantu?" Jake teased.

"And give him the free PR he was after? Not on your life." Carla laughed. "Is that it for the day?"

"Well, for you it is," Jake replied. "These last two appointments declined to be taped, although they had no objection to having a person from the media present. Say, why don't you stay, Carla? These talks today were mild compared to some I've had."

Carla glanced over at Kevin and Artie. "Well, I do have my car," she said. "I could drive home afterward, I guess." Carla did not relish the thought of driving home late, but she hated to miss out on these other interviews.

"Let me call Paul and let him know my change of plans," Carla decided. A collect call to Paul confirmed that he would be happy for her to stay on, so she bid

Kevin and Artie good-bye and followed Jake back down the hall and into another suite of offices.

Senator Kaye's secretary put a call through to her boss, then disappeared into his office with a steno pad. Jake leaned back in his chair and closed his eyes. "I doubt Kaye's going to come around, and I wouldn't even bother with him if I didn't think every vote was important," Jake said tiredly.

"You did wonders today with Fayrene Richardson," Carla said softly.

"Yeah, but she has a mind of her own," Jake said. "Wait till you hear this guy."

The secretary returned shortly and motioned for Jake and Carla to go in. For the next hour and a half Carla listened to enough of Senator Kaye's mealy-mouthed sidestepping to last her a lifetime. Of course Senator Kaye agreed with Jake, but after all he represented a tourist center and his constituents' livelihoods would be endangered if people didn't feel free to have a good time. Jake pointed out that the law being statewide would not affect just Kaye's district and that his constituents would be protected by the law, but at the end of the talk the senator would only concede to give the bill very serious consideration. Jake's lips were pressed tight as he left the office.

"He's scared to death of losing a lousy vote or two," he muttered as they headed for a water fountain. "And he's not representing his constituency either. A poll taken by their antidrunken driving group indicated that a vast majority of his constituents were in favor of a tougher law."

"Does he realize this?" Carla asked.

"Of course, but it isn't going to hurt him to sit up on the fence, now is it?" Jake replied tiredly. He rubbed the back of his neck and winced as a pain shot through his lower back. "I don't know why I saved this guy for last," Jake said as they walked into the office of Representative Malley.

At least this one doesn't beat around the bush, Carla thought a few minutes later as she listened to Jake and the representative. Malley, who looked and talked like a contestant for a J. R. Ewing look-alike contest, propped his feet on his desk and told Jake flat-out that he would never vote for a stronger bill to punish drunken drivers. He said that where he came from, a man who couldn't hold his liquor knew better than to drink with the big boys and that a man who could would be able to drive his car afterward. He said that a man had a right to drink as much as he damn pleased and that he would go on record as defending that right. Jake's tight lips were the only outward sign of his anger, but Carla sensed that he would have loved to punch Representative Malley in the face.

"I can't believe that guy," Carla said as they stepped out of the capitol building. The late-afternoon sun beat down hotly on the two of them, but Carla was so angry she didn't even notice. "Imagine, he really believes that people—no, make that *men*—have a right to go out and drink and then drive a car!"

"Calm down, Carla," Jake said tiredly as he put his hand up to her neck and rubbed it gently. "He's not alone, believe me. This way," he said, gesturing down the street. "I walked this morning."

Carla wrapped her fingers around his arm and lengthened her stride a little to match his. "You mean there are really other people out there who feel like he does?" she asked.

"Oh, yes," Jake assured her. "Remember, Texas has made a tradition of the he-man macho image. You know, the tough hombre who could hold the most liquor and love the most women and shoot a gun the straightest was the most admired. A lot of that attitude is still around. Those people consider it an affront to their personal freedom if you try to infringe on that hard-drinking image."

"I never would have believed it," Carla admitted as they lapsed into silence on the way back to the hotel. It's no wonder Jake felt bitter sometimes, Carla thought, if he comes across that attitude very often. The frustration Jake was bound to feel after an afternoon like this one would make a saint angry, and it was no wonder that after a while he had lost his objectivity and forgotten that drunken drivers were human too. Although Carla had not changed her mind in the least about using the Tyson tapes in her program, after today she could understand Jake's objections to them a little better.

Jake ushered her into the hotel lobby and gave her arm a little squeeze. "Would you like to have dinner with me tonight?" he asked as his tired eyes traveled over her face. "I'd like the company."

"I would too," Carla agreed, glad she had packed a lace-paneled sundress just in case. "I'll meet you in—what? Thirty minutes?"

"Make it an hour," Jake suggested. "I need to call the girls and after the day you put in, you could probably use a good long soak in the tub!"

"An hour, then," Carla said as she headed toward the elevator, a slight smile on her face at the prospect of dinner out with Jake.

Carla sank down into one of the plush chairs in the lobby and watched the patrons of the elegant old hotel as they came and went, trying to picture what the place must have been like during its heyday many years ago.

She had been sitting for just a few minutes when the elevator opened and Jake stepped out. His hair was still damp from the shower. He had changed into a navy sport coat and charcoal slacks but had skipped a tie this evening, and a tantalizing column of tanned throat peeked out of his conservatively buttoned shirt. He smiled as he spotted Carla, but his face was just as tired and discouraged as it had been when he left her an hour ago. He extended his hand and as she stood she had to fight the urge to plant a kiss in the middle of his throat.

"Sorry I'm late," Jake said as she slipped her arm into his.

"No, I was early," Carla said as they headed for the door. "I was entertaining myself by making up stories about the people who were walking by."

"Oh? What kind of stories?" Jake asked, steering her down the street.

"See that little couple over there?" Carla asked.

Jake nodded. "You mean the little old man in the bowler hat and the lady in gloves?" he asked.

"Yes, them," Carla replied, getting into the spirit of the game. "Well, they may look like an innocent old couple to you, but they're really international jewel thieves. They can get into a locked hotel room faster than you or I can get into our locked cars."

"And how about that couple over there?" Jake asked, pointing to a young couple across the street unfolding a stroller for their toddler.

"They make dirty films at night after the kids are asleep," Carla replied, deadpan.

Jake laughed as they rounded a corner and continued walking. "And her?" Jake asked, nodding toward a rather grimy-looking young woman who was crossing the street.

"Local president of the Moral Majority," Carla said. "I gather we're walking tonight?"

"I hope you don't mind," Jake replied. "The restaurant's only a couple of blocks away, and after a day like today, walking's sometimes the only thing that makes me feel better. Now, how about those two kids over there? Who are they?"

As Carla entertained Jake with her silly speculations, she wondered if lobbying always depressed him like this. Sure, this afternoon he had not gotten anywhere with Kaye or Malley, but he had made a real convert in Fayrene Richardson and he had mentioned several others who had come over to thinking the way he did about DWI legislation. Jake was laughing and talking and playing along with her game, but Carla could sense that inside, he was still upset about something.

Jake ushered her into a small restaurant that specialized in the continental cuisine that Carla adored. "More your style?" he teased as the headwaiter seated them at a small, candlelit table.

"I'll have you know that Burger Works made a convert that night," Carla informed him. "I've dropped by there twice when I had to work nights."

Jake closed his menu and took a sip of his water. "Do you have to work late often?" he asked.

Carla admitted that she did, and by the time the waiter had returned to take their order, they were launched into a discussion of some of the more interesting guests Kevin had interviewed on *Winners All*. Jake ordered a carafe of wine, which surprised Carla until she remembered that they hadn't driven to the restaurant. Jake laughed and talked and tried to hold up his end of the conversation, but by the time the waiter had brought her flounder and his steak Diane, he had fallen almost silent and Carla was left to carry the conversational ball alone. She tried to talk a little as she ate, but Jake's monosyllabic replies did very little to spur her on, so after a while she concentrated on her meal. In spite of the busy day he had put in, Jake was pushing his steak around his plate, and his eyes had taken on a distant cast, as though he were thinking about something else.

"Does it always get to you like this?" Carla asked softly as she nibbled on the end of a broccoli spear.

"What?" Jake asked.

"The lobbying," Carla said. "Does it always upset you this much?"

"Oh, it's never that pleasant," Jake said as he poured himself a second glass of wine and drank from it. "For every representative or senator who's behind us, they're are several more like the ones you saw this afternoon. Either they're too politically chicken to take a stand, or like Malley they hold some antiquated ideas about people having a right to get drunk and drive."

"But, Jake, you're in a blue funk tonight," Carla said. "Does it always do this to you?"

"No, it usually leaves me feeling frustrated as hell," he admitted as he finished off the wine in his glass. Perhaps spurred by the wine, he forked up a piece of steak and ate it.

"It's something else, then," Carla said. Jake nodded. "Want to talk about it?"

Jake shrugged. "It's silly, really," he said.

"Try me."

"I looked at a calendar in the room and remembered that today would have been Debbie's fortieth birthday," Jake said. "I had promised her a Caribbean cruise when she hit the big four-oh."

Carla's eyes widened with sympathy. "I'm sorry,"

she said quietly. "I would have understood if you had preferred not to come tonight."

"No, there's no point in sitting alone in that hotel room and brooding," Jake replied. "It's ironic. As crazy as I always was about her, she thought it would make a difference to me when she got older. She even made bad jokes about me trading her for two twenties when she turned forty. Then she didn't even get to make the birthday."

Carla shuddered in spite of herself, thinking of her own fortieth birthday to come in just two years. "She didn't have all that much time, did she?"

Jake shook his head. "I guess we should have gone on the cruise earlier," he said. "But we put it off until the girls were older and Debbie felt better about leaving them. We put off so many things that we should have gone ahead and done. We thought we had all the time in the world."

"But we all feel that way," Carla said. "At least we do until we have to face death."

Jake looked at her perceptively. "You've had to face it yourself, haven't you?" he asked.

Carla nodded. "Yes, once a long time ago," she said. "And it does leave you feeling differently, as you well know. But, Jake, Debbie had so much love and joy in those thirty-nine years she did have! She had you, she had her girls. She had a lot. And if her expression in that picture on your mantel is anything to go by, she was a happy woman. Think about that instead of all the things she didn't get to do."

Jake stared across the table at his dinner companion, then his hand crept out and covered hers. "Carla, you're a wonderful human being," he said softly as he gave her hand a squeeze. "You're right, and I'm feeling as sorry for myself tonight as I am for her." He finished off his glass of wine and, as he ate his steak, he talked a little bit about Debbie. Although in a way it hurt to hear Jake talk about the woman he had loved so much, Carla was glad to listen, because talking about her seemed to give him comfort.

They walked back to their hotel in the falling twilight, and as they climbed the steps, Carla caught a glimpse of them in the plate-glass windows—the elegant blonde on the arm of her distinguished dinner companion. They made a striking couple, and Carla felt an almost painful longing to be truly half of a couple with Jake, and not just a casual date.

"Would you care for another drink before you go up?" Jake asked, glancing toward the bar in the lobby.

Carla shook her head. "Thank you, no, I've had enough."

"I think I may have one more," Jake said as they asked for their room keys at the desk. "If I don't see you in the morning, I'll see you back in Corpus."

Carla nodded. "Good night, then," she said as she headed into the gift shop. She purchased the latest thriller to curl up with, since she had no desire to go out on the town by herself.

Once in her room, Carla pulled off her dress and laid it at the foot of the bed, then she slipped on her robe. She curled up in a comfortable stuffed chair and let the book take her away to a small Pacific island with a lovely young heroine, a handsome brooding hero, an evil villain, and a stash of stolen gold. The book lived up to its reputation, and a little over two hours later she closed it as the hero and heroine lived happily ever after. She set her travel alarm for seven, hoping to get back to Corpus by one or two, then on impulse called and had the desk ring Jake's room. She had not seen his car in Austin, and if he wanted to ride back with her he could save himself the cost of a flight. At least that was the reason she gave herself for calling.

The clerk at the desk let the phone ring a number of times before he gave up and disconnected the line. "I'm sorry, Mr. Darrow doesn't appear to be in," the clerk said.

"Is his key in the box?" Carla asked.

"No, it isn't," the clerk said rather primly.

I don't want to get in his room, you turkey, Carla thought. "Thank you," she said quietly as she hung up.

Carla sat on the side of the bed for a minute, thinking. Perhaps Jake was still somewhere in the hotel. The bar? Jake? Surely not, the way he felt about drinking. But that was where he had headed when she left him two and a half hours earlier. Carla bit her lip and hesitated for a minute, then she threw her dress back on and headed out the door. Jake had been very depressed when they had parted, and someone feeling as low as he was sometimes did things he wouldn't normally do. She would go and check in the bar just in case, and if she was concerned over nothing, then that was even better.

Carla strolled nonchalantly into the dim, tasteful bar. She ignored the speculative glances of some of the patrons and spotted Jake, sitting alone in the corner sipping a drink and staring straight ahead. As Carla made her way across the room, an efficient barmaid cleared three glasses off Jake's table and handed him another. No telling how many he's had, Carla thought as she slipped into a chair at Jake's table. "How are you?" she asked.

Jake turned bloodshot eyes in her direction. "Bombed," he admitted.

"*Jake,*" Carla ground out. "You're not supposed to get drunk."

"Why not?" Jake grinned defiantly. "I'm not driving,

136

am I? I'm not against getting snockered to the gills, I just don't believe you ought to do it in a car. Say, you don't have to drive either, do you? Want to get snockered with me?"

"Uh, I don't think so," Carla said as Jake picked up his fresh drink and drank deeply of it. He belched and Carla could smell the Scotch across the table.

"Jake, I think we better get you to your room," Carla suggested as the barmaid approached them. Carla shook her head at the woman and she backed away.

"But I'm not ready to go to my room," Jake protested. "I want to finish this snockering job."

"Well, for crying out loud, you don't have to do it in a public place!" Carla snapped. "Good grief, any one of a dozen legislators could walk in here right now and catch you like this. Then what do you think would happen to your effectiveness?"

Jake looked momentarily confused, then he grinned sheepishly and offered Carla his arm. "Care to see one tipsy old man to his room?" he asked.

Carla breathed a sigh of relief and took Jake's arm. Very slowly, so that Jake would not weave, they made their way out of the bar and into the elevator. Jake slumped a little as the elevator rose, but by the time they had reached his floor he was fairly steady on his feet. "See me to my door," he commanded her.

Carla nodded and followed him down the hall. Jake pulled his hotel key from his pocket, but after three unsuccessful tries he handed the key to Carla and watched as she unlocked the door and stepped inside. "Tricky lock," he explained as he followed her in. "Thanks for helping me up here." He reached out and before Carla could protest he had drawn her to him, his lips bearing down on hers. He bent her head back and kissed her thoroughly, his tongue touching her lips, her teeth, her tongue. Caught off-guard, Carla made no protest as his kiss went on and on, igniting her passions as well as his. They kissed and clung for long moments, and as Carla felt the evidence of his desire for her swelling against her body, she decided that Jake wasn't as drunk as he appeared to be. Finally, when she knew that she was just inches from total surrender, Carla murmured and shook her head. "No," she pleaded. "Please, no."

"Yes, Carla, please yes," Jake moaned as his hands gripped her shoulders in a gentle yet firm grip. "I want to kiss you and hold you."

"No, Jake, you've been drinking," Carla murmured as she tried to pull herself out of his arms. "You don't know what you want. You need to go to bed."

Jake pulled her close to the hard warmth of his body and held her gently against him, swaying just a little from the Scotch. "Carla, can you feel my heart beating?" he asked. "Do you know how much I want you?" His eyes pleaded with hers to understand. "Do you have any idea how badly I want you tonight?" As he cupped her head and started to pull his lips toward hers Carla could feel herself weakening. Dear God, she did want him. She wanted him more than she had any other man in her entire life. But was making love to her the right thing for Jake tonight?

Her eyes must have reflected her indecision, for Jake cradled her head next to his and rocked her back and forth. "You want me as badly as I want you," he crooned as he held her in his arms. "I can feel your desire just as you feel mine." He leaned forward and entwined his lips with hers, just nibbling her lips at first, then increasing the pressure until they were locked from their heads to their knees in a torrid embrace. Carla slid her arms up and around Jake's shoulders and tangled her fingers in his hair, pressing his head closer to hers as his hands closed around her waist. Jake kissed her for long moments as his hands tightened against her spine and held her to him. Then he released her lips and slid his lips to her temple. "Please," he begged as his tongue teased the lobe of her ear. "I need you tonight. Please."

He needed her. The thought echoed through her mind as he brought their lips together again. He needed her, and perhaps she could be some comfort to him. And he was right, Carla thought as her hands ran down the strongly sinewed muscles of his back. She did desire him, every bit as much as he desired her and more than she had desired any other man in her life. If giving way to that desire could bring the man she thought so much of a measure of comfort and relief from the torment of his grief, then she would do it. She would gladly take Jake Darrow to bed and let him make love to her.

Jake's lips left hers and sought the warm hollow of her throat. "I would love to make love with you," Carla rasped out as Jake's lips brushed the scented hollow of her throat. "Make love to me, Jake, please!"

His eyes heavy with drink and passion, Jake slowly and solemnly reached out and unbuttoned the bodice of Carla's lacy sundress, his fingers lingering on the soft skin of her midriff as he undid the lower buttons, then with clumsy but infinitely gentle fingers he pushed the dress off her shoulders and eased it down her hips. Carla stepped out of the dress and picked it up, tossing it across a chair as she reached out and pushed Jake's blazer off his shoulders. She caught the blazer and laid it across the same chair that held her dress, then she reached out and started flicking open the buttons that held Jake's shirt together. Soon the shirt joined the pile of clothing on the chair, and Jake's muscular shoulders and chest were bared to her eager gaze. She sought him out with her fingers and touched the soft curly hair that covered his chest.

Jake reached around Carla and with a swift motion he unhooked her bra and sent it flying across the room. "Damned shame to have to wear one of those things," he murmured as one finger reached out and touched one of Carla's high, firm breasts. "You're too small and perfect to bother."

Carla blushed as her nipple hardened from the fleeting touch. Jake bent his head and touched the other nipple with the tip of his tongue, the slight contact causing that breast to tighten into another hard point. Suddenly his thumbs gripped her slip, pantyhose, and panties, and he pulled them down her legs in one fluid motion. "No sense bothering with these either," he teased as he gently pushed Carla back onto the silken comforter that covered the bed. "You're beautiful, do you know that?" he asked as he swayed a little and sat down on the bed beside her.

Carla moved toward Jake to see if he was all right, but he stood back up and quickly shed the rest of his clothes, his fingers fumbling only a little. Is he going to be too intoxicated to make love? she wondered as Jake returned to the bed and the strong but not unpleasant smell of Scotch scented his breath. She could remember a couple of notable occasions in the past when alcohol had nixed a lovemaking session, but as Jake pulled her close and she could feel his arousal, her concern for their lovemaking was forgotten. Jake's arms wrapped around her body and he pressed her close to him on the fluffy comforter.

It's been so long, Carla thought as Jake's lips grazed the tender skin between her breasts. So long since a man has touched me like this. She shivered with pleasure as he took one small nipple in his mouth and rolled it around his tongue, sending shooting sparks of delight through her body all the way to her toes. His lips nibbled her other breast, teasing it into a hard, taut peak as Carla writhed in pleasure. Her own hands roaming, she stroked the hard muscles of his back and his waist, stopping to rest on a ridge in his skin that she suspected was his surgery scar. Her hands touched it once, twice, in a gesture of comfort before roaming lower to caress the hard tight muscles of his bottom. He feels so good beside me, Carla thought as her lips tasted the slightly stubbly skin of his chin.

It's been so long, Jake thought as his lips traveled away from Carla's face and down her chest and midriff. She's so warm, so soft, so right against me. I want her, he thought as his lips found the tender skin of her navel and tormented it with his tongue. She smells so fresh and she's so slender and gentle, he thought as he took a playful nip of her waist. His head was spinning a little as his fingers roamed the soft skin of her hips and inner thighs, but he shook off the sensation and continued to touch and caress the delightful creature below him.

Carla moaned and arched against Jake's hand as his fingers explored her intimately, drawing from her the very essence of her femininity. Take me, Jake, she thought as his fingers swirled in erotic patterns, driving her to even greater heights of pleasure. All conscious thought elsewhere, she gave herself over to the waves of sensual delight that were flooding her body. Take me, Jake, she thought as she strained against him. "Please, now!" she cried as Jake moved over her to make them one.

He entered her in a hard, eager thrust, drawing a gasp of surprise and pleasure from Carla's lips as his mouth bent down and kissed her softly. Then he was above her, driving, strong, pouring his desire and his passion into the woman who was with him. Spirals of delight twisted in his brain as he drove on, restraining himself from culminating this glorious act too soon, drawing out the pleasure as much for his own sake as for hers. He felt her move her hips beneath him, twisting and squirming and matching her movements to his. What a woman! he thought as he climbed higher and higher toward the spiral.

It's never been like this for me before, Carla thought as she clutched at Jake's waist and matched her movements to his. I've never been made to feel like this in my life. Pleasure tearing through her, she gave herself over to the rhythm of their movements, the shooting stars behind the lids of her eyes going brighter and brighter as she climbed with him toward the peak.

We're almost there, Jake thought as he felt her tense under him. She was almost at the crest, they both were, and they would take the plunge together, Jake could feel it, as he moved faster and faster, harder and harder. Then suddenly, as a name tore from his lips, they were over the crest together, plunging through a rushing waterfall of delight at the loosening of the pulsing knot in the center of his body. He felt her stiffen for a moment, then she was moaning and murmuring as her body trembled in his arms. Her body quivered as the tempest in her was spent, then she lay still beside him. Suddenly drained, Jake barely had the strength to gather her to him before he drifted off into oblivion.

Carla stared out the window at the light across the street. Her body reveled in the sweet aftermath of their glorious lovemaking, but her heart was a fist of pain. Jake had been a wonderful lover tonight, but she had found out in the worst possible way that he was not making love to her, at least not in his mind. Their lovemaking had been glorious, driving, fulfilling, until at the moment of delight he had called out a name: Debbie. It had been torn from his lips in a moan of frenzied anguish.

Carla reached up and wiped away the tears that were running from her eyes. What had she expected, anyway? Jake was fairly drunk, he had spent the evening thinking about Debbie and talking about her. But Carla had honestly thought he was making love to her for herself, and when he had uttered his dead wife's name it had nearly torn her in half. Oh, it didn't stop the culmination of physical pleasure, nothing could have stopped that, but suddenly their lovemaking had lost all its beauty and wonder. Jake had used her tonight. He had substituted her for the wife he had lost. It's not fair, Carla thought as she wiped her cheek on the pillow. I wanted him to make love to me tonight. I wanted to give him comfort. She turned over and looked at the sleeping, peaceful face on the other pillow. Well, how did she know? She might have done just that, even if she had gotten hurt in the process.

CHAPTER EIGHT

Jake blinked his eyes in the early-morning gloom and shut them again as he tried to block out the dryness in his mouth and the nausea churning his stomach. Hell, how much had he drunk last night? Too much, that was for sure. He had not gone into the bar intending to get drunk, but after his third drink it had seemed like a good idea. After that, though, his memory started to get fuzzy. He remembered admiring the cute bottom on the barmaid a couple of times, and then he remembered something about Carla coming down to the bar and arguing with him. She had brought him back up to the room and he had kissed her and they had taken off their clothes and they had made love. . . .

Jake groaned and tried to shut out the memory. No, it had all been a dream. He had not made love to Carla last night. He had just dreamed that he had. He wouldn't have cheated on Debbie that way. He loved Debbie. He had sometimes dreamed about making love to other women, but he had never done so. This time was no different. He was all right.

Jake groaned and turned over, freezing when he felt a movement in the bed beside him. Loathe to open his eyes, he lay still for a moment, then slowly opened his eyes a crack and stared at the tousled blond hair on the pillow next to him. Damn, it wasn't a dream after all. He had taken Carla to bed with him last night, had made love to her, had spent the night with her. It was no dream. Waves of guilt washed over Jake as he rolled out of bed and stumbled toward the bathroom. Groaning, he gagged a little on the toothpaste but drank down three glasses of tap water. He turned on the shower and stepped under the spray, soaping himself quickly and drying himself. He made quick work of shaving and darted out into the hotel room, hoping to get dressed before Carla woke up and he had to face her. He was angry—angry with himself and angry with her for what happened last night. They had no business becoming lovers.

Carla rolled over and opened her eyes. She felt for Jake's side of the bed and, finding it empty, snuggled back down into the covers for a minute while she listened to the sound of the shower. Was he feeling the effects of his night of drinking? Was he all right? She would have loved to have gone and joined him in the shower, but sudden shyness enveloped her. Not being sure of her welcome, she sat up on the side of the bed and reached around for her underwear. She found her panties and slip and pulled them on, then started looking around the room for her bra, trying to remember in which direction Jake had tossed it. She was peering around behind the bed when Jake marched out of the bathroom, naked as a jaybird with a sick expression on his face. Carla straightened and smiled tiredly at him. "Are you all right?" she asked softly.

"No, I'm sure as hell not!" Jake snapped as he blushed beet red. Carla jumped at the vehemence in his tone. He didn't seem sick, but he seemed horribly angry. Jake walked over to his suitcase, threw it open, and pulled out a T-shirt and a pair of briefs. As he turned his back to pull them on, Carla winced at the long scar that snaked from the middle of his back to his buttocks.

145

In the heat of their passion last night, she hadn't even noticed the long red line, but this morning she couldn't help but stare at the physical evidence of Jake's ordeal. Jake noticed her staring in the mirror and his face became even angrier. He pulled his T-shirt over his head, then turned around to find Carla staring at him. "What's with you?" he demanded. "Stop staring at my damned back and get some clothes on!"

Carla looked down at her half-naked body and her face reddened from hurt, embarrassment, and anger. "If I could find where you threw my bra in a fit of passion last night, I just might," she snapped. She turned her back and peered behind several pieces of furniture, then shrugged and pulled her dress off the chair. "If you find it, let me know," she said. "It was an expensive one."

"Will do," Jake replied sarcastically. "And I'll get in line behind all your other lovers when I return it. Tell me, is this how you get your lovers to come back and see you again?"

Carla's head snapped back as though he had slapped her. Why was he so angry with her? What had she done to deserve that kind of remark? She quickly got dressed and then rummaged around in her pocket until she found her room key. She turned to Jake. "I'd like to know what inspired that crack?" Carla demanded as she advanced on the half-dressed Jake.

Jake pointed his finger in her face. "You took advantage of me last night," he accused her. "Is that how you get your jollies, by making love to half-drunk men who don't know what they're doing?"

Carla laughed humorlessly. "No, actually I prefer that my men be sober, at least sober enough to know who they're making love to," she said. "But, Jake, why are you so angry this morning? So outraged? You knew what you were doing last night. Believe me, you knew

146

exactly what you were doing over there." She gestured contemptuously toward the bed. "You sure didn't need any lessons from me."

"Is that what you were trying to provide?" Jake taunted. "Did you think I needed your lessons?"

Carla's eyes widened and her face whitened. "Let me tell you something, Peter Purebred," she choked. "That's the third crack you've made about my morals, and those cracks are way off the mark. I don't sleep around, and if you hadn't been half looped last night you would have been able to tell. I'm not loose, Jake." She reached up and wiped two tears out of her eyes.

Jake stared at Carla's shattered face. In the early-morning light, without her makeup, she looked her age, with fine lines etching the corners of her eyes and faint shadows below them. Yet she was still appealing, with her hair tousled and her face bare, and a sharp stab of desire tore through him as he remembered the way she had felt beneath him last night. But those memories brought another cascade of guilt bursting through him again, as he remembered Debbie. He swallowed and looked over at Carla. In her heels she was a little taller than he was, and it unnerved him a little to have this elegant woman looking down at him in his underwear. "So why?" he asked bitterly. "If it wasn't for laughs, why?"

"Don't you remember?" Carla asked bitterly. "Or were you too drunk? I'll tell you why, Jake Darrow," she cried as her eyes brimmed with tears. "You begged me to, that's why. You said you needed me, that you wanted me, that you were lonely. And I felt compassion for you. You were lonely and you were hurting and you needed another human being, and I was here. And let me tell you something," she said as she moved closer to him and poked her finger in his chest. "Before you start knocking my morals, you might think about a man who makes love to one woman but calls her by another woman's name. You used me last night, Jake. You called me 'Debbie.' You pretended I was her. And that's about as low as you can get."

Sniffing loudly, she made no effort to hide the tears that coursed down her cheeks as she threw open the hotel room door and slammed it shut behind her, startling the porter who was unlocking the room next door. Sobs tearing through her body, she took the service stairs down to her own room, showered, changed clothes, and had checked out in thirty minutes' time. Slamming her car in gear, she didn't realize until she was already out of Austin that she hadn't eaten, but she was so upset she probably couldn't have eaten anything anyway.

She willed herself not to give in to her tears as she stared down the long highway that would take her back to Corpus. Jake had gone too far this time. She could forgive him for pulling away from her before, even though she had been angry at the time, and for getting angry over the Tyson tapes, but to make love to her and then attack her for it—this time he had gone too far. The man was poison, and she didn't need him. She was a person and her feelings and needs deserved the same consideration and respect that his did. Angry determination thinned her mouth into a firm line. From now on she would stay just as far away from Jake Darrow as she could get. He could hurt her too badly if she let him near her again.

Jake squinted into the afternoon sunlight that fell across the rolling coastal plains. In just an hour or so he would be back in Corpus, and tonight he had to do one of the hardest things he had ever done. He owed Carla an apology, a big one, and he just hoped she didn't slam the door in his face. After the boor he had been this morning, he wouldn't blame her if she never spoke to him again. And that would be his loss, not hers. He glanced down at the little bundle on the carseat next to him. He sure hoped she wanted her bra and pantyhose back badly enough to open the door tonight!

Carla wasn't loose. He had known that last night when he had possessed her. She wasn't a virgin, of course, but she had responded to him like a woman who had not been made love to recently. And it was obvious by her reaction this morning that she hadn't taken making love to him lightly either. God, how could he have done that to her? Thrown her affection and caring back in her face like that, after she had given to him out of the generosity of her spirit?

Debbie. It all stemmed back to Debbie and his continuing ties to her. He had lashed out at Carla because of his own guilt and feelings of having betrayed his dead wife. Even though Debbie was gone, their vows broken by death, he still *felt* as though he had been unfaithful to her. Last night should never have happened, but as Jake's drink-fogged memory began to clear, he had to admit that Carla had not initiated their lovemaking. He had, in part because he was lonely and hurting, but also because he was extremely attracted to her.

Jake's eyes glazed a little as he remembered the slender curves of Carla's body, and he wondered how one man could be attracted to two such very different women. Debbie had been short and her figure had been voluptuous, and once she had reached thirty she had fought the pounds continually. Carla was tall and almost too slender, but her hips flared gently and her breasts were perky and high, and he had loved the way she had wrapped her long legs around his waist. As he thought of the two women, he realized that though a part of him was still in love with his dead wife, a part of him was very much attracted to the very-much-alive Carla, who seemed to care for him in spite of the annoying barrier she kept around herself. He wanted to have some kind of relationship with Carla, yet he wasn't ready for what they had shared last night. But would she even be willing to see him again? Jake rubbed his eyes and flexed his back against the strain of driving all the way from Austin. He didn't know, but he had to find out. Tonight.

Carla stared at her keyboard and typed another question for the customs agent Kevin would interview tomorrow afternoon on *Winners All.* She rubbed the space between her eyes and tried to concentrate, but two long drives in three days, plus her tumultuous clash with Jake, had drained her reserves. She had been so upset she had eaten very little today, and the lack of food had made her weak. She racked her brain and had just thought of another good question when she heard a knock at her door. Damn, she thought, if I answer the door I'll forget the question. She typed it quickly, then as the insistent knock sounded again she stood up and peered through the peephole, stiffening when she saw Jake Darrow on the other side. She turned away, but Jake pounded on the door again. "I know you're there, Carla," he called through the closed door. "Your car's in your parking slot."

Carla placed the chain on her door and opened it just a crack. "Get lost," she said coldly. "I think you said it all this morning, didn't you?"

Jake flinched at the coldness in her voice. "No, I didn't say it all this morning. Let me come in and talk to you, please?"

"I've washed my hands of you, Jake," Carla said. "I don't need any more mornings like this morning."

"Please, Carla, I've come to eat humble pie," Jake pleaded as he saw the firmness of her features. He dangled a small laundry sack in front of her. "You don't get these unless you let me in."

Carla pointed down the stairs. "The line forms in that direction," she said coldly. "You can get in line right after my Tuesday night assignation."

"Damn it, Carla, *please,*" Jake begged. "Let me talk to you for ten minutes, then if you want me to go, I will."

Carla could feel her resolve wavering. Was ten minutes too much to ask? Then she could tell him to get lost with a clear conscience. That is, if you even want to, a little voice taunted her. "All right," she said, unhooking the chain and opening the door. She stepped aside and let Jake enter. He winced at the tired circles under her eyes, knowing he had put them there. "Ten minutes, no more," she said firmly.

Carla motioned to the armchair and sat down on the couch. Jake tossed the laundry bag on the coffee table and sat down on the couch beside her. He moved to take her hand, but she pulled away from him. He rubbed the back of his neck and sat forward, resting his elbows on his knees. "Carla, I'm sorry," he said quietly.

"About last night or this morning?" she asked coolly.

"Both," Jake admitted, then winced when he saw her flinch. "It wasn't because making love to you wasn't wonderful. That part of it was, and if circumstances had been different it would have been perfect. Please don't think I didn't like it, Carla, because I did."

Jake looked over at her but couldn't tell whether any of the ice was melting.

"If you enjoyed it, then why did you act like you

151

did?" she asked. "Why did you throw a fit this morning?"

"I felt guilty," Jake admitted. "I felt like I had cheated on Debbie, and I blamed you for making me feel that way."

"Wonderful," Carla said dryly.

"I know that was unfair," Jake said quietly. "I know she's gone, but I can't help the way I feel."

"What about the other women you've made love to since Debbie died?" Carla asked. "Have you treated them the same way?"

"There haven't been any," Jake admitted. "You know that! Damn it, why do you think I feel so badly? This is the first time I've even wanted to since I lost her!"

Carla stared up at him, her determination to show this man the door wavering. No wonder he felt guilty, if she was the first woman he had made love to since his wife had died. But the way he had talked to her this morning and the way he had used her, making love to her while he was thinking of Debbie, was unforgivable. "That doesn't excuse the way you treated me this morning," she said, her anger evident again.

Jake stood up stiffly and paced the floor. "I know that. Look, I would give anything if I could go back and take back all those things I said to you this morning. I'm sorry I threw your caring back in your face and I'm sorry I said you were immoral. Of course you're not."

"And how about using me last night?" Carla asked softly. "I think that hurts the worst of all. You made love to me pretending I was your wife."

"I wasn't pretending you were Debbie. I knew it was you!" Jake protested hotly.

"Then why did you call out her name?"

Jake sighed and took a deep breath, as though trying to make up his mind what to say, then he flopped down

152

in the big chair. "I guess it's because I associate sex with Debbie," he admitted. "I always called out her name. She's the only woman I'd ever made love to until last night."

Carla couldn't keep her mouth from falling open in surprise. "She was? You didn't?" Jake shook his head. "Even I—You mean you were a virgin on your wedding night?"

"I didn't say that!" Jake protested, blushing brightly. "Look, I'm trying to make you understand. Debbie and I started going together when I was sixteen and she was fifteen. We grew up together, did all the teenage petting and exploring together, and when we were in college and the time seemed right, we became lovers. We even used to make jokes about it, saying that we were probably the only two people in the state who had been to bed only with each other. Not that I minded, of course. Nor did she."

I'm sure she didn't, Carla thought as she remembered Jake's tender, virile lovemaking. She looked over at his embarrassed, tormented face, and she began to understand the way he had felt this morning and perhaps why he called out Debbie's name last night. His devotion and his bond to Debbie had been exceptionally strong, and one night in Carla's arms wasn't going to change that. But Debbie was gone now, and it was time for Jake to go on with his life and have other loves. "Jake, I'm sure you loved her and that you miss her, but you have no reason to feel guilty for making love to me. Nor was it fair for you to take out your feelings of guilt on me, when I have no reason to feel guilty for making love to you."

"I agree," Jake said softly. "And I'm working on that." He stared over at Carla's face and pleaded with his eyes. "Please forgive me," he murmured. "Can you?"

Carla shrugged. "I guess so." She looked across the room and saw Jake's face fall. "All right, I'll try very hard to forgive you," she said.

"Thank you, Carla," Jake said softly. "I'm not ready for an affair with you, but I'd like to see you again. How about this weekend?"

Carla stood as she shook her head. "No, I don't think so, Jake," she said firmly. "I don't think I should go on seeing you."

"Why not?" he demanded. "You said you would try to forgive me."

"I'll make every effort," Carla said as she stared out the window. "But I just don't think we should see one another any more."

"But why?" Jake asked. "I'd like to go on seeing you. I need that."

"That's right. *You* need this and *you* need that!" Carla spat out as she whirled around to face him. "*You* aren't ready for an affair, but *you* want to go on seeing me." She poked her finger in his chest. "But what about me, Jake? I have a few needs too, you know. Maybe it's selfish, but I wouldn't mind having you think a little about what might be good for me!"

Jake's eyes widened at her attack and he swallowed convulsively. "Good God, Carla, I'm sorry," he said as he ran his hand down the side of his face. "I have been a selfish bastard, haven't I?" He got up and put his arm around her. "So what do you need from me, Carla?"

Carla shrugged. "Last night wasn't too bad for starters," she suggested.

Jake stiffened and pulled away from her. "I'm not ready for that yet," he said. "I'm still too much in love with Debbie for that." He thought a minute. "But I

154

think it would be nice if we got to know each other as people. I would like to take you out to those fancy restaurants you look so at home in, to talk to you about your work and mine. To have you tell me about yourself, tell me all the little things I don't know about yet that have made you what you are. To enjoy you as a person. Don't you need that too?"

"I don't know," Carla admitted as she paced the floor. "Maybe I need more than that out of you. I may as well be honest with you, Jake. I have very strong feelings for you, stronger than yours are for me. I need more than to just be your friend. If that was all I needed, I'd be with Kurt. I need your closeness, physically and emotionally. Those are my needs, and I think we both know you can't fulfill those needs." She stopped and took a deep breath. "I think I may be falling in love with you. Hell, I don't know, I may already be there, and with you still in love with Debbie there's no way I can keep from being hurt. I don't need that, Jake. You hurt me enough this morning."

Jake stood and came to stand beside her. "Thank you for being honest with me," he said, reaching out and stroking the side of her face. "I want to go on seeing you, Carla. As selfish as it sounds, I'm glad you feel something for me. I just need some time, Carla, before I get involved in a full-fledged affair. But someday very soon I hope to reciprocate those feelings. I can't be your lover just yet, but I swear to God it won't be long. And I'll do my damnedest not to hurt you in any way, ever again. I may not succeed but I'll try. How about it? Are you willing to see me again?"

"How long before you're ready?" Carla asked. "Weeks, months, years?"

"I don't know," Jake admitted. "But I'm not putting you off, Carla, honest!" he added when he saw her face start to tighten. "I'll be your lover just as soon as I can."

Carla thought a minute and nodded, her face solemn. "Yes, Jake, I'll see you again," she said as Jake reached out and pulled her gently toward him.

"Thank you, Carla," he said as he stroked her back. He leaned down and kissed her softly on the lips, then deepened the kiss, holding her tightly to him. Carla moaned and clutched at his shoulders. They kissed and clung for long moments, then Jake released Carla's lips and smiled down at her. "You're a wonderful woman, Carla," he said softly.

"I thought we weren't going to have an affair," Carla said dryly.

"We're not," Jake agreed. "But I don't promise not to snatch a kiss or two now and then."

"Won't that make you feel guilty?" Carla asked a little sarcastically.

"Nope," Jake said cheerfully. "Not a bit. Now, how about dinner and a movie Saturday night?" he asked, releasing her.

"Sure, sounds great," Carla said as Jake kissed her nose once and headed for the door.

As a thought struck him, Jake turned around with a frown of concern on his face. "About last night," he said. "Neither of us took any precautions. Is it—could there be a problem?"

Carla shook her head quickly, her eyes becoming shuttered. "Don't worry about that," she said briskly. "There was no possibility of that last night."

"Are you sure?" Jake asked, wondering at the strange look on her face.

"Absolutely," Carla assured him, then the peculiar look left her face and she smiled. "See you Saturday."

Jake left her apartment and Carla locked the door

behind him, then she pushed open the sliding door and stepped out on her balcony. She sat down in the folding chair and stared out at the moonlight dappling the waves in the bay. Carla, you're a damned fool for giving in to him, she told herself angrily. Sure, he promised not to hurt her again, but that was about as likely as a snowfall in July. There was no way he could live up to that, when she was falling in love with him and he still loved Debbie. She was setting herself up for a whole lot of pain. But how could I say no? she asked herself as the soft sea breeze caressed her face, wiping away her anger. How could I turn away the man I'm falling in love with?

CHAPTER NINE

"Jake, did you enjoy the performance?" Jeannie asked brightly as Jake escorted Carla from the Civic Auditorium and Jeannie and Bradley walked alongside them toward the parking lot.

"Yes, I enjoyed it thoroughly," Jake said. "I didn't realize that touring Broadway companies are so much better than the local group!"

Jeannie and Carla both laughed. "Better not say that too loudly," Carla teased him as she put her fingers to her lips. "I saw the director of the local production company sitting just a few feet in front of us. He might not take kindly to hearing the local efforts maligned."

"God forgive anyone who steps on that temperamental so-and-so's toes," Bradley said dryly. "Shoot, our local company would be much better if it weren't for him."

"I agree," Jake said. "The last time my late wife and I went, it looked like some of the actors may have had some talent, but the staging and mannerisms were so terrible that what should have been high drama turned into melodrama and I had to fight to keep from laughing out loud."

Jeannie and Bradley started to laugh, and Carla blushed brightly. "We know the production you mean," Jeannie said. "Carla started giggling and couldn't stop. Kurt could have shot her that night."

Carla laughed at the gentle teasing and invited them to her place for dessert.

Sitting in the living room, the men were immersed in a discussion of politics. Jeannie followed Carla to the kitchen and pushed the door shut behind her. "So how serious is it between you and Jake?" she asked as Carla opened the cabinet and got out the ground decaffeinated coffee.

Carla raised her eyebrows. "Who knows?" she asked dryly.

"Which means that you know how you feel, but not how he feels, right?" Jeannie suggested.

"No, that isn't it," Carla said. "Unfortunately, I know just how he feels." She plugged in the coffee maker and poured the water in. "Jeannie, he's still in love with his dead wife. He told me so."

Jeannie shrugged. "Of course he is, and he always will be. But the question is how does he feel about you now?"

"How should I know?" Carla asked angrily. "He says that he wants to get to know me, spend time with me, but he backs off from any kind of real intimacy or commitment. He says he just isn't ready. But damn it, I am." She opened the refrigerator and got out a home-made strudel and placed it in the microwave.

"It takes time, Carla," Jeannie said softly. "It took me a long time to get over Joe." Joe was Jeannie's first husband who had died in Vietnam. "And I still love him a little, I guess. But that doesn't mean I don't love Bradley too." Jeannie looked at Carla strangely. "Don't you feel anything anymore for—"

"No, I don't," Carla said, more sharply than she had intended. "That was different, though."

"Yes, I guess it was," Jeannie agreed, pouring the coffee while Carla sliced the warmed strudel. "But

159

you've got to hang in there, Carla. Give the man time to come around. That is, if you think he's worth it."

"You always manage to hit the nail on the head, don't you?" Carla asked dryly. "Of course he's worth it, or we wouldn't have come this far."

For the next couple of hours, the four friends shared stories about their jobs and teased Carla about trying to make them all gain weight with her marvelous dessert. All too soon, Jeannie and Bradley wished Carla and Jake good night.

In spite of his teasing about his waistline, Jake returned to the kitchen and helped himself to another piece of strudel and a fresh cup of coffee. He returned to the living room and curled up beside Carla on the couch. "Quite a wine rack you have in there," he said as he dug into the strudel and sipped his coffee. "You don't have to stop serving it to your friends just because of me, you know," he said softly.

Carla shrugged. "Maybe my consciousness has been raised," she said. "And besides, what vintage would I serve with strudel?" She got up and poured herself another cup of coffee, then sat back down beside Jake. "Do you like Jeannie and Bradley?" she asked.

"Yes, they're two of the nicest people I've met in a long time," Jake said. "They're as nice as that Kurt you used to go with." They had gone out to dinner with Kurt and his new girl friend last weekend.

"Why, thank you to both compliments," Carla said as she sipped her coffee. "I thought you might enjoy meeting them."

Jake sighed and sipped his coffee, blowing a little on the hot surface. "I'd like to introduce you to a few of my friends sometime," he said. "I'm ashamed to say that I haven't seen a whole lot of a lot of them lately. The CCC's kept me so busy that I've lost touch."

"And then I've monopolized your time," Carla murmured.

"Now, don't you dare think that," Jake said as he reached out and patted her hand. "I've enjoyed every minute we've spent together. And I don't know of very many women who would make it a point to include a nine-year-old girl on at least a third of her dates."

Carla smiled. "Believe me, it's no sacrifice to include Sonia," she assured him. "I just wish Patty wasn't always too busy to come."

Jake laughed. "Her social calendar is somewhere between full and overflowing," he said. "But I do wish you two could have a chance to get to know each other better."

"Tell you what," Carla suggested. "Why don't you plan to bring the girls to dinner next Saturday evening? I'd love to repay some of your hospitality, and it would give Patty and me a chance to get to know each other a little better. You can bring your suits and swim after supper."

"No, I hate to put you to all that work," Jake objected. "We can go out to eat."

Carla laughed out loud. "Work? Jake, entertaining is my hobby! And I *love* to cook! I'd enjoy cooking dinner for you and the girls. Honest."

"In that case, we would love to come. About six?" Carla nodded her head.

Jake reached out and took her coffee cup and placed it on the coffee table. "I've got to go in a minute, but before I do . . ." He pulled her to him and held her head steady as he kissed her lips, gently at first, then as Carla arched herself to him, he groaned and gathered her close to him, opening his lips and savoring the sweetness of hers. She kissed him wildly, passionately, opening her mouth to his and savoring the sweetness within his depths. Her hands, with a will of their own, sought the hard muscles of his chest and his shoulders, touching and caressing Jake even as his hands traveled over the slender lines of her back and shoulders. Carla touched and caressed him, communicating her caring and her affection with every loving touch, and he savored her sweet giving even as he touched her with the same loving gentleness. Finally, as their passion threatened to burst the dam of reason, Jake pulled back and held her away from him. "I better stop while I still can," he said, fighting to control his erratic breathing. He leaned over and kissed her cheek gently, then got up and headed for the door. "It won't be long, Carla," he promised as he opened the front door. "I'm almost ready."

I wish to hell you would get off the fence! Carla thought as she stared at the closing door and remembered the way Jake had brought her to trembling ecstasy in Austin. Many more of his passionate kisses and she would be dragging him into her bedroom by his thick gray hair, ready or not! She touched her passion-swollen lips with the tip of her finger. You're being unfair to me, Jake, she thought as she picked up the dishes on the coffee table and carried them to the kitchen. You're stringing me along, promising more than you're willing to deliver, and that isn't fair.

Not that the last month had been all that bad, she reminded herself as she loaded the dishes into the dishwasher and turned it on. For the last month she and Jake had been getting to know each other as people, and she was becoming more fond of him every time she saw him. He had fit in beautifully with her circle of friends, and he had seemed to enjoy the dinner parties she had included him in. But she was becoming increasingly frustrated with his hesitancy about becoming intimate.

She wanted, needed warmth and caring from him now, and she needed to give the same to him. But she was afraid he'd never let her get past the shell he'd built around himself, and she didn't know how long it would take for him to realize that they both needed each other.

Carla quickly showered and pulled on a short nightgown trimmed in lace. She stared at herself in the mirror for a moment, at her long sleek body and her small high breasts, and she wondered briefly if Jake found her as attractive as he had found Debbie. Then she shrugged and turned back the covers. There wasn't much she could do about the physical attraction part; he either liked what he saw or he didn't.

Carla banged in the door and slammed it behind her. What a day to have to cover the Secretary of State! Paul had called her at ten o'clock the night before, interrupting a lively kiss she and Jake were sharing on her couch, to inform her that since she had met the Secretary once several years ago he wanted her to spend all day Saturday covering the Secretary's visit to Corpus. Jake had immediately offered to cancel their Saturday night dinner, but Carla wouldn't hear of it, and cooked an elegant chicken dish this morning before leaving for the airport. She pulled the chicken marengo out of the refrigerator and popped it into the oven to warm, then prepared the rest of the meal.

After changing into casual clothes, she set her table with her best silver and china.

She was just putting her rolls into the oven when the doorbell rang. "Coming!" she called as she hurried for the door.

Jake and his girls stood on the porch, the girls wearing coverups over their suits. Jake and Sonia were smiling, but Patty stood to one side with a scowl on her

163

face. She marched into Carla's apartment and sat down stiffly on a chair. Sonia wrapped her arms around Carla's waist and squeezed her tightly.

"Don't do that, Sonia!" Patty snapped. "You'll mess up her clothes!"

Sonia tried to pull away, but Carla pulled her closer and hugged her back. "Don't worry about an old pair of jeans," she said as she gave Sonia a warm hug and a kiss on her cheek. "How are you tonight, Sonia?"

"Just super!" Sonia enthused. "Boy, you sure look pretty! I thought we were going swimming. Are we?" she asked wistfully.

"You bet, just as soon as we've eaten," Carla assured Sonia. She opened her drapes and pointed down at the pool. "See? It's just down there."

"I'd rather swim at the beach," Patty said sullenly. "It's more natural."

Jake shot Patty a warning look and started to speak, but Carla caught his eye and shook her head. "Yes, I guess it is, if you prefer salt in your hair to chlorine," she said pleasantly. "I enjoy both."

"So do I," Sonia piped up. "Is supper ready?"

"Almost," Carla said. "If y'all want to have a seat, it will be ready in a minute."

"Dad, how long do I have to stay?" Patty asked suddenly. "Skeeter said we could go to the movies at eight."

"We've accepted Carla's invitation for the evening," Jake said firmly. "You and Skeeter can go to the movies another time."

"Aw, Dad, come on," Patty wheedled.

"Patty, that's enough!" Jake snapped sharply.

Patty slouched back into the chair while Jake followed Carla out to the kitchen. "I hope we're not too casual," he said as he looked at her elegantly set table.

164

"Oh, heavens no," Carla assured him as she got out the iced tea glasses. "My jeans are hardly dressed up." She followed his eyes to her elegantly set table. "I just wanted things to be nice for them."

Jake ran a comforting hand down her back to her spine, sending shivers of awareness through her. "It looks very nice, and I thank you," he said.

Carla poured tea into the goblets and got the salad she had made that morning out of the refrigerator. "I'll change into my suit after dinner," she said as she sprinkled the salad with her spicy dressing. "Even if the pool isn't 'natural' enough." She lowered her voice. "Jake, if she doesn't want to stay, I understand. I can feel the hostility a mile away."

Jake sighed and rubbed the back of his neck. "And that hostility won't go away if she stays away from you," he said. "It will if she gets to know you. Look at Sonia. She adores you."

"Sonia is also at the hero-worshipping stage. Patty's way beyond that."

"Give her a chance, Carla," Jake pleaded. "The same chance I want her to give to you."

"Of course," she said, placing her hand on his arm. "I'll give Patty every chance."

"Atta girl," Jake said as he carried the goblets into the dining room.

After Carla had placed the food on the table, she called the girls to supper.

Sonia hopped up and hurried toward the table. "Whatrwehaving?" she demanded as she skidded to a stop, narrowly missing the table with her shin.

"Chicken," Carla said as Patty slouched toward the table.

"Ooh, that's my favorite!" Sonia squealed, sliding into a chair. As Carla sat at the opposite end from him,

Jake passed the platter of chicken around the table. Patty took one small piece and handed it to Carla, who served herself and gave the plate to Sonia. Sonia looked at the chicken a little strangely, but she put two pieces on her plate and handed the tray back to Jake.

Patty and Sonia also took small portions of the bean casserole and salad, and one roll each. They're supposed to be starving! Carla thought as she looked at the small portions on their dishes.

Carla cut into her chicken and turned to Patty with a friendly smile on her face. "Have you been enjoying your summer?" she asked.

"Yes," Patty replied tersely.

"Uh, that's nice," Carla replied. "What have you been doing?"

"Summer band," Patty said.

Carla waited for the girl to elaborate, but Patty said nothing more. What should she say now? If she continued to question the girl, it might seem like she was submitting Patty to the third degree. Carla looked over at Jake helplessly.

He glanced over at Patty. "Maybe Carla would enjoy hearing about summer band," Jake suggested.

"Sure. We go two hours in the morning and practice, then we go back in the afternoon to march." Patty put a bite of salad in her mouth and chewed it slowly.

"What instrument do you play?" Carla asked.

"Clarinet."

Carla sighed, knowing from their taping that Patty could be quite articulate if she chose to be. The girl was letting her and Jake know in no uncertain terms that she did not want to be there. Carla glanced up at Jake and noted the nonverbal message he was sending Patty's way, a stare that the girl was ignoring. I'll make one more stab at it, Carla thought. "Do you have any long-term ambitions toward your clarinet or the band?" she asked.

Patty shook her head. "Not particularly," she replied as she bit into a buttered roll.

All right, young lady, two can play at this game, Carla thought. "That's too bad." She turned to Sonia and smiled at the younger child. "How about you, Sonia? Have any interest in the band?"

Sonia did, and she spent a good ten minutes telling them about her future ambitions to play the trumpet and march for King High School. Jake then admitted that he was a member of the Band Parents Association, and he talked a little about some of the fund-raising activities the group had been involved in. He even managed to draw Patty back into the conversation a little. Although her responses were a bit reluctant, she did talk a little about some of the out-of-town football games the band had gone on and some of the funny things that had happened on those trips. When Carla asked if Jake had made any of the trips, Patty said no, her mother had, and then she fell silent again. Carla could have kicked herself for asking the question, since she should have known that Debbie would have been a member of the Band Parents too.

Jake and Carla ate heartily of the delicious dinner, but except for the rolls, the girls just pushed the food around on their plates a little. Carla's disappointment grew by the minute as she watched the small portions not growing any smaller. What was wrong? Had she overcooked the meal? Undercooked it? Spiced it too heavily? She sampled each dish again. No, they were done to perfection. Why weren't the girls eating?

Finally, when she and Jake had each finished their portions and Jake had taken seconds, Carla asked if everyone was ready for dessert. When Sonia eagerly nodded yes, she gathered up their plates and carried them into the kitchen, then returned with a German chocolate cake. "Sonia, you said the other day that you liked cake, so here you go."

"What kind of cake is that?" Sonia asked as Carla cut her a piece.

"It has all sorts of things in it," Carla said as Sonia looked at the slice of cake.

The little girl took a hesitant bite of the cake, then eagerly took a second. "It's good!" she said. "It tastes a lot like Mom's used to."

"Cut me a big one, then," Patty said, enthusiastic for the first time since she had arrived. Carla cut the older girl a generous piece and handed it to her. Patty took a bite and nodded her head. "It sure is," she said. "It's like the ones Mom used to make."

Highest praise, Carla thought wryly.

"Yeah, it really does," Sonia said absently as she ate another big bite. "I was hoping the chicken would be like hers to." She turned wistful eyes on Carla. "Mom made the best fried chicken in the whole world."

Carla cut herself and Jake pieces of cake and sat back down. If she had possessed an ounce of common sense, she would have fried the chicken too and made potato salad, and taken a picnic out to the pool. Carla swallowed the lump that was threatening to rise in her throat and shoved a piece of cake into her mouth. She had wanted to please and impress the children, but she had not given her menu or her plans any thought. A nine- and a sixteen-year-old weren't going to enjoy the same kind of dinner party that sophisticated adults enjoyed. They would have much preferred a simple meal like their mother used to cook them. Even a career woman should have known that.

Carla turned to Sonia. "Tell you what. Next time

your daddy brings you over, we'll have some fried chicken. How will that be?"

"Fine," Sonia replied. "Can I have another piece of cake?"

Carla glanced over at Jake. He nodded, so she cut both Sonia and Patty another piece of cake. At least the cake had pleased them! The girls finished their cake quickly, then Sonia stood up and grabbed her father's hand. "Can we go swimming now?" she asked.

"Whoa, we need to help Carla clean up first," Jake protested.

"No, let's go on and I'll clean up later," Carla said.

"I'll help Carla, Daddy. You and Sonia go on down," Patty said suddenly.

Jake glanced down at the look on his daughter's face and started to shake his head, but Carla caught his glance and nodded for him to go on. If Patty wanted to talk to her, that was fine, because she could then say whatever needed to be said to the girl.

Jake shrugged and took Sonia by the hand, then Carla started clearing dishes off the table. Patty picked up the cake platter and carried it back to the kitchen. Carla scraped the plates into the trash and stacked them into the dishwasher while Patty returned to the table for another load of silverware. She handed the silverware to Carla. "Stay out of my father's life," the girl said suddenly.

Carla turned around and arched an eyebrow at Patty. "Pardon me?" she asked.

Patty stared at her defiantly. "You're trying to take Mother's place in his life, and that's wrong. He has Sonia and me; he doesn't need anybody else. He doesn't need you, so get lost."

"Bothers you, does it?" Carla asked slowly. "That your father's seeing me?" She put the last of the plates and silverware in the dishwasher and shut it. She started to turn it on, then decided that she would accomplish little by shouting over its noise. "Does it bother you to see him with another woman? Other than your mother?"

Patty's face turned a dull shade of red. "I don't like it, no," she admitted sullenly.

"Go sit down. We need to have a little talk," Carla said, pointing into the living room. Patty preceded her and flopped down on the couch. Carla sat down in the chair opposite her.

"You've laid your cards on the table, now I'm going to lay mine. First off, I know exactly how you feel because it nearly killed me the first time I saw my father with another woman after my mother died, and I was a whole lot older and tougher than you. So I do know how it hurts you, Patty."

"Then why are you seeing him?" Patty demanded.

"Because, contrary to what you think, your father *does* need me—well, not necessarily me, but he does need some adult companionship in his life. He needs friends and he needs to date."

"Are you sleeping with him?" Patty asked.

Carla carefully kept her face even. "Does your father know the details of your sex life? Or does he trust you and respect your privacy? Don't you owe the same respect to him?"

Patty had the grace to look shamefaced. Carla took a breath and decided to gently press her point. "Patty, surely you can see what losing your mother and starting up the CCC have taken out of your father. He not only has grief for your mother to cope with and the heavy responsibility of the CCC, but he has a business to run and he's trying to be both mother and father to you and Sonia. He needs an outlet, he needs to go out and have fun with other adults. He needs to get away and forget it all for a while. And that's where I come in. He can do that with me."

"But you're trying to take my mother's place in his life!" Patty protested.

Carla shook her head and smiled wistfully. "Patty, I'm not trying to take your mother's place in your father's life. I'm not that stupid. I couldn't take her place even if I tried, and I certainly have more respect for your father's feelings than that. Surely you realize that your father still loves her very much." Carla pursed her lips and delivered her final thought. "And instead of knocking me, Patty, you ought to be thankful I'm not trying to persuade him to make me the second Mrs. Darrow. A lot of women would be, you know."

Patty shrugged and got up. "I'm going to the pool," she said as she headed out the door and shut it behind her. Carla blew out a deep breath and walked toward the bathroom. Had she made any sense? she wondered as she changed into her sleek black maillot. Had she made even a dent in the girl's resentment and hostility? Could Patty understand Jake's need for feminine companionship, or was she too wrapped up in youthful resentment to understand?

Carla walked down to the pool and slid into the cool water. Jake was playing with Sonia in the deep end, and a bikinied Patty was playing on the lawn with a group of teenagers tossing a Frisbee. Carla struck out across the pool and swam laps for long moments, trying to work off her disappointment over the evening's failures. First she had prepared the wrong kind of dinner for the girls and then she had gotten nowhere with Patty. Maybe she just didn't have a way with kids, or at least with Jake's. She sat down on the side of the pool and Sonia swam up to her.

171

"Carla, did you see me swimming?" she asked eagerly.

"Yes, you were very good," Carla assured her. Well, at least Sonia liked her, even if she couldn't fix a meal the little girl would eat.

Sonia paddled off and Jake hoisted himself up to the side of the pool. Carla had to resist the impulse to reach out and stroke the broad chest with rivulets of water running off it. It would never do to display any kind of intimacy in front of the girls. Jake gazed across the lawn and his lips tightened as he spotted Patty jumping for the Frisbee. "What did she have to say?" he asked.

"She warned me off you," Carla said dryly, then reached out her hand and stopped him when he made a motion to get up. "No, don't say anything to her about it. We talked, and I gave her as good as I got."

Jake settled back down. "If I know you, she got an earful," he said dryly.

"I wasn't hard on her, Jake," Carla said quietly. "I told her that I wasn't trying to take Debbie's place with you, but I did point out that you needed to have adult friends and to date." Carla grinned impishly. "And I told her that she was better off with me than she would be with somebody who was bucking to be the second Mrs. Darrow."

Jake snickered under his breath. "I was right to trust you with it," he said. "Did you detect any softening on her part?"

Carla sighed as she watched the pretty girl run across the lawn. She saw Patty look in their direction, then look away. She couldn't see the expression on the girl's face, but she would have bet money that it had been harsh and bitter. "I couldn't tell, Jake. But I don't think so. I really don't think so."

172

CHAPTER TEN

"Jake, are you all right?" Carla asked as Jake limped up the stairs to her apartment and stood to one side while she unlocked the door.

"Sure, why shouldn't I be?" Jake said as he followed her and eased himself down on the sofa.

"Because you're limping worse than usual," Carla accused him softly as she sat down in the chair opposite him and stretched her miniskirted legs out in front of her. "You screwed your back up doing the twist with Jeannie, didn't you? You and Jeannie didn't have to get out there and dance like that." The Ryans had given a sixties party and Jake had gotten into the spirit of the party a little too much. "With a back like yours—"

"For God's sake, quit harping on my back!" Jake snapped, then he groaned as another spasm caught him. "All you ever do is ride me about my back. My back's fine."

"Sure it is," Carla taunted him softly. "It's so great that you're sitting over there in so much pain that your face is white. But no, we mustn't talk about Jake's bad back. That would be breaking the rules, wouldn't it?"

"What the hell are you talking about?" Jake asked as another spasm caught him.

"Lie down on your stomach. I'll try to ease some of the pain," Carla ordered Jake as she got up out of the chair.

"Honestly, I'm fine," Jake protested.

"Humor me," she said, looking him in the eye.

"Oh, all right," Jake said as he carefully eased himself down onto the couch. "But only if you explain what you meant by that crack about breaking the rules."

Carla knelt by the couch and placed her fingers over Jake's lower back. "You won't talk to me about your bad back," she explained. "You shut me out every time I try to talk to you about it."

"So what?" Jake demanded. "You know everything else about me. You even have it on tape. Hell, you know a lot more about me than I ever thought about knowing about you." He groaned as Carla's fingers worked out some of the tension.

"I—I guess that's true," Carla had to acknowledge. "But I just don't understand why your back is so taboo."

"Because maybe I don't want your pity. Maybe I would like to maintain the illusion of being whole."

"Thanks a lot," Carla said angrily. "I'm not about to pity you for anything, and as far as the other goes, why should you want to maintain an illusion for me? Damn it, we've been as close as two people can be! I want to be your lover, Jake! Lovers don't have illusions." She gave his back a hearty rub.

"Oww, not so rough!" Jake cautioned her. He lay still until she had worked out the worst of the stiffness, then he eased his legs around and sat up. Carla sat down beside him and he reached out and drew her close to him. "You're right, lovers don't have illusions," he said thoughtfully.

"So how bad is it?" Carla asked softly. "Really."

"I'm lucky to be able to walk at all," Jake admitted softly. "I was in traction for weeks. Most nights I sleep on a heating pad and sometimes I even have to take medication so I can sleep. Dear God, I hate that!" Jake knotted his hands in front of him.

"It's not a weakness to need an occasional pain-killer, under the circumstances," Carla said quietly as she touched his forearm. "But there's more to it than that, isn't there?"

"Yes," Jake said gruffly. "Every time it hurts me it reminds me of the first time it hurt. I was lying in the wreckage, hurting like hell, and I couldn't get to Debbie. I tried but I just couldn't move that night."

Carla reached out and took Jake's hand. "Don't torture yourself, Jake. It wasn't your fault you couldn't get to her."

"Yeah, I've told myself that over and over again. Maybe someday I'll learn to believe it."

"I'm sure your back will get better with time, if you take care of it. Maybe you should be more careful. Like tonight—"

"Damn it, what about tonight?" Jake demanded. "Aren't I entitled to have a little fun sometimes? Do I have to live like a semiinvalid?"

"I guess not, if you like pain," Carla snapped back. "Oh, Jake, I'm sorry," she apologized immediately. "It's just that it hurts me to see you in pain, and then until tonight you wouldn't even discuss it with me. Don't you trust me enough to talk to me about it?"

"As much as you seem to trust me to talk about your past," Jake said dryly. "Every time I try to get you to tell me about yourself, you clam up, and then you have the nerve to get upset when I won't talk about my back. I've known you for four months, and I know virtually nothing about you."

"I guess I just didn't think it was all that important. What do you want to know about me?" Carla asked quietly.

"Some basics might be nice," Jake drawled. "Like where you come from, where you went to school, what you were like when you were twenty-five, things like that. I've told you a lot of those kind of things about me, but you've always changed the subject."

Carla shrugged. "I was born and grew up in Dallas. Daddy's a mechanic for a Buick dealer and my step-mother's a secretary for an insurance firm."

Carla's face softened. "My dad and stepmother are very special people and I love them dearly," she said. "Anyway, I went to University of Texas at Arlington, got a degree in communications, and have been a career woman ever since." She smiled slightly.

"And what were you like at twenty-five?" Jake asked.

Carla shrugged. "Young. Young and naive and hope-ful. I've come a long way," she added with only a little bitterness.

"And that's all you're going to tell me, isn't it?" Jake asked angrily. "Just a few facts. Nothing about who you were, your feelings. You're not going to open up to me, are you? Do you realize how badly that hurts me?"

Carla carefully kept her voice calm. "I'm sorry you're hurt, but we have different ways of opening up, Jake. You're willing to tell me about yourself, except for your back, but you pull away from me in other ways."

"Like making love to you?" he asked softly.

"Yes," Carla said. "You're upset because I don't want to talk about things in my past that maybe weren't the happiest things in the world, but you're not willing to include me in your present. You're shutting me out."

"You're shutting me out too," Jake said flatly. He took a deep breath, then leaned over and kissed her on the lips. "But I don't want to shut you out any more, and I'm willing to open up with you. I'd like to make you my lover," he said. "I'm pretty sure I'm ready to take that step."

"Are you just saying that because we quarreled?" Carla asked shrewdly. "Are you just trying to make up with me?"

"No, I really am ready," Jake said. "And I hope, after we've become lovers, that maybe you'll be willing to open up with me and share whatever it was in your past that hurt you so."

Carla raised her head and stared into his eyes. "Are you absolutely sure you want to make love to me?" she asked. "What about your feelings for Debbie? I don't want any more scenes like the last one."

In response Jake took her by the shoulders and pushed her into the cushions of the couch. Eagerly he covered her lips with his and kissed her until Carla wanted to cry out with pleasure. "Is that the kiss of a reluctant lover?" he asked. "I haven't resolved all my feelings about Debbie, but I've come a long way. Before, I couldn't even touch another woman without feeling like a heel," he admitted. "Now touching you and kissing you feels right." He ran his hand down the side of Carla's face. "Yes, I'm ready."

"Tonight?" Carla asked.

Jake looked at his watch and shook his head. "It's almost midnight and Mrs. Lopez is out of town for the weekend," he said. "I hate to leave the girls alone much later than this."

"You're right," Carla said quietly, quickly damping down her disappointment. "You don't want to leave them alone all night." She sat up and rubbed her forehead. "Has Patty ever said anything more to you about us?"

Jake shook his head. "She's never said a thing. She doesn't have to." He sighed. "Damn it, I know she misses her mother, but you'd think she would try to understand just a little!" He sat up and ran his fingers through his rumpled hair.

"Maybe you should talk to her about us," Carla suggested. A couple of times she had sensed that Jake was deeply torn between her and the daughter he loved so much. Carla would have loved to ring the child's neck, except she remembered how she had felt at first about her stepmother. "Are you going to let on that things are changing between us?"

Jake shrugged. "I don't know. Hell, Carla, I don't know how to handle this! But I'm not going to let her stop me either. I need you, Carla, and I'm going to have you for my lover, if that's what you want."

"You know it is," Carla assured him.

"All right then. Next weekend I'm going to Houston and Dallas to speak to groups interested in forming coalitions in their cities. The speaking engagements shouldn't take more than a few hours. Can you get off and come with me?"

Carla nodded. "I'm off Saturday and Sunday."

"I'm flying back Monday about noon," Jake said. "Would that get you back in time to do your show?"

Carla nodded. "I'll have to check with Paul, but I don't see any problem."

"Maybe if you cover my speeches Paul will pay your way," Jake teased as he got up and went over to the telephone.

"No way," Carla said as he got out the Yellow Pages and opened them. "My days of covering you are over!"

Jake called the airline and made another reservation on all his flights, then called the hotel and changed his room reservation. When Carla asked him what her plane fare would be, he informed her that she was his guest. Before she could protest, his lips were back on

178

hers. By the time he had finished kissing her she had forgotten all about the plane fare. He promised to pick her up next Saturday about seven, then, after another lingering kiss, he was out the door.

Carl stared at the front door with a faint smile on her face. So it was finally happening. They were going to be together. "Well, Jake, it's about time!" she said out loud. The situation wasn't perfect by a long shot, not with Jake's continuing feelings for Debbie and his daughter's disapproval, but she would worry about that later. Despite the late hour, she stood in front of her closet for half an hour deciding which outfits to take with her.

Carla stared out the window of the rented Buick at the congested snarl on the Houston freeway. "Makes you appreciate Corpus, doesn't it?" she asked wryly.

Jake swore and dodged a young man on a motorcycle. "I swear, this is almost as bad as New York," he said as a little old lady in an Oldsmobile cut in front of them. "Why, that old—"

"Now, Jake," Carla admonished. "This isn't so bad. It's lots worse at rush hour. Especially Katy Freeway."

"Get caught in it one time?" Jake asked as he put on the signal light and tried to edge over into the next lane.

"Every day for ten years," Carla replied dryly. "I used to work for one of the affiliates here. Oh, look, there's our exit!"

And you just changed the subject again, Jake thought angrily as Carla chattered about the Galleria, the huge shopping mall adjacent to their hotel. He didn't think Carla was hiding anything important, but he was tired of her reluctance to talk about her past. He had opened up with her, even about the touchy subject of his back, and she simply refused to do the same with him. Her

179

refusal to talk about herself really hurt him badly. You're going to have to open up with me sooner or later, he thought grimly as he took their exit and drove through the clogged streets to the Galleria Plaza where he had reserved a suite. Although Carla had never complained about her moderate income and the thriftiness that she had to practice, he could tell that she liked elegance and luxury and thought that one of the nice suites would please her.

Jake parked under the driveway and a porter unloaded their suitcases onto a rolling cart. They both signed their names to the register without batting an eye, although Carla could have sworn the clerk winked at Jake when he thought she couldn't see. Although the August heat was wilting outside, the lobby was cool, and Carla could hardly wait to splash a little water on her parched face. As they boarded the elevator that would take them to their rooms on one of the upper floors, Jake caught sight of the two of them in a mirror, and he was suddenly ridiculously proud to have this beautifully dressed, elegant woman on his arm. He smiled to himself. Carla was as lovely on the outside as she was on the inside, no doubt about it. If only she weren't so secretive!

Carla gasped as she stepped into the luxurious suite. "Jake, this is lovely," she said softly as he came up behind her and put his arms around her.

"I thought you would like it," he said, nuzzling the back of her neck. The tip of his tongue touched her tender skin, sending prickles of awareness down her back.

"Are we going to commence this affair this morning?" she asked huskily as Jake's palms reached up to cup her breasts.

Jake made a production of looking at his watch, then

gasped out loud for real. "Damn, we have to be down-stairs in ten minutes! Do you need your makeup kit to get ready?"

Foresighted Carla had dressed for the luncheon in a cool summer suit and had put a few makeup essentials in her purse, so she was quickly refreshed and ready to go. They made their way back downstairs and found the meeting room, where a charming middle-aged couple introduced themselves as Ted and Martha Walton. Their college-age daughter had been killed by a drunken driver earlier in the year, and they wanted to start a coalition similar to the one Jake had organized in Corpus Christi.

Carla mingled easily as Jake stood with the Waltons at the door and greeted people as they came in. The guests drifted to tables and claimed a place to sit for the informal luncheon, and Jake signaled to Carla to join him and the Waltons at the head table. There were two other couples there also, and Carla enjoyed both the delicious pork chop luncheon and the delightful people she dined with. All the people at the table had lost a friend or family member to a drunken driver, and they were delighted to discover Carla's keen interest in their cause. Jake mentioned Carla's special, although he did not bring up their difference of opinion on it, and Carla hoped that he was over whatever objections he had at one time to her use of the Tyson tapes.

The Waltons introduced Jake to the assembled group, and Carla listened to him with admiration for the next hour and a half. Although Jake showed all the enthusiasm for the cause that he always had, on this occasion his burning urgency had been channeled into hard-headed practicality. These people were on his side, they shared his concern, so he wasted no time on persuasive rhetoric. Instead he gave a seminar on starting their own CCC from the ground up—how to form a non-profit organization, how to find a meeting place, how to lobby in Austin, how to call the public's attention to the cause, how to support tougher sentences without alienating the judges and the DA. As he talked, Carla realized for the first time just what kind of job it had been to organize the CCC from scratch, without benefit of the kind of advice these people were receiving, and her admiration for Jake went up just that many more notches.

There were thirty minutes of questions after Jake's lecture, then he and Carla left the meeting room and headed out into the Galleria. Carla had always enjoyed its collection of department stores and boutiques, although many of the stores were well out of her price range. They walked past Lord & Taylor and down into the original section of the mall. "Tell me, which shops are your favorites?" Jake asked as they gazed down on the huge ice rink nestled amid live trees on the mall's lower level.

"All of them!" Carla admitted. "Although I guess clothes are my weakness."

"Then let's buy you an imaginary wardrobe," Jake said as he reached out and held her by the hand.

Carla squeezed his fingers and pointed in the window of a youthful boutique. "How about that one?" she asked.

Jake took one look at the leather-studded jacket and started to laugh. "Only if you let me get you a motorcycle to go with it," he said.

They strolled through the mall, holding hands and pretending they were on a shopping trip. Carla drooled over a fur-trimmed cape in the window of Neiman's and Jake closely examined the selection in the shop of one of his competitors. Carla splurged and brought herself a stainless steel wok in one of the cooking shops, and Jake bought each of his daughters an imported leather shoulder bag for school. Carla's sharp eyes studied the fall fashions on the mannequins in the windows and, with Jake's interested prompting, she outlined to him what purchases she would make to update her wardrobe for the fall. He admitted that he was glad that very few of his customers had her clothes savvy—he sold more clothes when they gave everything away and started over!

After a couple of hours of browsing, they bought ice cream cones and sat down on a bench overlooking the skating rink. "Enjoying the window-shopping?" Jake asked.

"Sure am," Carla said as her eyes gazed across at the gold jewelry on display in the window of an exclusive jewelry store. Of course, the jewelry was well beyond her budget, but the craftsmanship was superb and Carla wanted to see the pieces up close. "I'll be back in a minute," she said as she got up and made her way to the window. She stared down at the bold, striking pieces. There were several wide gold cuffs and two chokers and several pair of geometric earrings in hammered gold. Carla admired the exquisite workmanship in the unusual pieces and felt a momentary wistfulness that such beauty was beyond her means. But there might be a way after all. Hurriedly she finished the ice cream and stuffed the napkin into the trash. Sometimes a store carried a similar line in silver, and if this one did she would be willing to go into hock for a pair of the hammered round earrings.

Jake nibbled his ice cream and watched the play of emotions cross Carla's face as she looked down at the jewelry—first admiration, then wistfulness, then excitement. Had she seen something she liked? Could she afford what she saw? Jake tossed the rest of his ice cream into the trash and followed her into the store.

Carla approached the counter and caught the eye of a bored salesman, who could tell at a glance that she had the taste to appreciate the fine pieces the store carried. "May I help you?" he asked.

"I'm interested in the hammered round earrings in the window," Carla asked. "Do you have them in silver?"

The salesman shook his head. "Our designer works only in gold," he said. "Would you like to see them in gold?"

Carla shook her head. "I don't think so," she said quietly, trying to mask her disappointment.

The salesman quickly assessed the situation. "Ma'am, there's a silversmith on the bottom floor who makes pieces similar to these, and his workmanship is excellent. Why don't you try there?"

Carla brightened. "I will," she said. "Thank you."

"Just a minute, sir," Jake said as he appeared at Carla's elbow. "Would you mind showing them to us in the gold?"

"Of course not," the salesman said, getting out his key and unlocking the window case.

Carla turned rueful eyes on Jake. "Oh, I hate to waste his time. Those earrings are several hundred dollars. I couldn't touch them, Jake. I'll go down to the silver shop."

Jake laid his hand on her arm. "Let me look at them," he said. "Humor me, Carla."

Carla shrugged and waited patiently until the salesman brought back the earrings. He held them out, and Carla reached out and took the box from him. She held the earrings up to her ears and peered into the mirror.

184

"They're beautiful," she breathed. "I'll definitely go down to the silver shop."

"May she try them on?" Jake asked.

"Oh, of course," the saleman assured him. Carla took off the costume earrings that she had on and replaced them with the hammered gold earrings. She peered into the mirror, admiring the earrings for a moment, then Jake turned her face toward him and stared at her. "They become you," he said. He pulled out his wallet and handed the salesman an American Express card. "She'll take them," he said.

"Jake, no, I can't possibly aff—" The rest of Carla's protest was stilled by the swift descent of Jake's mouth on hers. He kissed her in full view of everyone in the shop until he was sure her embarrassment was sufficient to quiet her protest, then he waited calmly for the transaction to be completed. Carla stood quietly, her face burning as she wondered how Jake expected her to pay him back in the near future. The earrings were five hundred dollars!

The transaction was completed quickly, and Jake picked up Carla's costume earrings and put them in his pocket. He then took the dumbfounded woman by the arm and led her from the jewelry store. "Happy August," he said as he kissed first one ear and then the other. "They're my present to you. No, not a word!" he said autocratically as she started to protest. "First off, I'm not making a habit of this. I wouldn't insult your independence by showering you regularly with fancy gifts. But damn it, you've given Sonia and me so much, and you would Patty too if she'd let you. I want to give you these, to thank you for the happiness you've given me and my little girl. All right?"

Carla nodded as she reached up and fingered the earrings. Suddenly they were more than just a work of art.

They were a symbol, if not of Jake's love, of his gratitude to her for caring. "I'll treasure them, Jake," she assured him, her protests forgotten.

"Carla, when can I have the shower?" Jake asked, sticking his head in the steamy door of the bathroom. "The reservations are for eight, and it's nearly seven."

"Coming," Carla called as she emerged from the steam, damp and naked but for a towel wrapped around her. "Sorry, I lay down for a moment and went to sleep."

"That's all right," Jake assured her as he admired the fetching sight she made with her hair wet and her body only partly covered by the thick terrycloth towel. She was a tempting sight and Jake felt desire curl in his lower body, but he was hot and sweaty from a workout in the Galleria's rooftop health club and he didn't think she would appreciate his sweaty masculinity just at this moment.

Carla confirmed his theory by turning up her nose a little. "Soap's that way," she suggested, pointing to the bathroom.

Carla watched Jake as he headed for the bathroom, shedding his clothes on the way. Shaking her head, she picked up the sweaty shirt and shorts. She found a sack to put the clothes in and opened her suitcase. She withdrew lacy underwear and pulled it on, then picked out the dress she had brought to wear tonight. It was a simple blue caftan in polished cotton and it had cost Carla an arm and a leg even at her discount boutique. She pulled it on and looked approvingly at herself in the mirror. Yes, it was worth it, she assured herself as she admired the way the gold earrings complemented the dress. She added the chunky wood and cord necklace she had brought and quickly made up her face. She wanted to look her best tonight. Tonight was special—before it was over, she and Jake would again be lovers.

Jake emerged from the shower wrapped in a towel as Carla picked up the hair dryer. Damp from the shower, the gray hair on his head and his chest glistened, and Carla set the dryer back down and reached out to stroke his chest lovingly. "I've wanted to do that every time I've seen you without your shirt," she said as Jake picked up her hand and kissed it. He laid her hand back down on his chest, and through the hair she could feel his heart beating wildly. He's as excited as I am, she thought as his heart beat a wild tattoo against her fingers. He let the towel drop and drew her to him, kissing her slowly as he ran his fingers through her damp hair. "Thank you for coming, Carla," Jake murmured against her lips.

Carla's hands slid around Jake's waist and she pulled his hips closer to hers. "We can call the restaurant and cancel if you wish," she murmured against his lips.

Jake kissed her once more and pushed her away. "No, I'd like tonight to be special. I want to wine you and dine you like the lady you are, and I want to show you off in that wild dress and your earrings. It'll just be that much better if we wait."

Carla nodded and pulled away, feasting her eyes on Jake's naked body. Good heavens, it was all she could do to keep from knocking him onto the bed and begging him to make love to her! But Jake was right. Tonight was special, and they deserved to savor every minute of the delightful anticipation. She sat down at the vanity stool and picked up her hair dryer. She was about to turn it on when Jake, clad in a pair of briefs, took it from her and switched it on himself, taking the brush from her. Carla sat, amazed, as Jake wordlessly made drying her hair a sensuous prelude to the love they would be making later on in the evening. Slowly he stroked her hair, holding it up and letting the warm air caress her sensitive scalp, then picking up another section of hair and curling it around the brush. Every brushstroke sent shivers down her body to her toes.

When her hair was dry, Jake kissed her cheek and finished dressing. Carla loaded her things into an evening purse and slipped into a pair of high heels that brought her to Jake's height. Jake had just finished with the buttons on his silk sport shirt when she stood up. "You look lovely," he assured her.

"You look wonderful yourself," Carla said as they left the suite. Downstairs the attendant brought them their rented car, and Carla gave Jake directions as he drove them to Kaphans, one of Houston's oldest and most respected seafood restaurants. They arrived on time, but the headwaiter explained that there would be a slight delay and pointed them to a comfortable bar. Jake ordered them both a glass of wine. Carla sank down next to him and slipped her hand into his. She was thinking of the night to come when she heard a strident voice calling her name across the crowded bar. "Carla! Carla Thompson! How are you, honey! My God, it's been years since I've seen you!"

Carla ignored the surprise in Jake's eyes as he mouthed the unfamiliar last name, and she turned toward the homely face that came with the voice. "Jane Ann, how are you?" Carla asked. "And Tommy?"

"Aw, hell, Tommy and I got divorced four years ago," Jane Ann said. "Once you and Mike broke the ice, there were three divorces on the block in the next three years. I don't know about the others, but, Carla, honey, I'm grateful to you!"

"Thank you." Carla laughed uneasily as she saw Jake's face start to darken. "By the way, Jane Ann, I'd like you to meet Jake Darrow. We're up from Corpus for the weekend."

Jake masked his hurt and anger and extended his hand to Jane Ann.

"How-de-do, Jake," Jane Ann said. "From Corpus? When did you move down there, Carla?"

"Nearly six years ago," Carla said.

"Well, hell, no wonder I haven't seen you in years. Gosh, it seems like just yesterday you and Mike were our neighbors. Saw him and Belinda just a few months ago. Those two boys of theirs are getting big now, and their baby girl's a real doll. Looks just like Mike. Belinda's gone back to work at the station to help him buy a bigger house for the family."

In spite of his hurt feelings and his anger, Jake felt Carla's body stiffen next to his. "I'm glad Mike and his family are doing well," she said calmly. "Did you and Tommy ever have a family?"

Jane Ann shook her head. "Nah, I'd rather have my horses any day. You don't have to send them to college. Listen, they just called my name. Great to meet you, Jake. Call me before you leave, Carla, and we'll have a real chance to get caught up." Jane Ann strode briskly across the room as her strident voice chided the waiter for the long wait.

Jake turned angry eyes on Carla. "You didn't even bother to tell me you'd been married," he said accusingly.

"I didn't want to talk about it," Carla bit out. "You have enough problems of your own without listening to mine."

"That's a crock and you know it," he said coldly. "You wouldn't have had to have given me a blow-by-blow account of your marriage. But not to even mention it, especially after I had asked you to tell me about yourself! That's really low, Carla. How long were you married, anyway?"

"Ten years," Carla ground out.

"That's a long time," Jake said. "And you didn't even think it was worth mentioning."

"It's a part of my past life," Carla said defensively, her eyes filled with pain. "I've been divorced for eight years now, and none of my friends in Corpus except for Jeannie and Bradley know I was ever married. I forget it myself most of the time," she said firmly. "By choice."

"You're not going to tell me about it, are you?" Jake asked as his eyes narrowed. "Not even now."

"Not tonight," Carla said angrily, then her face softened. "Jake, I know I've hurt you terribly, and I'll tell you about Mike and my marriage sometime, but I don't want to spoil tonight by dredging up a lot of old hurts. I want tonight to be for just you and me, and not a lot of ghosts from the past. *Please,* Jake, not tonight. Some other time, but not tonight."

"I'm going to hold you to that," Jake said as he nodded his agreement, although her refusal to confide in him still upset him. The waitress brought their drinks and he sipped his as his mind raced. Carla had effectively cut off any more information about her marriage, but she could not stop the questions that were bouncing around in his head. Whom had she been married to? What kind of marriage had she had? Why had she gotten a divorce? Why didn't they have any children? And why had she been so determined not to talk to him about it?

She must have been terribly hurt, Jake thought as he gazed at Carla's calm face. Whoever he was, he must have hurt her horribly. Jake's anger melted and he wanted to take Carla into his arms and heal her wounds

190

as she had tried to heal his. "All right, Carla, not tonight," he agreed. "But you must talk to me about it sometime."

"I will," she promised as she sipped her drink. So Mike had three kids now. Good for him, she thought. That's what he wanted. She waited for the bitterness to creep in as it used to when she thought of her ex-husband, but only a tired remnant of the remembered pain found its way inside her heart. I guess it's all well and truly behind me now, she thought as she turned to Jake and asked him a question about the agenda in Dallas tomorrow.

"Well, are you ready to go?" Jake asked, gazing across the table at Carla. Her face was glowing in the flickering candlelight and to him she had never looked more beautiful.

"Yes." She smiled across at him. She had put Jane Ann's intrusion and the argument out of her mind, and they had enjoyed a delicious dinner of crab imperial with all the trimmings. They had laughed and talked about various things during dinner, but every look, every word had been laced with a sensual awareness that was building to the evening's inevitable climax. It was now time to go back to the hotel, to play out the scene that had been building between them since early this morning. Jake signaled for the waiter and handed him a credit card. They left the restaurant just a few moments later, and Jake drove back to the hotel quickly.

As they rode the elevator to their floor, the distracted smile left Jake's face and Carla could tell that he was beginning to withdraw from her. Oh, hell, was he having second thoughts after all? Did he feel that he was wrong in making love to her? They stepped off the elevator and Jake felt around in his pocket for the key. He finally found it in his back pocket, and with trembling fingers he inserted the key in the lock and pushed open the door. He let Carla past him and pulled the door shut behind him, then sat down in a chair in the sitting room and put his hands in his lap.

Good God, what's the matter with me? Jake asked himself as Carla kicked off her shoes and put her purse in the bedroom. Here he was in a luxurious hotel suite with a beautiful woman who really wanted him to make love to her, and he was as scared as a teenager about to have sex for the first time. For the first time in his life he regretted the fact that he had not had a number of partners. Maybe if he had played around a little more as a young man, he would know what he was supposed to do now. He looked across the room at Carla, who was fussing with a brush on the dresser. Was she waiting for him to make the first move? Had her other lovers been better than he was? Could he satisfy her tonight?

Carla felt her heart sinking to her toes as she observed Jake's woebegone expression. He's changed his mind, she thought with exasperation as he stared across the room at her. He's sitting there thinking of a way to get out of it. I knew he wasn't ready for this. What do I do now? she asked herself angrily. For a moment she considered seducing him anyway—she knew she could do it—but he would hate her in the morning and she didn't think she could stand that. No, I'll let him off the hook, she thought disgustedly as she walked into the sitting room and sat down beside him. "You don't have to, you know," she said tightly. "I'll sleep out here."

Jake jerked himself out of his reverie. "I don't have to do what?" he asked.

"You don't have to go through with it, you know," she said.

Jake looked at her as though she had just flown in the window. "Have you changed your mind?"

Carla shook her head. "But if you have, that's all right."

Jake shook his head back and forth. "Whatever gave you that idea?" he said as he leaned forward and gave her a hard kiss on her lips. "I most certainly have *not* changed my mind!"

"But you looked so sad there for a minute, so scared!" she said, her anger fading. "I thought you were having second thoughts."

Jake blushed a deep shade of red and started laughing. "No, I was trying to figure out what I'm supposed to do next," he admitted. He turned embarrassed eyes on Carla. "I never had an affair, except with Debbie, and I'm a little nervous. You know more about this kind of thing than I do."

"Not *that* much more!" Carla sputtered indignantly. "And you did a pretty good job that night in Austin!"

Jake's face lit up like a Christmas tree. "Did I really? I was afraid that I might not have . . . well, you know."

"Oh, Jake, you really don't know, do you?" Carla breathed. "You have to be the best lover I've ever had, not that there have been that many, and that includes my former husband. Even as soused as you were that night." She leaned forward and ran her tongue around the edge of his ear. "Why do you think I could hardly wait to make love to you when you were sober?"

Jake shivered at the touch of her tongue on his ear, then he slipped his arm around her and settled back into the cushions. "So what do we do now? Strip and go to it?"

"Jake, you're priceless!" Carla squealed. "Just a minute, let me think." Jake ran his hand up the smoothness

193

of her thigh and she giggled. "Just a minute, I'm trying to remember what comes first!"

"I think I've figured it out!" Jake cried. His hand ran all the way up her leg until it encountered the softness of her hip.

"Jake, give me a minute!" Carla cried as she jumped up and ran for the bedroom, Jake on her heels. He caught up with her just as she reached the bed and fell across it with her, wrapping her in a tender embrace as his lips locked with hers. They kissed and touched for long moments, their lips and tongues mingling as Carla felt the heat of his body next to hers. Finally Jake drew away and smiled down at her. "All right now?" she asked.

Jake nodded. "I'm sorry about the nerves earlier," he said. "I'm fine now."

Carla sat up and climbed off the bed. "Five minutes," she said, pulling a silken swath from her suitcase and running toward the bathroom. She quickly wiggled out of her clothes and into the long filmy gown she had brought, but somehow the diaphanous flutter of fabric did not suit their present playful mood. She stripped off the nightgown and wrapped one of the big pink towels around her body. Jake looked as though he could have devoured her in the towel earlier this evening, so she knew it would appeal. She quickly rinsed the makeup off her face and applied a light scent to the hollow between her breasts, then she shut off the bathroom light and went to stand in front of Jake, who had removed his clothing and was resting under the covers.

Jake stared with undisguised appreciation and pleasure as Carla glided across the room to him. Clad only in a soft terry towel, she looked as innocent and vulnerable as a child, yet there was nothing childlike or innocent in her expression. She was a woman, she was all woman, and she wanted him. Her clean face glowed with excitement and joy and anticipation, and her lips were slightly parted, waiting for the touch of his lips on hers. God, why had it taken him so long to make love to her again? She had been right. They should have become lovers weeks ago.

"Come here, Carla," Jake said, extending his hand to her. Boldly she reached out and clasped his hand with her own, allowing him to pull her toward the bed. With fingers that trembled just a little from nervous anticipation, Jake drew Carla to the edge of the bed and pulled out the little flap of towel that was tucked between her breasts, then tossed the towel across the floor, baring her body to his eager gaze. He had been too looped that night long ago in Austin to appreciate the soft creaminess of her arms and legs, the tender uptilt of her high, firm breasts, the pale softness of her neck and shoulders. He had failed to notice the enticing way her body narrowed into a tiny waist or the funny little swirl of peachy down at her navel. He had not appreciated the slender curving of her hips or the smooth length of her thighs. Jake held Carla's hand, not drawing her any closer, as he drank in the sight of her body for long moments. As though under a spell, Carla stood quietly, obediently, letting him learn her body with his eyes. "You're divine," he said finally.

The sound of his words broke the spell. Jake drew Carla toward him and scooted over on the huge bed as she slipped in beside him. He started to push her down into the pillows but before he could stop her, she had flipped the sheet off his body and had pushed him down. "Let me look at you," she said. "Let me touch you, like I've wanted to touch you for the last two months."

Delighted by Carla's boldness, Jake lay back. Carla's eager lips bent down and brushed his, but before he

195

could deepen the kiss her lips had drifted lower, touching and caressing his bare shoulders and chest. She nibbled her way down to his nipple, where her tongue teased it and tormented it until it was a hard bud. She took a quick swipe at the other one but did not linger, leaving Jake vaguely unsatisfied until he realized that she had other destinations on her mind.

Once Carla had explored Jake's muscular chest to her fill, she let her hands and her lips drift lower, delighting in every discovery she made about his hard, sensual, arousing body. Her fingers found the flat muscles that held his waist firm and tormented them until they were taut under her touch, then she found the tense muscles of his stomach and caressed them until Jake was positively writhing under her touch. As she tormented him with her fingers she tormented herself with her eyes, feasting on his beautifully proportioned body, his strong legs, his slim thighs, the strength and arousal in his slim hips. He wanted her tonight. And tonight he knew who he was making love to, who was touching him with her fingers and her lips. He knew that Carla was his lover, and she knew that he wanted her.

Jake let Carla touch and caress him until he possessed only a tiny sliver of control, then with tender strength he turned her over in bed and began to touch her body eagerly, to explore her the way she had explored him. Her small nipples felt wonderful to his lips; her stomach smooth to his palm. He slid his hands down and spanned the width of her waist with his fingers. "You're so tiny," he whispered. "I can reach around you with my fingers."

Carla moaned and arched her body toward him, glorying in the feel of his lips on her breasts, his hands around her waist. Almost mindless with pleasure, she drifted, letting Jake touch and torment her as he wished. His nervousness had been for nothing. He was a wonderful lover. He was strong, he was tender, he knew how to touch her so that he drove her almost out of her mind. The gentle hand that stroked her stomach drifted even lower, and Carla gasped as knowing fingers found the center of her femininity and pleasured her until he could sense that she could take no more. "Now, Carla," he whispered as he parted her legs with his and made them one.

Carla had thought their lovemaking beautiful that night in Austin, but that evening was only a sample of the emotions and sensations Jake could bring forth in her. He moved over her, slowly at first, drawing out the sensual pleasure of his touch, then faster and faster, carrying her away with him to the pinnacle of pleasure. Carla gasped and moved with him, matching his every move with one of her own, so that they rocked and writhed in tandem in their own private heaven. Together they moved, faster, now slower, as Jake built the momentum slowly for the both of them. They scaled the cliffs of pleasure together, as under Jake's direction they came step by step to the summit. Carla could feel the tension tightening within her, slowly and then more quickly, until she could feel her body rushing out of control. As she crested the summit of pleasure, she felt Jake stiffen above her, and together they tumbled over the top of the cliffs and down the hilly slopes of the other side.

Jake rested his forehead on Carla's for a minute, then he kissed her eyelids gently and snuggled down beside her. "You're wonderful," he said as he reached up and brushed a strand of hair off her face.

"So are you," Carla assured him. "You have no reason to ever be nervous or unsure with me." She snuggled her face into his shoulder and draped her arm across his stomach. "I could stay like this all night."

"No, you can't," Jake said as he turned her face toward his and covered it in a long, lingering kiss. "We'll have champagne sent up and then in a few minutes we'll do it all over again."

Carla laughed as Jake sat up and picked up the telephone. "If I'd been thinking, we'd have had the champagne first," he said.

"I'm not complaining," Carla assured him as he dialed room service.

When he hung up, he turned to her, an expression of concern on his face.

"I hate to mention it, but this is the second time we've made love without protection," Jake said. "I forgot about it earlier, just like I forgot the champagne. Are you all right?"

"Yes, I'm fine," Carla said quietly.

"I mean, are you sure? I know you didn't use anything tonight," Jake persisted. "Or are you on the Pill?"

"No, Jake, I didn't use anything tonight and I'm not on the Pill," Carla said in a small, tight voice. "I'm all right because my tubes were tied years ago."

CHAPTER ELEVEN

Carla sat up and slid slowly out of the bed, then she walked over to her suitcase and got out a peach-colored robe and tied it on. Lost in a wave of painful memories, she did not even notice the look of shocked disapproval on Jake's face. She ran a brush through her hair and pushed on a pair of house shoes. "I'm well enough covered in this robe to answer the door," she said. "I'll get the champagne. You can stay where you are." She walked into the sitting room and sat down on the couch to wait for the knock. She didn't care about the champagne any more, but she wanted a few minutes by herself to think. She knew that if their relationship was going to be one of complete honesty and trust, Jake deserved to know about Mike and her marriage. But it was hard for her to dredge up the past, to talk about the disappointment and the heartache that she had put behind her so successfully. After all these years, it still hurt to talk about it.

Jake stared throught the open door at Carla as she sat quietly waiting for the champagne to arrive. He wished now that he had not pressed her to tell him about her birth control status. She was an intelligent woman; he should have trusted her when she said that everything was all right. But why would she have taken such extreme measures? Why would a lovely woman like Carla have that done to herself? Was she that afraid of becoming pregnant and having her career disrupted? Jake's eyes narrowed as he thought of the love Debbie had lavished on their two girls. Was Carla so selfish that she refused her husband children? Was that why he had left her and had a family with another woman?

No, that just didn't add up. Carla was too warm, too loving a human being to do a thing like that. Even if the thought of children would not have overjoyed her, in the generosity of her spirit she would have given her husband children if he had wanted them. Besides, she had had a genuine fondness for Sonia that had nothing to do with her relationship with him. Carla had taken Sonia to her heart and seemed to have an almost wistful love for his little girl. So it wasn't that Carla disliked children or had no interest in them. It had to be something else.

Jake pushed himself up off the bed and found a thick velour robe in his suitcase. He glanced into the sitting room and his heart twisted at the pained sorrow he saw in her eyes. Damn, he should have kept his mouth shut. His persistence had brought back something very painful to Carla, something that had spoiled the beautiful intimacy they had shared. But wasn't that what intimacy was all about—sharing? Wasn't that what she had encouraged him to do with her? Jake pushed the door of the sitting room open a little wider and stared at Carla's troubled face. He was going to ask her to talk to him tonight, to tell him about her troubled past, and he hoped for the sake of their relationship that she trusted him enough to do so.

Jake sat down on the sofa beside Carla and took her hand. "I'm sorry I upset you," he said quietly. "If I had realized that I was getting into a painful area, I would have kept my mouth shut."

Carla shrugged. "That's all right," she said flippantly. "Wouldn't want Carla to come up pregnant, now would we? Heaven forbid! I'm sure that's the last thing you want," she added sarcastically.

"Carla, I'm sorry if I offended you," Jake said softly. "I wasn't thinking of myself. I assumed that the thought wouldn't have pleased you at all."

"No, Jake, I'm sorry," Carla said. "That remark was bitchy and uncalled-for. You were being considerate, not wanting to get me pregnant. Not that there's any possibility of that," she added bitingly to herself.

She's bitter about it, Jake thought. So it wasn't a voluntary thing. "Carla, I want you to tell me why you were sterilized," Jake said, gently but firmly.

Carla shook her head. "It's in the past," she said. "It's over."

"No, it isn't," Jake replied. "You're still bitter about something, even though you don't talk about it."

"I'd rather forget it," Carla said as a knock sounded on the door.

Jake got up and answered the door, then he put the champagne in the bedroom and sat back down beside Carla. "I know you think I'm being pushy, Carla, but I think I need to know whatever it is that happened to you. Look, I'm your lover now, and I've shared everything with you. You know about my marriage, my sorrow at losing my wife, the way I'm struggling to bring up the girls. You know when I'm angry and when I'm bitter. You even know how much I hate having a bum back! I haven't held anything back, yet I've known you four months and I didn't even find out until tonight that you were married for ten years!" Jake reached out and took her hand. "If we're going to have any kind of relationship, and I do want one with you, we're both going to have to share our thoughts, our feelings, our pasts—everything."

"And I haven't done that," Carla said. "Jake, I'm sorry. You're right, I should have shared my past with you long before now." She got up and walked aimlessly around the couch. "But I thought that you had enough troubles without having to think about mine. And I'm over mine now. It all happened so long ago."

"What happened, Carla?" Jake asked.

"Mike, marriage, and all the babies we lost," Carla said. "Mike and I married while I was still in school, then when I graduated we moved to Houston and went to work for one of the affiliates." Carla sat down in a chair across from the couch. "Mike was a reporter and I did the weather, and before too long he had worked his way up to anchorman. We loved each other and we were happy." Carla shrugged. "I thought I had a good marriage."

"And then?" Jake asked.

"We tried to start a family," Carla said. "Oh, I didn't have any trouble getting pregnant, but I sure had trouble staying that way. The medical term is 'chronic aborter,' which is a polite way of saying that I can't hang on to a pregnancy for more than three or four months. We tried for five years to have a child. I lost one every year, would get well and start over, and lose another one."

"That's bound to have been hard on your health," Jake said disapprovingly.

Carla shrugged. "Of course it was, but Mike and I wanted a child. The doctor tried to get us to quit after the fourth miscarriage, but we begged for one more chance, so when I got pregnant the last time I went to bed. That pregnancy lasted six months, then I delivered a little girl who lived for three hours." Carla thought a minute. "When is Sonia's birthday?"

"March," Jake said grimly.

"My little girl would have been just a couple of months older if she had lived," Carla said quietly. "Anyway, I hemorrhaged and they tell me that I came close to dying. The doctor told me that another pregnancy would kill me and that there was no way I could have a child anyway, so I got well and then let him tie my tubes."

"Is that why you got a divorce?" Jake asked.

Carla nodded. "Mike stuck around long enough for our joint insurance policy to pay the hospital bills, and then he left me and married Belinda a few months after our divorce was final. I heard later that she was already five months' pregnant when he married her. I guess he wasn't taking a chance on it happening to him twice," she added bitterly.

"So you moved to Corpus Christi and made a new life for yourself," Jake said.

Carla nodded. "I left that station immediately, of course, and went to work for another, then when Paul called me a couple of years later with the job at KGBD, I jumped at it. I decided that if the family I had always wanted was out, then I would be the best damned producer in Corpus Christi." She smiled faintly. "And I think I've made it. You know what Paul thinks of my work, and I've won several awards in the last six years." She shrugged. "Those awards aren't very warm on a cold winter's night, but they beat having nothing."

"Have you thought of marrying again?" Jake asked.

Not until I met you, Carla thought to herself. She shook her head. "No, I really haven't," she answered. "And it's not because I'm bitter about men because of Mike. Nine out of ten would have stayed with me and adopted a child. No, I guess the right man just hasn't come along." Until now, she amended to herself.

Jake stood and moved until he was behind Carla's

chair. He placed his hands on her tense shoulders and started kneading them gently. "How did you cope with all of that?" he asked. "It would have destroyed a lot of women."

"It's like any other grief, Jake," Carla said. "It nearly did destroy me at the time. I had crying jags for almost a year, and something as stupid as seeing a new mother with her baby could set one off. But I'm over that now. It took a long time, but I've put it behind me." The firmness was back in her voice, and Jake could tell that the conversation was over.

"Well, I just think you're a hell of a brave lady," he said as he put his hands on her shoulders and lifted her up out of the chair. He moved around the chair until he was facing her. "Brave, and beautiful, and so very womanly," he said as he kissed her tenderly on her lips.

"You don't think I'm less of a woman because I can't have children?" she asked softly.

Jake shook his head, horrified at the thought. "Oh, Carla, no!" he assured her. "I think you're a brave woman for trying so hard!" His lips tightened in a grim line. "I wouldn't have let it go on," he said. "If it had been my wife, we would have adopted after the second or third miscarriage."

"But then, you're a very loving, very special man," Carla said softly, sliding her arms around his shoulders. *And I love you,* she said to herself. *I love you so much, but I can't tell you that just yet, because you're not ready to hear it.*

Jake wrapped Carla in his arms and rocked back and forth with her. "Are you all right?" he asked. "I'm sorry I brought up so many unhappy memories."

Carla nodded. "You needed to know," she said softly. "So let's think about other things for the rest of the evening. The past is over, it's here and now and I'm with the most wonderful man in the world." She stepped back and untied her robe and let it fall into a rumpled heap at her feet. "Make love to me again," she said as she stood naked before him. "I need you tonight." She reached out and untied Jake's robe and pushed it to his feet. "I need your warmth, your tenderness." She moved toward Jake until the tender tips of her breasts brushed the curling hair on his chest.

Jake's arms wrapped around Carla and he pressed her to his naked body. "Oh, Carla, I need you too!" he said as he held her close. "I need your gentleness, your passion, all that you give me." He framed her face with his palms and kissed her lips lovingly. "And I want to give you the same. I want to hold you and love you and make all the hurts of the past go away. Can I do that for you?"

Carla nodded, her eyes suspiciously bright. "Yes, you can, Jake. You most certainly can!"

Jake took Carla by the hand and led her toward the wide, rumpled bed. "I want us to have that champagne," he said as he sat Carla down on the side of the bed and reached for the bottle. "We've both been victims of circumstances beyond our control, Carla. I want us to drink to the days to come, that our futures might hold more joy than our pasts have given us."

"I think we should drink to that," she agreed. Suddenly the cork flew from the bottle and champagne bubbled forth. "Here, pour," Carla said, holding a goblet under the bottle. Jake filled it, then Carla held up the second one.

Jake picked up the goblet and clinked it against Carla's. "To the future," he said.

"To the future," Carla said as she sipped the champagne. The sparkling wine was delicious, but some of the bubbles got up her nose and she sneezed violently, spilling a little champagne on Jake's bare chest.

Jake laughed as Carla blushed. "Sneezing like a kid," he teased. "That's the first time I've had fancy champagne spilled all over me."

"Sorry, let me clean it off," Carla said as the rivulets ran down Jake's chest. She leaned over and began to kiss the trail that the drops of champagne had left, making her way down Jake's broad chest. "This is delicious," she said softly as she pushed Jake down in the sheets and deliberately poured a little more of her champagne in the middle of his chest.

"Yow, that's cold!" Jake complained, but he made no protest when Carla followed the champagne with her tender lips, kissing the trail that it had left. She continued to kiss him even when the champagne was gone, touching and caressing his chest and his shoulders with her lips and her fingers. She raised herself and found Jake's lips, lightly flavored with champagne as were her own, and brushed against them gently. Jake put his finger in her champagne glass and drew a circle of champagne around her mouth, kissing his way around the circle of moisture. "Umm, champagne *is* delicious this way," he agreed as Carla put her finger in the glass and drew a similar circle around his lips. She kissed off the sweet taste of the champagne, then their lips locked together as they shared a deep, tender, caring kiss that shook Carla to her toes.

"Let me love you," Jake murmured as he rolled over and pressed Carla down into the sheets, his mouth drinking from the beauty of her lips and her body. He felt passion for Carla, of course, but since her revelation of the hurt she had suffered in the past, he felt fiercely protective of her too. He wanted to take care of her and take her away from everything that could hurt her, and he communicated those feelings as he kissed Carla and touched her intimately. He wanted to hold her, to cherish her, to shield her from any more hurt. Carla shivered as his lips traveled lower and found one of the aching buds of her breast. He tormented it until it was hard with desire, then with infinite gentleness and caring he found the other breast and caressed it until it too was hard with delight.

As Jake's lips continued to move lower, Carla could only marvel at the way her heart swelled with love for him. Their lovemaking earlier in the evening had been wonderful, of course, but it had been primarily a joining of passion, two people driven by a strong physical desire to become one. But now, now that she had broken down and shared with him the hurt and the sorrow of the past, it was like they were joining on a mental and an emotional plane also, two hearts and minds joining as well as two bodies. Jake had cared, had really cared that she had been hurt in the past, and his touch revealed the same longing to ease her hurt that she had felt about him for the last four months. Every kiss, every caress said "I care." And Carla poured her love and her caring into her kisses and caresses as she returned kiss for kiss, touch for touch, letting him know that she wanted to hold and comfort him too. Eagerly she stroked the skin of his back and the smoothness of his hips, touching and caressing the strength of his thighs and the back of his legs. Slowly she slid her hands upward, until she encountered the strength of his masculinity, and with daring fingers she explored it, letting Jake know in no uncertain terms how much she wanted him.

Jake groaned and moved away from her. "Just a minute," he whispered as his lips traveled down her chest and onto the smoothness of her stomach. "I want to give you pleasure tonight." His lips tormented the soft indentation of her navel, encountering a small scar that must have been her surgery scar, then traveled lower, past the barriers to the final intimacy. Jake gently parted her legs with his hands and found the center of her desire, his gentle ministrations building the tension within Carla. She moaned and tried to pull away, but Jake anchored her hips with his hands and continued to torment her. He wanted to give her this pleasure, he needed to give to her unselfishly, the way she had given her caring and her healing affection to him. He wanted her to know what a man's unselfish loving could be like. The pressure built up, higher and higher, until crashing waves of satisfaction overtook Carla and she arched and moaned beneath him, shooting stars of pleasure going off behind her eyes. Never, never had a man made her feel the way Jake had made her feel, and she had never known that kind of satisfaction was even possible.

But Jake was not through with her yet. Slowly, tenderly he primed her body again, kissing and touching and caressing until Carla, who had thought her capacity for pleasure was spent, was on fire for him again. He would not let her pleasure him the way he had pleasured her, saying as he stroked her hips and the tender warmth of her womanliness that he wanted tonight to be hers alone. This time when she was ready he parted her legs and made them one, kissing her lips as he claimed her. Carla reeled with the force of the physical rapport they shared and with the emotional joining that went with it. They moved together, their hearts and their bodies joined, in a dance as old as the stars yet new for them. Carla whispered Jake's name over and over as the passion soared between them yet again, carrying them both to a place they had never shared before. At the moment of delight Carla called out Jake's name and heard her name echoed on his lips. Waves of pleasure and release rocked her as she gave herself over to the storm that tore her from within.

They rested in the swirling aftermath for a moment, then Jake rolled off her and held her close. Spent, Carla started to tell him that she loved him, but she shut her eyes for a moment and drifted off to sleep before she could say the words.

Jake reached down and pulled up the covers, then he stared down at the woman who slept so trustingly in his arms. Her revelations tonight had startled him and had given him a whole new picture of the woman who was coming to mean so much to him. It had nearly destroyed her when she lost that last little girl and that bastard had left her, but instead of folding up, she had gone on with her life. And to think that once he had accused her of never having been hurt! Yes, she had been hurt, at least as badly as he had. Even though Debbie's death had hurt him, his loss had been a clean kind of pain, and he had plenty of happy memories to go with it. Carla had to get over not only the loss of her desperately wanted children, but the betrayal of the man she loved.

But she had done it. She had gotten over the hurt and the loss and she had made a good life for herself in a new city. And that had taken courage. Do I have that kind of courage? he asked himself. Can I put Debbie's death behind me and go on like Carla has? He wasn't sure, since he knew he was still in love with his dead wife. He deliberately made himself think of her and what they had shared, and yes, the pain, the hurt, the loss was still there. He still loved her, still missed her, still wanted her back. He wasn't over her yet.

But it wasn't as bad as it used to be. Some of the pain was fading. Maybe it is happening, Jake thought as he kissed Carla's forehead. Maybe I can put it behind me and go on. For the first time, he could envision a happy future without Debbie, and the thought surprised him very much.

Jake blinked then opened his eyes and stared at the telephone on the nightstand. Damn, what time was it? Groaning, he reached out and picked up the receiver, afraid that it might be Mrs. Lopez saying that one of the girls was sick. Or maybe it was the wakeup call he had requested. Yes, that was it. "Hello," he mumbled into the receiver.

"Jake, this is Paul Simmons," Paul's voice boomed into the receiver. "May I speak to Carla, please?"

What on earth? How did Paul know where he and Carla were? He reached out and shook Carla's shoulder. "Carla, telephone," he said as Carla lifted bleary eyes to his face.

"Who?" she asked rather grumpily.

"Paul Simmons," Jake replied, irritation showing on his face.

"What on earth does he want?" Carla asked as she took the receiver from Jake's hand. "What can I do for you at seven o'clock on Sunday morning in Houston?" Carla asked irritably. "How did you know where I was?"

"I knew you were with Jake, so I called Jake's house and asked Patty where he was. Carla, I'm sorry to disturb you two right now, but I need you to come back to Corpus this morning. We have a tropical storm brewing in the Gulf that Chad thinks is going to make into a full-fledged hurricane. Unless it changes course it's headed right for Corpus." Chad was the independent meteorologist that the station had hired, and Carla had very little faith in his ability.

"Paul, that's ridiculous! That turkey couldn't predict

210

a windstorm if it blew out the candles on his birthday cake," Carla protested as she sat up and shoved a pillow behind her back. She let the cover slide to her waist, and her nipples hardened in the chill of the air conditioning. "There is no earthly reason for me to hurry back today."

Paul sighed. "Look, I'm sorry for interrupting your weekend, and if I didn't think I really needed you to help cover this storm I wouldn't have called. I just feel strongly about this one, Carla. Trust an old newsman's instinct, will you? Tell Jake I'm sorry. I'll see you later today. I've got to call Kevin now."

Carla hung up the telephone. "Paul must think it's serious," she said. "He didn't talk my ear off like he usually does." She flopped back against the pillow and clenched her fingers into fists. "Damn, damn, damn! I wanted to go to Dallas with you, Jake!"

Jake reached out and unclenched her tight fists. "I'm sorry too," he said. "I'll call Manny Holmes in Dallas and cancel."

Carla shook her head vigorously. "Oh, don't do that!" she protested. "There's no point, honestly."

"But if the Weather Bureau says there's a danger—"

"That's just it," Carla said. "The Weather Bureau's said nothing. Paul hired this clown to have an independent opinion. So far he's been wrong four times out of five. Here," she said as she picked up the telephone. "Call the local bureau. See what it thinks."

Jake got out the telephone book and dialed the local number, but all he could get was a forecast recording. "Look, maybe I ought to go on back just in case," he said as he hung up the telephone. "Your meteorologist might not know anything, but Paul's hunches have always been good."

"Until he hired that yo-yo," Carla said. Jake lay back

211

down beside her and she pillowed her head on his chest. "Jake, I'm going back because I have to, but there's absolutely no reason for you to cancel Dallas. Damn!" she said as she nuzzled the curling hair of his chest, "I wanted to spend the weekend with you so badly!"

"So? We still have most of today," Jake chided her. "I'll take a later flight to Dallas, and you can take a late one back to Corpus."

"Sounds great," Carla said as she stroked Jake's chest with her fingers.

"How about a little breakfast and then we can go out to NASA," Jake suggested. "You can show me around."

Carla nodded as her fingers worked lightly down Jake's chest. At first her touch was only meant to caress and comfort, but passion began to build between them both, the same passion that had burned so brightly between them last night. Jake turned over and bore Carla down into the sheets. "I think we better plan on making that a very late breakfast," he said as he captured her lips and covered her body with his own.

As Jake had predicted, it was nearly noon before they made it down to the elegant coffee shop for a breakfast of pecan hotcakes smothered in thick syrup. Then they got in the car and Carla directed Jake to NASA, where they took the self-directed tour with an automatic tape recorder. Jake marveled at the small size of the earlier capsules and Carla teased him that he would have been the perfect size to have been one of the first astronauts. She confessed that it had always been a daydream of hers to be the first woman astronaut and that she admired Sally Ride and the other women astronauts greatly. They wandered the huge grounds and peered here and there until they absolutely had to leave. As it

212

was they had to hurry through the airport so that Jake would not miss his flight. He was taking the flight to Dallas, and Carla would take the next flight to Corpus just a few minutes later.

They tossed Jake's luggage on the conveyor, and then they hurried toward his gate. "Are you sure there's no danger?" Jake asked as they hurried through the crowded airport.

Carla shook her head. "Believe me, I would be the first to tell you to come home to your girls if there was any reason to do so. I'm certain there's not!"

"All right then. I'll call you from Dallas—if they want me to, I may stay an extra day or two, but I'll call you if I do." The gate opened and passengers started to file through, but Jake stopped and kissed Carla full on the lips before he rushed toward the plane.

Carla watched until Jake had disappeared down the tunnel, then she took her own suitcase and checked it in. Her flight was called just a few minutes later, and a sudden depression weighed her down as she rushed through the tunnel to the plane. She sat down and obediently buckled her seatbelt, but refused the drink the flight attendant offered her and stared listlessly out the window of the airplane.

She loved Jake. She had fallen deeply in love with him, but the thought gave her no pleasure. Jake and I have about as much chance to succeed as a couple as a snowball has in hell, she mused. For although they had been as close as two people could be and had shared the ultimate of physical intimacy, Jake had never come out and told her that he loved her. He couldn't do that, since he still loved Debbie.

Carla sank back into her seat and fingered the hammered gold earrings that she had not taken off last night. Jake had given them to her out of gratitude and not the love she wanted and needed so badly from him. He was grateful to her, he wanted closeness and caring from her, but his heart still belonged to Debbie, and Carla was afraid that it always would.

And then there was Patty. If she hadn't known before that Carla was spending the weekend with her father, she knew it now, thanks to Paul's telephone call. Patty resented her, she had made that clear, and Carla had very little hope for her and Jake's relationship as long as his elder daughter made her displeasure known. A parent couldn't disregard the hostility of a nearly grown child indefinitely, and sooner or later it would start to bother Jake.

Carla sighed and stared out the window at the fluffy clouds below the airplane. Paul, why did you have to call me back to town today? Why couldn't you have left Jake and me in our happy fantasy a little longer? It was a shame, Carla thought as she picked up the magazine she had bought in the airport. It was a shame that Patty resented her so and that Jake was incapable of returning her love. Because she loved him, she loved him a lot, and she loved his children too. With him, not only could she have had a wonderful husband, she could have had the family she had always wanted so badly and had given up on all those years before.

CHAPTER TWELVE

Carla shifted in her chair and listened with half an ear to Paul as he outlined exactly what everyone's responsibilities were going to be during the hurricane that was due to hit Corpus by the end of the day. It had been three days since Paul had called her back to Corpus, and in those three days their meteorologist had proven to be correct. Corpus Christi was going to be hit by a major storm. As Carla has suspected, she would spend part of her time at the station writing news reports, but Paul also wanted her to be available to do some on-location spots. Carla wasn't overly thrilled at having to go out during the worst of the storm, but the reporter in her sensed a good story and that made it worthwhile.

Paul was giving the cameramen specific instructions when his secretary came into the conference room and tapped Carla on the shoulder. "You have a telephone call from Jake Darrow. He says it's urgent."

Carla got up out of her chair and followed Janet to the office. She had just spoken to Jake in Dallas last night, to warn him of the severity of the storm and to tell him to come on home. What could be so urgent that he had asked Janet to call her out of a meeting? She picked up the receiver. "Yes, Jake, what is it?"

Jake's voice was crackly over the wire. "Carla, I can't get back to Corpus before the storm hits. All of last

215

night's flights were full and they've canceled all of today's flights. I need you to take care of the girls."

"Jake, I can't do that!" Carla protested. "I'm scheduled to work for the duration of the storm. You know that!"

"Yes, Carla, I know that!" Jake said. "Look, I wouldn't bother you except that I'm desperate. Mrs. Lopez took off yesterday for the inland and left the girls alone."

Carla muttered a rude word about Mrs. Lopez under her breath. "Jake, I want to help you and the girls, but what can I do? I have a responsibility here."

"All right, then, let me call Paul's wife and see if she can get them."

"She left for San Angelo yesterday," Carla said in a flat voice. "Look, Jake, I'll make sure they're safe. I don't know what I can do, but I'll do something." She looked up as Paul walked in the room. "Just a minute," she said to Jake as she put her hand over the receiver. "Paul, the Darrow girls are alone and Jake can't get back from Dallas. He wants me to look after them. Can I possibly bring them down here?"

Paul made an expressive face. "No, the last thing we need down here is a couple of giggly, hysterical kids. Isn't there anybody else he can get to take care of them?"

"If there was he wouldn't have called me," Carla said flatly.

Paul thought a minute. "See me through the noon news, and then you can go."

"Thanks, Paul," Carla said. "Jake? Paul's let me off the hook once the noon news is over. The storm's not due to hit until six or later so that should give me plenty of time to get to the girls."

In spite of the static, Carla could hear Jake sigh in

216

relief. "Thank you, Carla," he said as he hung up the telephone.

Sonia looked out the window at the dull gray waves slapping the beach. "I wish Daddy was here," she said as a particularly high wave broke on the beach and splattered over the sand.

"Yeah, I do too," Patty admitted as she stood beside the window. "He's supposed to be home by three." She looked out at the giant trees swaying in the wind.

"Will that give him time to put up the storm windows before the storm hits?" Sonia asked.

"Probably not," Patty admitted. "Maybe we should do it ourselves. Daddy keeps them in the garage." She reached out and ruffled Sonia's hair, trying not to notice how scared her little sister looked. "Are you ready to help me?"

Sonia looked out at the windy backyard with doubt in her eyes. "I guess so," she said doubtfully. "I really wish Daddy was here."

So do I, Patty admitted to herself. But it would never do to let Sonia know that she was almost as anxious as she was. Plastering on a smile, she was just opening the door to the garage when the telephone rang. "I'll get it!" she called. "Hello? Daddy! Are you at the airport already?"

"No, hon, I'm not," Jake said from his hotel room in Dallas. The bright sun pouring in the windows was so different from what he knew was happening in Corpus. "I'm still in Dallas. All flights to Corpus were canceled, and I'm not going to be able to make it home by the time the storm hits."

Patty swallowed a lump in her throat. "Well, we'll be fine here," she said. "I'll take care of Sonia."

"Patty, I called Carla just a few minutes ago. She's

217

coming to stay with you as soon as the noon news is over."

"No!" Patty cried, all her resentment of Carla voiced in one single word. "Daddy, we don't need her."

"Don't be ridiculous, Patty," Jake said irritably. "You're just children, and you need someone to stay with you. I would have gotten Paul's wife, but she left town yesterday."

"But, Daddy, Sonia and I will be fine," Patty protested. "We don't need Carla to come and stay with us." Jake could hear Sonia talking in the background. "No, Sonia, we don't need her," Patty said in a muffled voice. "Don't be such a scaredy cat."

"PATTY!" Jake roared, his patience gone. "Are you still there?" he demanded.

"Yes, I am," she said rather defiantly.

"Now, young lady, you listen to me and you listen good. I know you don't like Carla, and after the way you've acted around her, I'm sure the feeling's mutual. But she very kindly agreed to come and stay with you and Sonia, who would like her there even if you wouldn't."

"But what about my feelings?" Patty wailed.

"I don't give a *damn* how you feel! You're to be polite to Carla, do you understand? You're to treat her nicely and do your part to see that her stay is pleasant, or you won't go anywhere or do anything for the next three months! *Do you understand?*"

Patty gulped. "Yes, Daddy," she said in a quiet voice.

"Fine. I'll see you tomorrow. Put Sonia on the telephone."

Patty handed the receiver to Sonia. "Carla's coming," she said flatly. "I better go get out the storm windows."

Carla picked up the overnight bag she had just packed and headed out the door of her apartment. The stinging rain hit her in the face and the wind blew her raincoat apart, drenching the front of her dress before she could pull it back together. Oh, well, she had packed several changes of clothes in case she had to stay with the girls for more than just one night. She pulled her coat around her and fought the whipping wind all the way to her car.

In spite of the deserted streets, it took her twice as long to make it to Jake's house as it would have normally. The wind, which had risen steadily since morning, whipped her car back and forth on the pavement, and the pouring rain had turned the streets into minor rivers. As she made her way through the storm, she wondered what her reception from Patty was going to be. She was sure that the teenager was not overjoyed to have what amounted to a baby-sitter stay with her, and Carla was afraid that the girl would sulk the entire duration of the storm. Carla just hoped that she could keep hold on her own temper until the storm was over and not tell the girl just what she thought of her. As she pulled into Jake's driveway, she glanced over at the angry gray waters of the bay as they swelled and churned, and she wondered briefly if, as usually happened during a hurricane, some idiot would try to go surfing out there and drown.

Carla rang the doorbell and pounded on the door, but neither of the girls answered. She swore under her breath. She ran around to the back of the house, soaking her shoes in the process, so that she could look through the plate-glass windows into the family room and bang on the back door, but when she rounded the house she found the girls outside, valiantly fighting the wind and the rain to hammer up the prefitted plywood that covered the windows during a hurricane. Patty was standing on a metal lawn chair and trying to hold the plywood high enough to cover the window, but she was just too short and the wind was too strong. Sonia was holding the chair steady and trying to support the board, but she too was just too small to manage.

Carla hurried forward and gestured to Patty to get down off the chair. Patty could not disguise the relief in her frightened eyes as she got down and held the chair so that Carla could stand on it. With her additional height and Patty holding the bottom half of the plywood, Carla managed to get the first plywood board nailed in fairly quickly. They moved down the patio, nailing board after board, Carla becoming as drenched as the girls in the process. They boarded up the windows in the front in a similar fashion. When they had boarded up the last window, they dragged the lawn chairs into the garage and shut and locked the garage and back door. After the roar of the wind and the rain and the ocean outside, the kitchen seemed strangely quiet.

"Oh, Carla, thank you!" Sonia said as she wrapped her soaked arms around Carla's equally wet waist. "We'd have never gotten those up!" Sonia's face was white with fear and her lower lip trembled.

Carla glanced over at Patty's exhausted face. "How long have you girls been trying to get those windows up?" she asked.

Patty glanced up at the clock. "Three hours," she said, her voice unsteady.

Carla muttered a rude word under her breath that made Patty and Sonia both jump. "I'm sorry, girls, I wish I could have gotten here sooner," she said.

"T-that's all right," Patty said in a rush. "I'm just glad you're here. I'll put you in Daddy's room, since the guest room faces the ocean and last time the windows broke in there." She picked up Carla's suitcase and motioned for her to follow.

Jake's luxurious bedroom was done in emerald green and white, but Carla took no time to admire her surroundings. "Girls, we better get changed into something dry, then we can turn on the television and see how the storm's progressing." She reached up to unbutton her raincoat and snagged the fabric on one of her three broken fingernails. "Damn, I guess I'll have to cut them off."

"I have a nail repair kit you can use if you like," Patty spoke up. "I'll bring it down with me after I've changed."

"Why, thank you, Patty," Carla said.

Patty nodded, smiling faintly. "Come on, Sonia, I doubt that Carla wants an audience while she changes," she said as she put her arm around her little sister and led her from the room.

Carla unconsciously expelled the breath she had been holding. So Patty was not going to be difficult, after all. Thank goodness! A sulky teenager was the last thing she needed. I bet her daddy fussed at her, Carla thought as a wicked smile crept across her face. Well, Jake, it was about time you took her in hand, she thought as she stripped off her wet clothes and changed into jeans and a cotton top.

Carla wandered downstairs and was just turning on the television set when Patty came down in dry jeans. She handed Carla a manicure set with fabric and glue for repairing broken nails. "Will this do?" she asked, her voice neutral.

Carla looked down at her broken nails. "I lost the pieces in the rain. I think I better just cut them off and polish them."

Patty peered down at Carla's hands. "I'm sorry you tore your hands up on the windows," she said. "It's a shame you broke the nails."

Carla glanced up, thinking Patty was being sarcastic, and was surprised to find genuine regret on her face. "Oh, they'll grow back," she assured Patty. "And it beats a room full of broken glass from the windows, doesn't it?"

Patty nodded as Carla clipped one of the broken nails. "Want a cola?" she asked.

"Don't mind if I do," Carla said as she clipped a second nail.

As Patty wandered off toward the kitchen, Sonia ran down the stairs and cuddled up on the couch beside Carla. "Carla, I'm scared," she said as she watched the spot on television that Kevin was doing. Kevin was standing in front of the flooded causeway giving a report of the damage so far.

"I don't think you should be," Carla said softly as Patty handed her a cola. "I reported Celia in 1970 and it was a lot worse than this."

Patty did some quick mental arithmetic. "Are you really that old?" she asked. "Sonia said you were thirty-eight, but I thought she must have gotten it wrong."

"I'll be thirty-nine in December," Carla volunteered.

"Told you so," Sonia said knowingly. "See? I knew."

Patty shrugged. "You just don't look it, that's all."

"That's because I sleep in a freezer," Carla said, deadpan.

"Do you *really?*" Sonia demanded.

In spite of herself Patty giggled. "Right there in the bedroom, huh?" she asked.

"Right there in the bedroom," Carla assured her. Patty's face split into a grin, and before she could help herself she laughed out loud.

Carla and the girls spent the afternoon drinking soda and watching TV as the storm raged on outside. The wind howled and they could hear the roar of the water in the bay, but the storm windows prevented them from looking out. A few times Patty and Carla wandered into the living room and peeked out the peephole in the front door, but it was too dark for them to see anything, and the storm was just too bad for them to open a door and look out. After Patty had broken down and laughed at Carla's joke, she had gradually become a little more friendly, but Carla couldn't tell whether the girl was really thawing or if she was just glad to have anybody, even Carla, there with her in the storm.

About six, as the full fury of the storm beat the house with wind and rain, Patty asked Carla and Sonia if they were hungry. "Yes, Patty, I am," Carla said. "Would you like me to fix you something? I'll keep it simple."

"That's all right, I can fix us something," Patty said. "But if you'd like to come help—"

"Sure thing," Carla said as she and Sonia followed Patty into the kitchen. "I missed lunch and I'm starving."

"Yeah, Daddy said that you eat like a truck driver," Sonia piped up.

"*Sonia,*" Patty groaned. "Do you have to tell everything you know?"

Carla laughed as she tweaked Sonia's nose. "Don't feel bad, Patty, it's true," she said as Patty opened the refrigerator. "I probably outeat you." Carla stopped and bit her lip, wondering if Patty was going to take offense at her remark.

Instead of becoming angry, Patty started laughing. "If you do you must cost Daddy a fortune on a date," she said. "Most of the time I could eat a horse."

Carla joined in the laughter, glad that Patty had not reacted badly to the joke. The girl was just taking a couple of thick steaks from the refrigerator when the lights flickered and died and the kitchen was plunged into almost total darkness. Sonia instinctively moved closer to Carla and took her hand.

"Patty, do you have any candles or a flashlight?" Carla asked.

"In the drawer just behind you," Patty said. Carla turned around and fumbled around in the drawer for a minute before she unearthed some candles and a cigarette lighter. A couple of flicks of the lighter and the kitchen was bathed in the soft glow of candlelight. "I'll take one of those out in the garage and find the big battery lamp," Patty said.

Carla handed Patty one of the candles, and in just a few minutes the teenager returned with a couple of large battery camping lamps. She set one on the kitchen counter and picked up the steak. "Too bad," she said wistfully as she put the steak back in the refrigerator.

"Yeah, I know," Carla agreed as she eyed the disappearing steak. "What else do you have?"

The refrigerator was amply stocked with cold cuts, so Carla and Patty made a heaping tray of sandwiches. Sonia found a bag of chips in the cupboard, and the three of them sat down to the kitchen table and dug in. With a few well-put questions, Carla drew Patty out for the first time, and by the time the meal was over, the girl was chattering happily about the new year at school, which had just started last week, and all her new classes. Patty kept up a stream of conversation while they washed the dishes in cold water, then Carla suggested that they find something to do to pass the time before bedtime. Sonia suggested Monopoly and Patty found a transistor radio so they could listen to the weather reports while they played.

Sonia went bankrupt within the hour and found herself a Nancy Drew mystery to read. Patty and Carla, both astute players, sat on the floor of the family room and made and lost money until nearly ten, when in a all-or-nothing proposition Patty gambled her entire fortune and won. With genuine admiration for the girl's skill, Carla handed over the rest of her money. "Boy, can you play that game," she said.

Patty smiled shyly. "Thanks. Daddy taught me how. He and Mom used to play pretty often. We could both beat her, but sometimes I can beat him." Patty paused a minute. "Does it bother you when I talk about Mom?"

"Heavens, no," Carla assured the girl. "Why on earth should you think that?"

"Well, you are Daddy's girl friend now," Patty said hesitantly. "I just thought it might bother you to hear about Mother."

"Oh, Patty, don't you ever feel like I don't want you to talk about your mother," Carla said. "You and Sonia may talk about her any time you want to, and I'd be delighted to listen."

Sonia got up from where she was curled up on the couch and sat down beside Carla. "Do you like me and Patty?" she asked.

Carla nodded, a film of tears misting her eyes. "Yes, I do, very much," she said quietly.

"Then why don't you have kids of your own?"

"Sonia, Carla isn't married," Patty said quickly. "She couldn't have any kids if she isn't married."

"But that didn't stop Aunt Marge. She wasn't married when Jimmy was born. I heard Mom tell Daddy one time."

Patty's face flamed and Carla started to giggle.

"Would you like some Desenex to brush her teeth with?" she asked Patty.

Patty rolled her eyes as Sonia looked from one of them to the other. "No, really, Carla, why don't you have any kids?" Sonia persisted. "Is it because you aren't married?"

Carla shook her head. "No, Sonia, I used to be married. I just couldn't have them, that's all." She smiled wistfully at Sonia. "I would have loved to, though." Amazing. She had had to force herself to admit her sorrow to Jake, yet telling the girls was the most natural thing in the world.

"What a bummer," Patty said in a low voice. "I want several when I'm grown."

"I hope you have them," Carla replied sincerely. "I think you'd be a wonderful mother." She made a production of checking her watch. "I don't know about you, but my sandwich has worn off. Is there anything else to eat over there?"

"Are you hungry again?" Patty asked, then she blushed. "I didn't mean—"

"Yes, believe it or not, your daddy's truck-driving friend is ready to eat again," Carla laughed. Patty admitted that she could eat again too, so they made a foray through the kitchen and found a sack of doughnuts that Mrs. Lopez had bought just before she left. They made a feast of those and then Carla insisted that they go upstairs and try to get some sleep. They were just climbing the stairs when they heard a loud thump and the sound of broken glass, and wind started whipping out of the door to the guest room. Carla muttered a curse word and started running up the stairs, Patty on her heels. "You were right about that window," Carla shouted over the roar of the storm as they stared into the room. A large branch had fallen against the window

226

and shattered the glass, the gaping hole letting in the wind and the torrential rain.

"Is there anything we can do to keep the rain out?" Patty shouted.

Carla thought quickly. "Isn't there another piece of plywood out in the garage?" she asked.

Patty nodded. "Yes, but that wind's too strong for you to nail it up," she said.

"I want to try," Carla insisted. She shut the door while Patty went for the plywood, nails, and hammer. While Patty held the lamp, Carla struggled valiantly to nail the wood over the hole, but the wind was just too strong. She could not get the plywood over the hole, and finally a particularly strong gust caught her and knocked her almost all the way across the room and down to the floor.

Patty stepped into the room and half-dragged Carla out. "Come on, it isn't worth it," she said, pushing the door shut behind her. Carla sat on the floor of the hall, momentarily dazed, as Patty dragged a heavy armchair out of Jake's room and propped it in front of the door. "There, that ought to do it," she said as she knelt beside Carla. "Say, are you all right?"

Carla nodded. "Sorry about the furniture," she said. "It's going to be ruined."

Patty shrugged. "Furniture's replaceable. I'm just glad you're all right." She helped Carla to her feet. "You're soaked again," she said. "I'll get you some towels."

She's turning out to be a really nice person, Carla thought as Patty scurried off. Patty returned a couple of moments later with fresh towels, and Carla spent a quick few minutes cleaning off under a cold shower. She had put on her nightgown and was turning back the bed when Sonia appeared, holding a stuffed dog in her arms. "Can I sleep here?" she asked. "I'm scared."

"Sure," Carla said as she turned back both sides of the large bed.

"Thanks," Sonia said as she climbed up on the bed. "Mom used to let me sleep on her side when I got scared."

"Do you still get scared?" Carla asked.

"Sometimes. But it's just not the same without Mom. At least, it wasn't until tonight. Night, Carla."

Carla extinguished the lamp and got into bed beside Sonia, but the battle with the storm had left her tense and unable to sleep. She was glad that she had been able to take care of Jake's children tonight, even though in a way it made her lack of a family seem just that much more poignant. She stared across the darkened room at Sonia's dim features, her face sweet in sleep. I'm glad I was here to help you, child, she thought.

Carla was lying still, listening to the pounding storm, when over the sound of the wind and the rain she heard the sound of footsteps and something being dragged across the floor. Carla sat up. "Patty, is that you?"

"I didn't mean to wake you," Patty said. "I thought I would make a pallet here by the bed. It's spooky in there by myself."

"Here, get in," Carla said as she slid over.

"No, I brought an air mattress," Patty said. "I'll be fine down here." She spread a blanket over the mattress and pulled the other one over her. She and Carla lay still as the wind and the rain lashed the house.

Carla stared into the darkness, conscious of the fact that Patty had not gone to sleep.

"Carla?" Patty said suddenly. "Are you asleep?"

"No."

"Do you like my dad a lot?"

Carla swallowed. "Yes, Patty, I do. I like him a lot."

"That's good. You're not like what I thought you'd be. Night, Carla."

"Night, Patty." Well, thank you, child, Carla thought as she smiled into the darkness.

Jake pulled up in front of the house and parked his rented Ford. The fury of last night's storm was over, but at dawn a light rain was still falling over the city. Once it was certain that the storm was not going through Houston, Jake had flown there late last night and had spent most of the night on the road, driving down the coast and around the storm, which was headed to the northwest. His eyes were red-rimmed from a lack of sleep and the pain in his back was intense, but all he cared about was getting back to Carla and his children. He got out of the car and limped to the house as quickly as his tired legs would carry him.

Carla's car was in the driveway, a tree branch across the hood giving evidence of the power of last night's storm. With fingers that were only slightly unsteady, Jake unlocked the front door and stepped inside. "Patty? Sonia?" He walked into the family room and tried to turn on a light, but the electricity was off. As he made his way through the gloomy room, he almost tripped over the Monopoly board that was still in the middle of the floor. He limped up the stairs and stuck his head in first Sonia's room, then Patty's. "Carla? Girls? Where are you?" He glanced at the chair propped in front of the guest room door and spotted the water oozing out from under it, then hurried down the hall and poked his head in his own door. "Carla? Girls? Are you all right?"

In response three heads slowly came up and three pairs of sleepy eyes turned toward him. "Jake, how did you get back?" Carla asked, her voice thick with sleep. Patty and Sonia just blinked at him.

His feeling of relief was so intense that Jake almost sagged against the doorframe. "I drove. Y'all are all right, then?" he asked weakly.

"Yes, but we're tired," Patty admitted. "The sound of the storm kept us up all night."

Jake stepped into the room and kissed both his girls on the cheek, then he reached out and caressed the side of Carla's face. "I'm so glad," he said. "Thanks for coming, Carla."

Carla nodded as she slid back down in the bed and turned over. "Why don't you go sleep for a while in Patty's room?" she asked. "You look beat."

By the time Jake had pulled his heating pad out of the drawer and taken a pain pill, Carla and the girls were asleep again. Jake stood in the doorway for a moment staring at the three of them, a tender smile playing around his lips, then he limped down the hall and in a few minutes he was asleep himself.

"I sure hope your apartment isn't too badly damaged," Patty said as she leaned over the seat. Carla had wanted to go to check her apartment before she reported for work this afternoon. Miraculously, the station had maintained power throughout the storm, and, now that Jake was back, Paul wanted her to come in about two.

"So do I, Patty," Carla said.

"It's a miracle the house wasn't more badly damaged," Jake said as he maneuvered the rented car through a thick layer of mud on the street. "I'll have to replace everything in that room, though."

"I probably won't be so lucky," Carla murmured as they turned the corner and pulled into her apartment's parking lot. As they climbed the steps to her apartment, Carla could feel her heart sinking. The plate-glass window in front was shattered, and Carla knew that her living-room furniture was bound to be ruined.

It was, as was the dining-room set. Carla bit her lip and fought back the urge to cry. She had saved so long for that set! She sniffed back the tears and turned too-bright eyes on Jake and Patty. "Let's see what shape the bedroom's in, and then you can take me to the station."

"Pack a bag to bring with you," Patty said. "She can stay with us, can't she, Daddy? Since the guest room's a mess, I'll sleep with Sonia."

Jake nodded and Carla smiled weakly as she made her way through the broken glass to her bedroom. Miraculously, her expensive wardrobe was untouched, and in minutes Carla had packed a bag and a makeup kit, which Patty took from her to carry. "I'll move a few of my things so you'll have room to hang yours," she said cheerfully, then turned to her father. "She's all right, you know." Patty scampered out the door and ran down the muddy stairs.

Jake's mouth fell open and Carla smiled faintly. "I guess you know you just got paid the highest compliment in the teenage vocabulary," Jake said.

"I'm glad," Carla said. "But what on earth made her change her mind about me?"

"Well, I guess my little heart-to-heart talk got through to her and she realized she'd better stop fighting the inevitable. Besides, you were there when we needed you," Jake said as he reached out and kissed Carla on the temple. "And you don't know how much that means."

CHAPTER THIRTEEN

Carla blotted the light lipstick that she had applied and looked at herself in the mirror. You look like a woman in love, she thought as she smiled at her glowing reflection. Her cheeks were rosy and her eyes had taken on a permanent glow. She slipped on her shoes, picked up her purse, and went into the living room to wait for Jake, who was supposed to pick her up in just a few minutes to go to his house and watch her special on television tonight. She sat down on the new couch that the insurance money had purchased and admired the new dining-room set that had arrived just that day. Jake had driven her all the way to San Antonio last weekend to pick it out, and they had spent the night in the historic old city, sharing the closeness and the caring that had been growing between them for the last month. Carla could feel herself falling more deeply in love with him by the day, and, although he hadn't come out and said that he loved her, she could sense caring and affection on his part. He'll say it soon, she thought. He's getting over Debbie. He's learning to love me, even if he doesn't realize it yet.

Because Jake had fired Mrs. Lopez, Carla had spent the entire week after the hurricane with Jake and the girls. The other reason was that her apartment had to be recarpeted and repainted, and she was just grateful that hers had been one of the first apartments to be repaired, for although she enjoyed being with Patty and Sonia, their constant presence had left her and Jake very few private moments. She had been pleasantly surprised, however, at how well she had fit into their lives that week, making their breakfasts and fixing them all a quick supper when she arrived from the station. Patty had remained Carla's fan, and Carla was quickly growing to love the older girl as much as she did Sonia. Even after she had moved back to her own place, she fixed supper for Jake and the girls a couple of times a week, and she alternated simple dishes that would please the children with more sophisticated meals that would educate their palates. Then Jake would insist on seeing her home, and they would fall into her bed for hours of passionate lovemaking, holding each other in the quiet of the night. Their mutual passion had only grown stronger in the month they had been lovers, and Carla marveled at the depth of her response to Jake and his tender lovemaking.

Carla peeked out the window and spotted his car turning into the parking lot, so she grabbed her purse and locked the door behind her and ran down the stairs, arriving at the curb just as Jake slowed to a halt. "Sorry I'm so late," he said as he drew her to him and kissed her firmly on her slightly parted lips. "I got a long-distance call from my buyer in New York about an order of spring shirts."

"Isn't late September a little early to be worrying about spring shirts?" Carla asked.

Jake shook his head as he pulled out of the parking lot. "No, it isn't. I guess I need to teach you a little more about my business. I know quite a bit about yours. By the way, does this program have a title?"

"*A Tragedy for All,*" Carla said.

Jake said the title under his breath. "Hey, I like that," he said enthusiastically.

"I hope you like the show just as much," Carla said quietly. She had finished putting the show together by August, but Paul had waited a month to air it, when the new fall shows were starting to come on and interest in television was higher. Carla had watched the show recently with the local reviewer, who had given it highest marks in the paper this morning. Paul was sure it meant another state award for her, but Carla was most concerned with Jake's reaction to the program. After all, she was telling *his* story, his and the story of those like him.

And Don Tyson's story too, she reminded herself as Jake turned up the street that led to his house. She and Jake had never spoken of the argument they had so long ago about her use of the Tyson tapes in the program, but she assumed that he had gotten used to the idea. She felt that Don's story was in a way the most powerful portion of the program, and that it inspired a feeling of "My God, that could be *me*" in the viewer. At least she hoped it did.

Jake pulled into his driveway and they entered his house together as Patty and Sonia greeted them at the door. "Hurry, you two, the show's due to start in five minutes," Patty said. "Carla, I made popcorn and bought some sodas. Is that all right?"

"As long as you don't throw popcorn at the television," Carla teased. She turned to Jake with laughter dancing in her eyes. "I wish Representative Malley had let us tape him. I'd have let her throw popcorn at him."

"I can think of a better place to put his popcorn," Jake quipped as they walked together into the family room. Jake and Carla sat down on the couch and Sonia curled up between them as Patty set the popcorn and sodas on the coffee table. Carla picked up a handful of popcorn and nibbled it as she waited for a detergent commercial to be over.

The opening visuals were graphic. Two cars, mangled beyond recognition, sprawled across the causeway as Kevin's voice intoned the name of the victim of the crash. Another wreck, this one on the highway that led to Victoria. A sports car and a semi. The dead driver of the sports car had .13 percent alcohol in his bloodstream. Another crash scene, this one right in the middle of downtown. Two people dead. Patty shuddered at the torn carcasses of the automobiles. "Did it look like that when Mom died?" she asked.

"Yes, Patty," Jake said tonelessly as the program paused for a commercial.

Carla glanced over at Jake and down at the girls with a frown of concern on her face. In her enthusiasm, she had not realized until just now how upsetting the program was bound to be for this family. She poked Jake on the arm. "Are you sure the girls should watch this?" she whispered. "Is it going to upset them?"

Jake shook his head. "They've learned to live with the reality of it," he said grimly.

The first portion of the show outlined the problem of the drunken driver in the nation and locally. Skillfully written and edited, the program cut from clips of local officials stating their position to random interviews with the "man on the street." Even with the publicity the drunken driver had gotten over the last two years, the overall ignorance of the typical citizen was appalling. When asked to estimate how much a person could drink and not be legally drunk, half the people interviewed guessed about twice the alcohol that would actually be required to raise the concentration in the bloodstream to .1 percent, the legal level of intoxication. The segment ended with the inevitable drinking test, in which Kevin and news director Pete Garcia became progressively more intoxicated as their driving was tested repeatedly, and their poor responses after their third and fourth drinks in an hour were duly recorded and analyzed. "Kevin felt rotten the next day," Carla said as the program cut to a commercial. "You can hold it a lot better than he can."

"I didn't know you drank anymore, Daddy," Patty said.

Oh, no, thought Carla. "Y'all are next," Carla said to change the subject. "You girls are about to become stars."

"Our librarian's taping the show so we can have a copy at school to use in the health classes," Patty said.

The three Darrows watched intently as their interview was aired. There were brief clips of Jake working in the stores, speaking to the Rotary Club, lobbying in Austin, with the history of the Corpus Christi Coalition woven into the narrative. Then Jake was being interviewed by Kevin, his determination to stop the carnage on the highways positively vibrating from the set. Then the girls came on, talking about what losing their mother had done to them. Last was Jake's impassioned declaration of love for his dead wife and his grief at losing her, as he explained why he had founded the CCC and why he continued to fight to have the drunken driver taken off the road. Carla glanced over at Jake and was not surprised to see tears glistening in his eyes. He was reliving it all over again tonight. Carla reached down and pushed a napkin into his hand. Jake wiped his eyes quickly and was composed by the time the interview was over and the girls had turned around. "Daddy, you were great," Patty said proudly.

"So were you, punkin," Jake said. "Both of you." He reached out and pulled Sonia into his lap.

Patty got fresh soft drinks from the kitchen during the longer commercial break, then the second part of the telecast began. The first footage was of the accident scene that had claimed Harvey Beadle. There were films of the firefighters trying to free the dead man from his mangled car, of Don Tyson's wrecked pickup truck, of Don himself, sitting on the curb with a glazed stare on his face. Carla could feel Jake stiffen beside her as the camera did a closeup of Don's cut face. "That's the way it always is," he muttered. "The damn murderers get away scot-free."

Carla started to refute the statement, but the program cut to a few shots of Harvey Beadle's funeral, then the Beadle interview was shown. As Lenore Beadle and her children described what losing Harvey had done to their lives, Carla's heart went out to them all over again. Jake had mentioned just the other day that Susan had quit college and was working full time to help out financially, and Carla hoped that someday the girl would get to go back to school. In a last-minute change in the program, Carla had included that fact, showing that some of the disappointments in this kind of tragedy did not happen until some months later.

"That was good," Jake said as the program cut to a commercial.

"Yes, it was," Carla said, sipping at her soda and wondering how Jake was going to feel about the next segment. This was the segment that would either make or break the show, as far as she was concerned. If the viewers could understand what the accident had done to Don Tyson and his family, then hopefully they would understand what the tragedy could do to them too if they drank and drove.

Carla sat silently and watched as Donnie Tyson's little face filled the screen and Kevin's voice-over said that this little boy's father had killed a man. Then a shot of Don Tyson on the night of the crash was inserted, and then the interview with Don and Cindy themselves, as they described the sickening guilt that was eating them alive. Patty commented that Don looked thin in the interview, and Carla said that the young man had lost a lot of weight right after the accident and had lost even more since. Carla could feel anger emanating from the man next to her, but her attention was captured by the hollow-eyed images on the screen. Don and Cindy looked so young, so scared, and so miserable as Don admitted that he had been drunk. His anguish showed in his eyes as he wondered out loud what would happen to his wife and children if he had to go to jail. As Carla, Jake, and the girls sat in silence, Kevin's sober voice ended the program with a moment of reflection.

"The tragedy we have shown you so graphically tonight is not only Harvey Beadle's tragedy or Jake Darrow's tragedy or the tragedy of every victim of a drunken driver. It is Don Tyson's tragedy too, and the tragedy of the man who took Debbie Darrow's life, and the tragedy of every driver who drinks and drives and kills. The drunken driver is not a monster, not an alien being unlike the rest of us—he *is* us. People just like you, and me, and Don Tyson, who drink and drive even though they know better. The solution to this problem does not lie entirely with Jake Darrow or the legislature or the courts—it lies with you and me, with all of us. We have to stop drinking and driving, and by doing so see that this tragedy for all concerned is put to an end." The picture faded and the program cut to a final spate of commercials.

"He didn't seem like a killer," Sonia said thoughtfully. "He seemed rather nice."

"He *is* rather nice, Sonia." Carla sighed. "And that's the worst part of this whole mess."

"He's a killer!" Jake snapped angrily.

"How old is Cindy Tyson?" Patty asked, ignoring her father's outburst.

"Not very old," Carla said. "Eighteen. Nineteen at the most."

Patty made a grim face. "Awfully young to be married to a jailbird," she muttered.

"If he gets that far," Jake said sourly. He stood Sonia on her feet and turned angry eyes toward Carla. "Come on, I'm taking you home. We have to get up and go to work in the morning," he said.

"I liked the show, Carla," Sonia said as Carla stood up.

"I did too," Patty said loyally as Carla followed Jake to the door. "Night, Carla."

Carla said good night and followed Jake out to the car. He opened the door and slammed it behind her, then got in on his side and slammed the car into gear. "Damn it, Carla, I can't believe you put that killer on there like that! Hell, now you've got all of Corpus Christi feeling so sorry for him that we'll never get a conviction! How stupid can you be?"

"I beg your pardon, Jake, I am *not* stupid," Carla said coldly. "In fact, I'm a whole lot smarter than you'll ever be! You're so tied up inside with hatred for Don and the others like him that you couldn't even see what I was doing! Spare him a conviction? Don sat there tonight and *admitted* that he had been drinking and that he was guilty of killing Harvey Beadle. He's going to be convicted, Jake."

Jake swung the car around a corner, narrowly missing a car parked along the curb. "Watch your driving, Jake!" Carla snapped. "At this moment you're no more in control of your car than Don Tyson was his."

Jake immediately slowed down. "He's going to get off," he sneered. "He's going to throw himself on the mercy of the court, and do the 'oh, look at me, I just had one too many and now my wife and my kids are going to starve to death if I have to go to jail' routine that I've seen so often I could puke! He's going to play on the judge's and the jury's sympathy and get a light sentence like they all do." He braked for a red light.

"He has a *life* sentence, Jake," Carla said quietly. "It haunts him, or couldn't you tell?"

"Well, it ought to," Jake said bitterly. "And now he has everybody in Corpus Christi feeling sorry for him."

"I doubt that," Carla said bitingly. "Jake, I can't believe that you missed the entire point of the last half of the show! I was trying to show that either tragedy could happen to anyone. That viewer is going to be thinking, 'yes, I could get hit by a drunken driver and killed—but I could also have a few too many and kill somebody, just like Don Tyson did.' That viewer is going to look at Don Tyson and think that it could have been anyone, that it could be him if he drinks and drives."

Jake turned into the parking lot of Carla's building and ground the car to a halt. "Yes, and they're all going to be ready to go light on Tyson, thinking that if they were in his shoes, they would want somebody to be light on them."

"Jake, that's ridiculous!" Carla said as she got out of the car and slammed the door. Jake got out on his side and slammed his door too, then they walked stiffly up the stairs to Carla's apartment.

"And why is that ridiculous?" Jake demanded as Carla closed the front door behind them. "That's what

240

happened to Debbie's murderer. He paraded a string of character witnesses in front of the jury, and in spite of his record he was sentenced to one year. *One lousy year!* In exchange for Debbie's life. She died and he was out in six months!" He turned around and rammed his fist into the wall. "Damn, damn, *damn!*" he screamed.

Carla stared, white-faced, as Jake vented his fury on the wall, then as the anger began to fade from his eyes her own ignited.

"Carla, I'm sorry about—" he said before she cut him off.

"Oh, *shut up!*" Carla cried, advancing on him. Startled by the fury in her eyes, Jake stumbled backward until he backed into the couch and flopped down on it. Carla poked one trembling fingernail into the middle of his face. "Now you listen and you listen good. You're not mad about Don Tyson or Harvey Beadle and we both know it. You're still bitter about Debbie, you're so bitter that you're letting it eat you alive. And, Jake, that's wrong!"

"Hell, yes, I'm still bitter about Debbie! I always will be! I loved her and I always will! Damn it, I'm not going to let myself forget!"

"Yeah, that might be a little bit too brave, now mightn't it?" Carla taunted. "You might have to give up a little bit of that delicious bitterness and get on with the business of living, and that might be hard, mightn't it? Oh, no, it's easier just to stay bitter and let it corrode your insides to the point where you can't even admit that Don Tyson and people like him are human beings too—stupid human beings, but they are human. Blanket hatred is so much easier."

"Damn you, how can you stand there and say those things to me? You talked to me, you talked to my kids, you *know* how much it hurt us to lose Debbie! And now

241

you have the gall to tell me not to hate, not to let it eat me alive! Well, why don't you try it sometime? We'll let you feel a little grief—"

"I *have* felt grief!" Carla yelled as she held her outstretched fingers in front of Jake's face. "Five babies, Jake. I mourned five babies, and then I had to get over having the man I loved walk out on me because I couldn't make him a baby, so don't talk to me about grief! Yes, I've known it, but I've also had the guts to put it behind me and go on." Carla stopped and took a deep, gulping breath. "You are a coward, Jake Darrow. A sniveling coward. You could let go of a little bit of your bitterness and go on. Hell, you could have a second chance with me, if you had the guts to let go of Debbie and get on with your life."

"I am not a coward," Jake said coldly. "I can't very well—"

"Oh, yes you can," Carla said quietly. "You sure as hell can. I did it so I know. You could let yourself get over her and get on with the business of living, if you really wanted to. But you don't. You'd rather stay buried in the past. Well, Jake, I don't want to share the past with you." She threw open the front door. "I'm tired of breaking my heart over a coward. When you get up the guts to go on with your life, come over and see me."

Jake stared at the open door with disbelieving eyes, then he walked through it and slammed it behind him. Carla sank down into the sofa and stared into the empty room as her anger raged. Damn him! Damn the narrow-minded coward to hell! He could have a second chance with her, but he was too hardheaded to get over his grief and take it.

Carla sat for a long time as her anger turned to a deep despair. Jake wasn't getting over Debbie, after all. Even after all her loving, after all the caring they had shared, he could sit there and tell her that he still loved Debbie and that he always would. And the bitterness—Carla knew there was no way she could learn to cope forever with that. It's hopeless, Carla thought as two tears welled from her eyes and ran down her cheeks. He'll never get over her. He'll never let go of that bitterness. She sniffed in an effort to forestall tears, then jumped as the telephone rang. She cleared her throat and answered it calmly, hoping against hope that it might be Jake calling to say he was sorry.

"Carla? This is Paul. Listen, the calls have been pouring into the station. Corpus loved it."

I'm glad somebody did, Carla thought. "Uh, that's great, Paul," she said.

"Carla, are you all right?" Paul asked.

"Fine, fine," she assured him. "I'm glad it was a success."

"So am I. Listen, I just got a call from the DA's office. The Tyson trial was set this afternoon for Wednesday of next week. I want you and Kevin to cover it and to do a follow-up on the nightly news."

"Do you think I should be the one to cover it?" Carla asked. "Jake's bound to be involved."

"All the more reason to have you cover it. Say, how did Jake like—"

"Paul, I have a pan that's running over on the stove. Got to run!" Carla banged down the receiver hurriedly. The last thing she wanted to talk about tonight was whether Jake had liked the show.

Carla and Kevin climbed the steps of the courthouse and stepped inside the sleek new building. "Well, are you ready to see how this all ends?" Kevin asked as Carla checked the roster for the court in which Don Tyson was to appear this morning.

"I wish I were anywhere else but here," Carla said as the tension mounted in her stomach. "That judge is going to find Don guilty and sentence him to prison, you know that." The judge Don had drawn was fair, but he had a reputation for sentencing DWI manslaughters to prison, if only for a short term.

"Don could have asked for a jury," Kevin said. "It's his lawyer's choice to have the judge decide the case."

Carla shrugged. "I guess he wouldn't be any better off with a jury," she said. "Especially since he's clearly guilty." They stepped into the elevator, and with a trembling finger Carla punched the button for the second floor.

"It's not just the trial, is it?" Kevin asked softly. "You're worried about facing Jake again, aren't you?"

Carla swallowed and nodded. She had cried herself to sleep the night when Jake had left her apartment in anger, and the next morning Kevin had noticed her swollen eyes and offered to buy her a pizza after *Winners All.* Over a pepperoni pizza Carla had poured out her anger and her heartbreak. Kevin had been understanding and supportive, telling her over and over that Jake would be back around, that he would get over his anger. But Carla wasn't so sure. And besides, his anger over her special wasn't really the issue between them—it was his continuing bitterness over Debbie's death and his inability to put his dead wife and that portion of his life behind him and go on that had driven them apart. If he was not willing to face the fact that his wife was dead and go on to a new life with Carla, he wouldn't be back and she didn't want him back, although the thought of living her life without Jake hurt.

Carla and Kevin stepped off the elevator and stood in the crowded hallway outside the courtroom. Artie stepped out of the crowd, the minicam parked on his shoulder. "Quite a crowd out here," he commented. "Thanks to the program, everybody in town's here for the trial."

"I hope it doesn't turn into a three-ring circus," Carla commented, thinking of Cindy Tyson and her children. They didn't need any more publicity disrupting their lives.

"It has every indication of turning into just that," Artie said. "Jake Darrow and the Beadles just got off the elevator."

"I guess they've come to make sure the system gets its pound of flesh," Carla said just loudly enough so that Jake couldn't help but hear her as he walked by. He shot an icy look in the direction of Carla's rigid back, which she sensed but did not see, and marched into the courtroom with the Beadles.

Kevin whistled under his breath. "Boy, if looks could kill Darrow would be on trial for murder in there, not Tyson," he said.

Carla's anger deflated and she regretted her catty remark. Jake and the Beadles were right in hoping that Don would be punished for his crime, because that was the only way this kind of thing was ever going to be stopped. And Don did deserve punishment. "Come on, let's go sit down in there," she said to Kevin. They walked into the courtroom and sat down, leaving Artie and his camera in the hall. He would shoot tape after the trial was over. Carla and Kevin sat down across the courtroom from Jake and the Beadles. A few minutes later Cindy Tyson came in alone, her face pale but her head held high, and right after her Don and his attorney walked in and sat down at the table in front of the bench. Don was carefully dressed in a new suit, but even from where Carla sat she could see the bitterness and the aging in his face when he turned around to speak to Cindy. He knows he's going to be sent up, Carla thought. She hoped against hope that the judge might see fit to levy a stiff fine instead, but with this judge she knew it was unlikely.

The bailiff called for the court to rise and the judge came in. He called the court to order and, since there was to be no jury selection, the trial began almost immediately. The prosecuting attorney made his opening statements, stressing the fact that the defendant had freely admitted to drinking too much the afternoon of the accident in which Harvey Beadle was killed. Don's attorney then made his opening statements, again freely admitting that Don had been drinking that afternoon, but arguing that the fight with his wife had impaired Don's judgment to the point that he was not aware that he had drunk too much to drive a car.

Carla shifted in her chair and jotted a couple of notes in her notebook as the first witness, the policeman who had made the arrest, took the stand. He identified Don as the driver he had pulled from behind the wheel of the truck that had hit the Beadle car, and told what he could as to the nature of the accident. Next came the policeman who had administered the Breathalyzer test, in which Don's alcohol concentration had been .125 percent fifteen minutes after the accident.

The prosecution spent the rest of the morning presenting evidence that Don had indeed been intoxicated at the time of the accident and that the accident had indeed been his fault, and then the court adjourned until two. Carla and Kevin jumped up and headed for the doors, Kevin hoping to avoid the crush of people and Carla hoping to avoid Jake. They were successful, and they joined Artie in the van for a short drive to one of the restaurants that lined the bay. They ordered, then Artie brought up the subject that was uppermost in

Kevin's and Carla's minds. "So how's it going for Tyson?" he asked.

Carla shrugged. "Fair to middling," Kevin said.

"Unless that judge feels awfully sorry for him, he's going to get it," Carla admitted. "He *was* driving while intoxicated, extenuating circumstances or no."

"Yeah, he was sure drunk that night," Artie said.

"But is the judge going to buy the bit about emotional stress and all that?" Kevin asked. "That's the question." He reached out and toyed with his fork. "You know, I do feel sorry for him."

"I feel sorrier for Cindy and the children," Carla said softly. "It's one thing to say Don ought to have to pay for his crime. And God knows, he certainly should. But Cindy's going to pay for it too, and those two innocent babies, and they didn't have anything to do with it."

"Don't look, but we have company in the restaurant," Artie murmured under his breath.

Carla felt cold prickles flow down her back. "Jake?"

"Yeah, and the Beadles are with him. They look rather pleased at the moment."

"I'm sure they do," Carla said tiredly. Jake and the Beadles sat down at a table near the door and didn't even see the news team, but for once Carla's appetite had vanished. When her meal came, she just pushed the delicious shrimp around on her plate and ended up giving three to Artie. Kevin picked up the tab and the three of them stood up and walked across the floor toward the door.

Carla had hoped to avoid Jake and the Beadles, but Lenore waved, and they had no choice but to walk over and speak. "I saw you covering the trial this morning," Lenore said cheerfully. "It's going well, don't you think?"

247

"Yes, I'm sure you feel that it is," Carla said quietly. "Susan? Gary? How are you?"

They assured her they were fine, and they spoke of Susan's new job, then Carla's eyes reluctantly slid to Jake's, where they met his hooded gaze. "Jake," she said curtly as she nodded her head in greeting.

"Carla." The chill in his voice told her he had not forgiven her for the truths she had hurled at him last week. Carla recoiled inwardly at the coldness in his voice and his manner, then her anger took over and she stared at him haughtily.

She wished the Beadles a good day and they made their way back to the courthouse. Court was declared in session promptly at two, and the defense attorney spent the afternoon making a case for Don. He called the young man to the stand and Don recounted his argument with Cindy and his flight to the Last Watering Hole. He testified as to their financial problems and the strain that his young marriage was under. Then Cindy took the stand and tearfully told the court how she had nagged Don that afternoon to buy her a house they couldn't afford. A psychologist hired by the defense attorney testified as to the severity of the strain that Don had been under that afternoon, saying that the drinking had been a perfectly understandable response to the situation. The defense rested its case at about four, and after closing arguments the judge declared a one-hour recess in which he would make his decision.

Carla and Kevin spent the recess in the lobby, milling around and drinking coffee from a vending machine. Susan Beadle went downstairs to get herself a cup, but her brother, mother, and Jake were nowhere to be seen. When the recess was almost over, they trooped back into the elevator and into the courtroom. The judge strode in promptly and called the court to order. He asked Don to stand, then spoke out for the packed court to hear.

"I, Judge Phillip Wilkes, find the defendant guilty of involuntary manslaughter in the death of one Harvey Beadle."

The verdict surprised no one. The court continued to hold its breath, since the sentence was the only issue at stake here.

"Young man, the next part of this procedure involves sentencing you, and that's the hard part of all of this, because I do sympathize with the problems that struggling young couples face and realize that you were under pressure that afternoon.

"But, regardless of the circumstances, you did break the law and you did take a man's life. You owe society a debt for that. Mr. Tyson, I'm sentencing you to three years at the state prison in Huntsville. Sentence is to begin immediately. This court is adjourned."

Don blinked but did not flinch when a prison guard stepped forward and placed handcuffs around his wrist. Cindy Tyson swayed and would have fainted if the man standing next to her had not reached out and caught her. "Tell Artie to shoot some footage and call the station with the verdict. That girl needs some help," Carla called back to Kevin as she pushed her way through the courtroom toward Cindy.

CHAPTER FOURTEEN

Cindy had slid back down in her chair, shock draining all color from her face. "I thought they would understand," she whispered. "I thought they would let him go."

"I'm sorry," Carla said as she sat down in the chair beside Cindy. "Cindy, I'm so sorry."

Cindy turned bewildered eyes on Carla. "What am I going to do?" she asked. "I don't have a job!"

"You can worry about that tomorrow," Carla said as she glanced over at Don and the guard. "Look, you better go tell Don good-bye. They're taking him away."

"Oh, *no!*" Cindy cried, leaping out of the chair and pushing her way across the courtroom. She threw her arms around Don and held him tightly. "Oh, Don, I love you," she said brokenly. "I love you so much! I'm sorry, Don. It's my fault. It's all my fault."

Don shook his head and looked down at his wife sadly. "I'm sorry, hon," he said, glancing at his handcuffed wrists. "It wasn't your fault. It was mine, all mine." He swallowed back the tears that were threatening to fall. "Sell the house and move back in with your mother. The money will help you start a new life." He reached down and kissed her once, fiercely. "Tell the babies I love them," he said as the guard led him away.

Cindy watched with trembling lips as they took Don through the doors of the courtroom, then she collapsed in a torrent of tears against Carla's shoulder. "What am I going to do without him?" she sobbed over and over.

"Come on, Cindy," Carla said as she fumbled around in her shoulder bag for a tissue. She gave it to Cindy, who wiped her eyes and blew her nose. "Let's go face the reporters and then I'll take you home. You can worry about everything else tomorrow."

Cindy sniffed and let Carla lead her toward the door. They walked through the swinging doors and were immediately met by two reporters from one of Carla's rival stations. Carla asked whether, as a favor to her, they would not bother Cindy. They agreed reluctantly and Carla started making their way toward the elevator when they heard Jake's voice booming from the other end of the hall, where a cluster of reporters and cameramen surrounded him and the Beadle family. "Tell me, Mrs. Beadle," one of the local newspaper reporters asked when Jake had finished speaking, "how do you feel about the Tyson conviction?"

Carla tried to hurry Cindy past, but the young woman turned and headed toward the cluster of reporters. Carla could not see Lenore Beadle, but she heard her angry voice ring out. "Three years isn't very long in exchange for my husband's life. That man should have been sent away for a lot longer than that."

Carla felt Cindy flinch beside her, but the young mother continued to push her way into the crowd. She stopped just behind the first row of reporters, with Carla right behind her. "How about you, Mr. Darrow?" the reporter asked. "How do you feel about this sentence?"

"It's a farce," Jake said coldly. "Tyson will be out on parole in eighteen months. That's a crime against Harvey Beadle. Tyson's a killer, a murderer, and as such he should have been sent up for life."

"No!" Cindy Tyson cried. "No, you're wrong, you're so wrong," she cried over and over. The reporters' attention turned from Jake to the sobbing young woman. "No, please no! Don's not a murderer, he wouldn't even go hunting because he hated to hurt things! He made a mistake, damn it! And now he's going to have to pay for that mistake. But my husband's not a killer!" She sobbed over and over.

"Oh, God, those bastards from KLSU are still taping," Kevin muttered disgustedly into Carla's ear. "This is going to be all over the ten-o'clock news," he said, as he walked away hurriedly.

Cindy continued to sob brokenheartedly as the cameraman from KLSU shot a closeup of her ravaged face. When the man stopped taping, Carla stepped out into the quiet pool of hardened reporters and cameramen, some of whom were visibly shaken by Cindy's distress. "You are a bastard, Jake Darrow," she said in a clear, cold voice. "A bastard and a heartless fanatic. Don Tyson deserves his punishment and he will take it like a man, but neither he nor his wife deserve the kind of public attack that you just made on him. Don Tyson's wife and children, who are now totally without support for the duration of Don's term, are innocent and have to live in this town, and they do not deserve having Don's name slandered on the ten-o'clock news."

The crowd was standing openmouthed with astonishment and Jake was staring at Carla in disbelief, but Carla was much too angry to notice. "And furthermore, Jake Darrow, you're a hypocrite of the highest order. You drink, I've seen you do it. I've even seen you drunk. And I want to know, Jake, if you can honestly stand here and say that before your wife was killed you never did it yourself. Never went to a party and drove home after you'd had a few and were feeling good. Can you

252

say that, Jake? Can you honestly say that *you* never drank and drove?"

Jake swallowed and looked across at the furious face that demanded honesty from him, then slowly shook his head back and forth.

"No, you can't say it, can you? I don't think any of us here could say it," Carla bit out. "So it seems a little hypocritical to be calling Don a killer. It could have been any of us."

Lenore Beadle spoke up quietly. "Carla, Harvey didn't drink," she said. "Our church doesn't allow it."

"Tell me, does your church teach compassion and forgiveness? Or does it teach revenge, Lenore?"

As Carla turned on her heel, a man in the corner started clapping his hands, and then a second person started, and soon the whole crowd of reporters was clapping enthusiastically. Her face burning, Carla took Cindy's hand and led her toward the elevator. She had not meant to publicly humiliate Jake the way she had, but she had come to the end of her patience with him. His hatred and bitterness had made him lose his sense of fairness. He was out for revenge, not justice. She pushed Cindy into the elevator and when it ground to a halt, she hustled the young woman out of the building before any of the reporters followed them. "Do you need a ride home?" she asked.

Cindy shook her head. "My car's over there," she said, pointing to a commercial lot.

Carla saw Cindy to her car, then she made her way back across the street to the courthouse parking lot. As she got into her car, she heard a voice calling her name. Turning she saw Jake running down the courthouse steps. "Carla, wait!" he called.

Carla shook her head, turning on the ignition with trembling fingers. No way was she going to face him again this afternoon! She shot out just as Jake reached the edge of the lot. "Carla, wait, I want to talk to you!" he called angrily.

The hell I will, Carla thought as she gunned the car, narrowly missing a white Mazda as she stopped to pay her parking fee.

Jake raced across the parking lot and pulled open her door just as the attendant handed her her change. "Carla, I have to talk to you," Jake wheezed. "What you said—I'm not—"

"Get lost, Jake," Carla said coldly. "You're a fanatic and a hypocrite and a cruel man, and I don't need that kind of person in my life." She reached out and slammed her door shut, narrowly missing Jake's fingers. Jake barely had time to jump backward before Carla hit the gas and whirled out into the street.

Jake stared after her car as it disappeared down the street. God, she had torn a strip off him, and in front of every news reporter in Corpus Christi. Had she planned to embarrass him like that, accusing him of being a hypocrite in front of the media? No, her anger had been too real, her fury too deep, to have been calculated. She had reacted suddenly, out of the depths of her heart, when she had told him what she thought of him.

And if the round of applause that had greeted her was any indication, she was not the only one who felt that way about him. He would be willing to bet that her tirade, rephrased and cleaned up a little, would be the subject of at least one ten-o'clock editorial. Jake turned around with sagging shoulders and shuffled toward his car, his face pinched into a frown. Had he, in his quest for justice for the victims of drunken drivers, turned into a fanatic? Had he lost his sense of proportion? Did he come across as vengeful, as out to get the pound of flesh that Carla had accused him of wanting? More important, *was* he becoming vengeful?

Jake's mind whirled as he got into his car and started the ignition. Drunken drivers did kill and should be punished. No one was arguing about that, not even the man who was convicted today. But Jake could not shake the image of Cindy Tyson, tears streaming down her face, saying that her husband was so gentle he couldn't even stand to go hunting. Was this man in the same class as a professional hit man or a mass murderer? Or was it like Cindy had said—he had made a mistake? "Damn it, I don't know," Jake said angrily into the silence of his car as he drove home. For the first time since he had started the CCC, he was confused and unsure of his motives.

And what about Cindy and the children? Jake shook his head back and forth picturing Cindy's ravaged face again while changing his clothes for dinner. The girl wasn't as old as Susan Beadle, she probably wasn't more than a couple of years older than Patty, yet now because of a childish argument with her husband she was faced with raising two children by herself for however long the state imprisoned Don. He knew she wasn't his responsibility or concern, but he couldn't shake the image of her tear-washed face or the sound of her sobs as he ate with his two daughters that evening. Patty and Sonia had chattered about their day at school and had argued about who had to do the dishes, and then Patty had taken the car and gone to one of the local shopping malls to buy Sonia a pair of new tennis shoes. Jake kept picturing Patty in Cindy Tyson's position, and the image made him very uncomfortable.

Once the girls were back he told them he was going back out. "Oh, are you going to see Carla?" Sonia piped up.

"No, punkin, I'm not," Jake said, wincing when Sonia's face fell.

"She hasn't been to see us in a week," Sonia complained. "Is she mad at us or something?"

"Not exactly," Jake hedged.

"Did you have a fight over her show?" Patty asked.

"That and other things," Jake admitted.

"Does that mean we can't see her any more?" Patty asked quietly.

Jake blinked and swallowed. "I don't mind if you see her," he said slowly. "Not at all. That is, if she wants to see you."

"She'll want to see us," Patty said confidently.

"Are you ever going to see her again, Daddy?" Sonia asked.

"Yes, but not just yet," Jake said as he kissed both girls on the cheek and shooed them off to bed. He copied the Tysons' address onto a piece of paper and headed across town to their home. Yes, he would see Carla again, but not now. She wanted no part of him at the moment, and after the way she had talked to him this afternoon he felt very much the same way about her. Besides, he had to prove something, to himself and to Carla, before he saw her again.

Jake got out of the car and walked up the sidewalk to the Tysons' front door, where he heard the sound of a baby crying through the open window. He rang the doorbell and in a minute the front light went on. "Are you another reporter?" Cindy called through the open window.

"No, I'm Jake Darrow," he said. "May I come in and talk to you?"

"Go away," Cindy said dully. The baby screamed louder and Cindy banged shut the window.

Jake rang the doorbell for a second time, then a third.

On the fourth ring Cindy threw open the door. "What do you want?" she demanded as the baby cried harder.

"Let me in and then go quiet your baby," Jake said gently. "I'm here to tell you I'm sorry for this afternoon."

Cindy shrugged, but she let him in. Jake stepped into the cluttered living room and sat down on the inexpensive but fairly new sofa. Probably isn't paid for yet, he thought as the little boy from Carla's special peered around the door.

"Hi, I'm Donnie," the child said.

"Hi, I'm Jake," he said as Donnie came in, trailing a worn blanket behind him.

Donnie sat down in the middle of the floor and put his thumb in his mouth. Jake watched the child for a few minutes, then the crying at the other end of the house stopped and Cindy appeared in the door of the living room. She hesitated until Jake pointed at the chair across from the couch, then she sat down in it. Donnie clambered up into her lap. "I want Daddy," he said. "Where's Daddy?"

Jake watched Cindy take a deep breath and fight back her tears. "He's gone away," she said softly. "He'll be gone for a long time, but he loves you very much and he'll be back someday."

"I want my daddy!" Donnie protested, starting to pucker up and cry. Cindy rocked him back and forth as she looked bleakly across at Jake. "How do you explain prison to a two-year-old?"

Jake watched the miserable young woman cradling her sobbing child, and he hurt for her more than he wanted to. Finally Donnie's sobs quietened and Jake cleared his throat. "I'm very sorry for the remarks I made this afternoon about your husband. They were way out of line."

Cindy shrugged. "If the situation was reversed, I'd probably feel the same way." She thought a minute and she stuck out her chin. "But I wouldn't say it, though."

"No, I'm sure you wouldn't," Jake replied. "I understand that Don was the sole support of the family. Have you thought about getting a job?"

Cindy nodded her head. "I'll look, of course, but I'll probably have to go on welfare. I dropped out at the end of the tenth grade to marry Don. He wants me to sell the house and move in with my mother." The girl made a small shudder of distaste. "Three years of 'I told you so.' "

"Maybe that won't be necessary," Jake said. He got out one of his business cards and handed it to her. "If you can find someone to keep your children, I could use you at Darrow's Duds Tuesday through Saturday. Base pay is minimum, but I pay a commission to my salespeople too, and most of them take home a livable wage."

Cindy stared at the card as though it were a snake. "I —I couldn't," she said haltingly. "Mrs. Beadle works for you. I couldn't face her every day!"

"Lenore's at the other store," Jake said. "You wouldn't have to face her."

Cindy looked over at Jake with a bewildered expression on her face. "Why are you doing this? You hate our guts!"

Jake shook his head. "I hate what your husband did, but I don't hate your guts or those of your children. Come on to work, Mrs. Tyson. It will be a way to keep your home."

"All right," she replied. "But why are you going out of your way to try to help me of all people?"

"I'm proving something to myself and to someone else," Jake said candidly. "Someone who matters to me said that I was vengeful, and I want to prove to her, and to myself, that I'm not. Fair enough?"

"Fair enough," agreed Cindy.

Jake pulled his jacket together to ward off the chill November wind and unlocked the back door of Darrow's Duds. God, what a week! He had spent three days in San Antonio helping to set up a coalition there, and then he had spent an entire day at the downtown store trying to straighten out a botched-up suit order from New York. Honestly, he was going to have to cut back some on his CCC commitments and devote a little more time to his business and his children. There had been several foul-ups lately at the stores that would not have happened if he had been there, and his daughters were beginning to complain that they saw more of Carla than they did him.

Jake took off his jacket, then he sat down and started to tackle the pile of paperwork that sat in the middle of his desk, but his mind kept drifting. Thank goodness Carla had continued to see the girls after they had quarreled. They had soaked up her love and her caring like a couple of little sponges, in some ways substituting her affection for their mother's. Jake was grateful to her for caring for the girls, but in a way he was envious of his children. He had not seen Carla since that traumatic day in the courthouse six weeks earlier and he missed her. He missed the love and affection she had showered on him. It had been love she had given him, he finally realized. Now that she was angry with him and had ordered him out of her life, he could see that she had loved him. But how did she feel about him now? Had he completely destroyed everything she had felt for him?

And what about his feelings for her? Jake doodled a large *C* on an important invoice and drew a rose through the center. He loved her. Fool that he was, he had not realized it until she was no longer a part of his life. His feelings of love for her were different from the kind of love he had shared with Debbie. He had loved Debbie with the sparkling sunshine of spring, but with Carla it was more like the blaze of an autumn sunset— warm, caring, beautiful. She had come into his life for a while and brought her own special brand of joy. She had taken away the sting of grief and brought him happiness. And it had taken her absence for Jake to see that.

The shrill ringing of Jake's telephone interrupted his reverie. Jake was expecting a call from his buyer in New York, so he picked up the receiver and identified himself rather than waiting for Becky to answer. "May I speak to a Mrs. Cindy Tyson, please?" a nasal voice asked.

"Just a minute, I'll see if she's here," Jake said before putting the caller on hold. It was nearly opening time and Cindy was probably already at the store. She had learned the routine quickly and was now one of his better salespeople, carefully hiding her private woes behind a friendly smile for her customers. In fact, she hid her private troubles from everyone, including him, and only the increasing tiredness in her face and the deepening circles under her eyes revealed some of the strain she was under.

Jake stepped out onto the sales floor and spotted Cindy sorting a stack of shirts. "Cindy, telephone," he said. "You can take it in my office."

"Thank you," Cindy said as she hurried toward the office. Jake followed her back more slowly and sat down in Becky's chair to wait for Cindy to finish with her call. He wasn't really trying to eavesdrop, but since the door was open he couldn't help but overhear part of the conversation. Cindy was begging for a little more time until she could make payments again. Apparently she was unsuccessful, for she mumbled the last few sentences and hung up the telephone, then folded her arms across his desk and laid her head on them.

Jake poured two cups of coffee from the coffee maker and walked into his office. "Cindy, would you like to sit for five minutes and drink a cup of coffee with me?" he asked.

Cindy jerked her head up and nodded. She wasn't crying, but she looked hollow, defeated. "Thank you," she said as she took the steaming cup. She sipped the coffee, wincing when a little of it burned her tongue. "Mr. Darrow, may I have a few extra minutes today at lunch? I have to take my keys to my next-door neighbor."

"Certainly," Jake said. "Is one of the children ill?"

"Not this time," Cindy said. "Donnie's over his cold. No, the furniture company's repossessing the living-room furniture since I can't come up with the payments." She shrugged. "That's all right, I always did like the carpet anyway."

Jake winced at her pathetic attempt at humor. "What about making other arrangements? Reducing the payments?"

"You've got to be kidding!" Cindy said. "Remember, I'm not just any young woman struggling to make it on her own. I'm the wife of a convicted felon. We're considered very poor risks. Hell, I couldn't borrow the money for a gallon of milk."

Cindy started to get up, but Jake motioned her back down. "Give me the name of that furniture company. I'll talk to the loan manager and see if I can do anything." Cindy wrote down the name of the company and handed it to him. "Have you talked to Don about any of this?" he asked.

261

Cindy shook her head. "What can he do?" she asked bitterly, then her face crumbled. "Besides, he won't even see me."

"I noticed that you've never asked for the day off to go and see him," Jake said. "Why not?"

"He wants me to get a divorce and get out of Corpus and start over without him," Cindy said. "He wrote me a long letter the second week he was there and said that we deserved better than being saddled with a convicted felon for the rest of our lives. He says that his life is ruined, but that's no reason to drag me and the kids down with him."

"How do you feel about that?" Jake asked softly.

"I love him, but he may be right," Cindy said dully. She stood up and headed for the door. "Thanks for the coffee."

Well, there goes that marriage, Jake thought as he stared at Cindy's retreating back. Don would shut her out and she would eventually go ahead and get the divorce, and two more children would be without a father. Damn, when would it all end? Does it ever end? Jake picked up the telephone and spoke to the manager of the furniture company on Cindy's behalf, then he got the number of the state prison in Huntsville and put a call in to the chaplain.

Carla pulled up into the driveway of Jake's house and tooted her horn. Jake's car was not in the driveway, but she did not want to take a chance on him being there and answering the door. She had not seen him since she had told him off in front of the reporters at the courthouse, and she was not sure of what her reception would be. Two stations, her own and one more, had carried editorials that night that had said in essence much of what she had said to Jake, and had called for more public education as to the dangers of driving while intoxicated and less emphasis on name-calling and punitive action. Carla heartily agreed with the editorials, but they had probably infuriated Jake, and since she had been the one to voice the thoughts first, he probably blamed her. In the dark of the night, Carla admitted to herself that she loved Jake and probably always would, but she knew now more than ever that she couldn't take his continuing bitterness over his wife's death and his unreasoning hatred of the people he held responsible.

Patty and Sonia ran out of the house and hopped into her car. "Carla, thanks for coming," Patty said as Sonia scooted over and sat in the middle so Patty could ride in front too.

"Yeah, Dad left town again this morning," Sonia piped up.

"Oh? Is he helping another group organize a coalition somewhere?" Carla asked, hoping her voice sounded casual.

Patty frowned and shook her head. "No, he drove up to Huntsville this morning," she said. "Something to do with Don Tyson."

I would have thought he had done enough, Carla thought caustically.

"Yeah, Dad said Cindy talked to him yesterday about Don. I don't know any more than that."

"Why would Cindy have anything to say to your dad?" Carla asked, genuinely puzzled.

"Well, she works for him now," Patty said. "She went to work for him right after her husband was sent up."

"I didn't know that," Carla said slowly as she braked for a red light. So maybe Jake wasn't the monster she had accused him of being. Or maybe her little talk had shamed him into doing something for Cindy. Either way, she was glad that Cindy was working and not on

263

welfare. "So what do you girls want to do this afternoon?"

"It's too cold to go to the beach, so how about a movie?" Patty said.

"I already thought of that, but when I checked the listings there wasn't anything suitable for you girls. Come to think of it, there wasn't even anything suitable for me." Carla laughed.

"That's all right. Why don't we just wander around in the mall and pretend we're shopping?" Sonia asked.

Carla nodded, thinking sadly of the last time she had played that game, then she reached up and fingered the gold earrings. She had worn them every day since Jake had given them to her, even after they had quarreled and parted ways. Patty suggested the new mall on the outskirts of town, and before long they were wandering around in the spanking-new mall looking at the Christmas merchandise that was already out, even though the holiday was six weeks away.

The three of them had a wonderful time looking through the Christmas party dresses, and Carla made a mental note of one she wanted to come back to buy for Sonia's Christmas present. Patty tried on a blue jumper that was out of Carla's price range, but didn't like it anyway, although Carla thought it was darling. Carla had learned that Patty had very definite taste in clothes, and even Carla had trouble guessing what the girl would like. Patty would get books or a gift certificate for Christmas! They bought ice cream for an afternoon snack, then Carla asked the girls if she could go and look at the new hats in one of the department stores. The girls were more than happy to go try on hats, so they headed into the store.

Carla found the millinery section and she and the girls *ooh*ed and *aah*ed over the new winter hats. Carla tried on a pillbox and Patty tried on several western hats, giggling at the Annie Oakley look her long hair and the hats gave her. Carla turned her nose up at the pillbox, but fell in love with a gray fedora and promised herself she would come back and get it after her next paycheck. Sonia tried on several hats but always made a face at herself in the mirror. "I wish I could look like you in a hat," she complained. "This stupid old hair of mine is wrong."

"Do you really think so?" Carla asked. "I thought you liked it."

Sonia shrugged. "I've been trying to get her to cut it for months now," Patty said. "It doesn't suit her face." The thick golden curls tended to overpower Sonia's tiny features.

Carla nodded her head as she took the hat off Sonia's head and placed it back on the stand. "Yes, as pretty as the hair itself is, it isn't right for her face."

"Can I cut it?" Sonia asked. "Can we get it cut?"

Carla bit her lip and turned to Patty. "What do you think?" she asked. "What will your father think?"

"Oh, Dad couldn't care less," Patty said. "I've been pretty much in charge of Sonia's clothes and hair since Mother died."

"Oh, I want to cut it, Carla," Sonia begged. "I want to cut it short like yours! Then we would look alike."

Carla's heart melted inside. "Would you really like it to look like mine?" she asked. Sonia nodded. "All right, then, let's go find a salon that will take you without an appointment."

The hair emporium at the other end of the mall did not require an appointment, so in just a few minutes Sonia was perched up in the chair, enshrouded in a cape, as a young hairdresser cut and snipped away at her long curls. He had studied Carla's cut and had

265

agreed that with a few modifications that style would look darling on Sonia. Carla and Patty watched as Sonia's thick hair was cut and then blown dry in a bouncy wedge. The hairdresser showed Sonia how to blow her hair herself, and then the little girl held up a mirror to her face and turned her head this way and that. "I love it," she said simply.

"So do I," Patty agreed.

Carla insisted on paying for the cut, then, even though they had eaten ice cream just a couple of hours earlier, she took the girls to an inexpensive steak house, where they ordered thick steaks and munched away happily at the salad bar. It was nearly eight when Carla pulled up in front of Jake's house. Jake had just pulled up in the driveway, and as he stepped out of his car he rubbed his back as though he were in pain. Carla longed to get out of the car and rub his tired back herself, but she resisted the urge. Nevertheless, she walked the girls up to the front door.

"Daddy, we're home," they chorused as Jake got out the key and opened the door.

Jake turned around and smiled at his children in the darkness. He looks tired, Carla thought. Tired and older. He had no business making that drive to Huntsville.

"Hello, Carla," he said quietly. "How have you been?"

"Fine, just fine," she said.

"Would you like to come in for a cup of coffee?" Jake asked.

"Sure," she said.

Jake stepped into the darkened house, his girls after him and Carla following him more slowly. He flipped on the lights in the entry and then the ones in the family room. Sonia scampered in front of him and pointed to her new haircut. "We got my hair cut, Daddy," she said, turning her head this way and that. "Don't you think it's pretty?"

Jake froze in his tracks and stared down at his younger daughter. "What on earth have you done to yourself?" he demanded.

CHAPTER FIFTEEN

Sonia's happy smile faded. "I got a haircut, Daddy," she said. "Don't you think it's pretty?"

"No, I do not," Jake said coldly. "Sonia, how could you do such a thing? Your hair was beautiful! It was just like your mother's. She always wore hers long." His face tightened. "It makes you less like her."

Carla whitened as Sonia burst into tears. "I didn't like all that hair! I wanted it short!" she cried. "Daddy, I wanted to be like Carla!" Choking on sobs, Sonia ran from the room.

Jake turned around slowly. Carla had tears running down her face too. "I—I'm sorry, Jake," she said. "We should have asked you first but I thought—Patty said you wouldn't care." She reached up and brushed the tears off her cheeks, but they kept falling anyway. "She said she wanted to look like me, Jake. You have no idea how much that meant to me." She turned on her heel, her tears turning into choking sobs as she pulled the door shut behind her.

Jake stared at the closing front door, then turned around to face Patty. "Go ahead and yell at me too, Daddy. It was my fault as much as theirs," she said.

Jake rubbed his hand across his face. "I'm not going to yell at you, Patty. I've already done enough damage for one evening." He shucked off his jacket and headed up the stairs. "Now I've got to see if I can undo some of that damage."

Jake knocked on Sonia's door, and when she didn't answer he opened the door and stepped inside. Sonia was stretched across the bed, crying quietly. Jake sat down on the side of the bed and took the child into his arms. "Punkin, I'm sorry," he told the sobbing girl. "It's all right. I don't mind about your hair, honest."

Sonia's sobs stopped suddenly and she pulled away from him. "Daddy, do you really like it? I wanted it to be pretty like Carla's."

Jake reached over and picked up a brush that was sitting on the dresser. He flicked it through Sonia's hair a couple of times and looked at her thoughtfully. "Yes, I do like it. It does make you look like Carla." And it did. He had never noticed it before, but with her finely sculpted features and her blond hair, she could have been Carla's little girl. No wonder Carla had become so fond of her. He took Sonia's face between his palms and kissed her on the cheek. "Sonia, I'm sorry for what I said before. Your hair is lovely and you feel free to look and be as much like Carla as you want to." He got up off the bed. "Have you and Patty had supper?"

"Carla took us out for ice cream and then out for a steak," Sonia said.

Jake smiled to himself. Carla had certainly learned about the legendary teenage appetite! Ignoring the rumbling in his own stomach, he stripped off his business suit, showered, and dressed in a pair of jeans and a pullover sweater. He headed back down the stairs and found Patty and Sonia parked in front of a cable movie. "Girls, I'm going out for a while," he said. "Don't wait up."

"More business?" Sonia asked.

Jake shook his head. "I have to go tell Carla I'm

sorry," he said. "I hurt her pretty badly tonight. Will you girls be all right?"

They nodded and Jake left the house. As he drove toward Carla's apartment, a knot of apprehension formed in his stomach. He had hurt her so many times. In his struggle to get over his grief for Debbie, he had said so many things, done so many things that had hurt Carla. And now, now that he was ready to put the past behind him and go on, had he said and done one thing too many? Had he destroyed the love she had felt for him at one time?

Carla sat curled on the couch, tears still streaming down her face even though she had been gone from Jake's house almost an hour. It was hopeless. It was utterly hopeless. That scene at Jake's house had convinced her of that. He still loved Debbie, he would always love her. He would never have room in his heart for anyone else. In the weeks since the trial, Carla had harbored the faintest hope in the back of her heart that he would change, that he would be able to put the past behind him and go on, but now she knew that would never happen. If he worshipped Debbie to the point that he insisted on making his daughters living monuments to her, then she didn't have a chance.

She went into the kitchen for a tissue, then decided that maybe a hot cup of coffee would help. She was just plugging in the coffee maker when she heard a knock on the door. Figuring it was her next-door neighbor, she ignored the knock, but it sounded a second time, this time harder. "Carla, it's Jake. Please let me in!"

Jake! Carla looked out the window but could not see his expression on the dark porch. "What do you want, Jake?" she asked tiredly through the window.

"To beg your forgiveness," he said. "And if you don't

270

let me in, I'm going to do it right here on the front porch and embarrass you in front of all the neighbors."

May as well get it over with, Carla thought, unlocking and opening the door. Jake winced when he saw her tearstained face, which she made no effort to hide. He sat down on the couch. As Carla sat down on the chair and faced him, fresh tears welled up and spilled from her eyes. "Say what you have to say and go home," she said, trying to wipe her eyes with her fingers. "I've had just about as much of you as I think I can take."

Jake reached out and tried to take Carla's hand and winced when she pulled hers away. "I hope you don't mean that," he said in a strange voice. He got down on his knees in front of her chair. "Carla, please forgive me," he begged. "For tonight and for Austin and for all the other times I've hurt you."

"Why?" Carla sniffed angrily. "Why should I keep on ignoring the hurt and forgiving you?"

Jake swallowed back a lump in his throat. "Because I love you?" he asked. "I do, you know."

Carla shook her head. "That isn't possible," she said. She got up and brushed past Jake and headed into the kitchen for another tissue, then blew her nose and sat back down.

Jake was sitting on the edge of the couch when she returned. "Why isn't it possible?" he asked softly.

"Because you still love Debbie," Carla said bitingly. "You always have, and you always will. Tonight was proof enough of that."

Jake stood up and put his hands in his pockets. "I do love you, Carla," he said. "Tonight was just a knee-jerk response, a response left over from a time when I really would have been upset about the hair. I told Sonia that I was sorry, and I told her she could look and be just as much like you as she wanted to be."

271

"But you still love Debbie," Carla said flatly. "You haven't denied that. Yet you say that you love me. How can you love two women at once, Jake?"

Jake walked slowly across the room, deep in thought, then he came back and sat down on the edge of the couch. "I can't deny that I still love Debbie—or I guess I should say Debbie's memory. A part of me will always love that memory, Carla. She gave me almost twenty-five years of happiness and my two children. I'll always love her for that.

"But the pain of losing her is fading, Carla. I don't wake up in the night and reach for her anymore. I don't feel that frantic kind of panic when I realize she isn't coming back. I don't want to put my head down and cry at the supper table when I look over and she isn't there. I'm ready to put her in the past and go on—with you, Carla."

"You haven't acted like you felt that way," Carla pointed out. "You haven't acted much like you love me the way you loved her."

"I don't love you the way I loved her," Jake said. "No, I didn't mean it like that!" he protested when Carla flinched. "Let me try to explain. With her, it was like daisies in the spring. It was a youthful love, and while it did mature, we took it for granted. Nothing was ever going to happen to it. And then something did and it nearly killed me.

"With you, it's like the blaze of an autumn sunset. I *know* what I have. I can look at you and appreciate what love's all about. I know a little more about the cost, the sacrifice involved in loving me like you do. It's hard to compare the way I felt for her to the way I feel for you, but believe me, I know love when I feel it and I do feel it for you, Carla. I love you very much."

Angry confusion was written all over Carla's face.

"But if you love me the way you say you do, why do you continue to be so bitter over Debbie's death? That's what I can't take, Jake, all the bitterness. I worked so hard to get rid of all my bitterness after Mike left me, and I just can't take it in you. I didn't like what it was doing to me, and I can't stand what it's doing to you."

"I'm working on that," Jake said as he sat back against the cushions of the couch. "Carla, I'm not just bitter over Debbie's death. If she had died of pneumonia, of cancer, of a heart problem, I could have accepted that. It would have been like that was fate, or God's will, or something like that. It was the useless way she had to die, and the fact that the man who hit us had such a lenient sentence, that rankled me. It still does.

"But, Carla, a lot of the bitterness was because I saw that man, and a lot of other drunken drivers, get off scot-free, with maybe a short term or just a fine. Thanks to the CCC, a lot of that has stopped. They're being sentenced to prison, they're being punished now. Believe me, they're not getting off like they used to. They're paying for what they've done."

Carla looked over at Jake with surprise at the fervent tone of his voice. "What made you change your mind?" she asked. "Just a few weeks ago you would have put every one of them in cement shoes and thrown them into the bay."

"I still think they should be punished for what they've done," Jake said quickly. "They do have a price to pay, and as much as I hate the thought, for some people in this society the threat of punishment is going to be the only thing that stops them from drinking and driving. But I never realized, Carla, until I hired Cindy Tyson, just what kind of price they are paying."

"The girls told me she's working for you," Carla murmured.

273

"Yes, I hired her mostly to prove to you, and to myself, that I wasn't bitter or vengeful. That justice was my sole motive in fighting for stiffer punishment. Well, anyway, I just never thought of all that happens when a man's sent to prison. His kids lose a daddy, his family loses his support, he loses his self-respect. Hell, do you know what I was doing in Huntsville today? I was up there trying to convince Don to let his wife come visit him! He's got the notion that they would be better off without him and Cindy's about to decide he's right. I don't think I got anywhere with him, though. I'm afraid two more kids are about to lose a parent."

Carla swallowed and stared over at Jake. He must have come a long way in getting over his bitterness to do what he had done today. "So where do you and the CCC go from here?" she asked warily.

"I've talked to some of the other members of the CCC and we're going to start a counseling program for the families of the drunken drivers. And we'd like to expand into doing public education—you know, going into schools and businesses and teaching people to recognize when they've had enough to drink, and how to cope with stress without driving to a bar or reaching for the bottle. What do you think about that?"

"That's all well and good," Carla said neutrally. "I'm glad you're getting over your unreasoning hatred for drunken drivers."

"Is that all you have to say?" Jake asked.

"What am I supposed to say? I *am* glad you're getting over the way you feel about drunken drivers, and I'm glad your organization is broadening its scope. But that really doesn't have that much to do with you and me."

"I think it has everything to do with you and me," Jake argued. "That was most of the problem, wasn't it?

274

The bitterness I felt over Debbie's death and the bitterness I felt over the whole issue of drunken driving were tied together. I'm getting over both of those."

"But what about my feelings?" Carla cried as she stood up and paced the floor. "All I've heard for the last six months is what *you* were feeling, what *your* needs were! I was ready for a deeper relationship with you as long ago as June, but we had to wait until *you* were ready for a physical relationship with me. We had to wait until it was right for *you.* Then, after we had become lovers, you had the gall to tell me that you still loved Debbie and always would. That was after we had become *lovers,* Jake! After I had given myself to you completely! You never stopped to think how that might make me feel. You completely rejected my love and my caring that night. And I'm tired of that, Jake. I'll be damned if I'm spending the rest of my life trying to meet your needs, when you won't try to meet any of mine."

"It wasn't entirely my fault that I couldn't meet your needs, Carla," Jake said quietly as he got up and stood by the couch. "I know that my reluctance to have an affair with you hurt you last summer, but you were so secretive about yourself. And that secretiveness hurt me, Carla. It probably hurt me as much as my bitterness over Debbie hurt you. How do you think I felt when I found out from your friend that you'd been married for ten years? How do you think I felt when you had to force yourself to confide that you couldn't have children? You accuse me of not meeting your needs, but except for wanting to be my lover, you never trusted me enough to share yourself with me." He reached out and took Carla by the shoulders. "If I had known about Mike and the babies, I could at least have shared the hurt the way you did sometimes with my grief for Debbie. But I didn't know, Carla."

"You knew tonight," Carla accused him softly as she pulled away from him. "You knew tonight that I couldn't have kids, and how much little Sonia means to me, and you still didn't want her to cut her hair like mine." She stared at him stonily.

"I said I was sorry for that." Jake sighed as he looked at her implacable face. "But it isn't just tonight, is it? I've hurt you once too often. I've trampled on your love one too many times. Hell, I was afraid of that. I managed to kill everything you felt for me. I'm sorry, Carla." He walked to the door and opened it, then turned around, tears streaming down his face. "You know, I thought when Debbie died that I had felt the worst pain that a man could know, but I was wrong. There's nothing quite like losing the woman you love and knowing it was your own fault. Good-bye, Carla." Jake stepped through the door and shut it behind him.

Carla stared at the door as the thoughts raced through her head. In spite of the pain, in spite of the hurts he had inflicted on her, she still loved him. And he was walking out of her life because he was convinced that her love for him had died. She couldn't let him do that! Carla wrenched open the door and raced after him, catching up with him at the foot of the stairs. "Oh, Jake, don't go!" she cried, throwing herself into his arms. "It was my fault too, it was both our faults, but I don't want to lose you. I still love you, of course I do." Tears streamed down her face as she held Jake in her arms.

Jake's arms tightened around Carla and he clutched her to him, his arms trembling with emotion. "Carla, I'm sorry, I'm so sorry I've hurt you," he said over and over. "How could I keep on hurting you so much when I love you like I do?"

"I hurt you too, didn't I?" Carla said, burying her face in his shoulder.

Jake nodded. "But I think that's over now." He took her by the hand and led her back up the stairs, and the two of them curled up together on the couch. "I promise that from now on I will meet your needs, Carla, if you will promise never to hold back anything from me."

Carla nodded. "It's hard for me to communicate what I want to someone else," she admitted. "That's a lot of why I never wanted to talk to you about Mike or the children we lost."

"Then that's got to change," Jake said firmly. "I want you to tell me, right now, how you feel and what I could do for you right now."

"I—I'm all right," Carla said.

Jake shook his head back and forth. "Nope, you have to do better than that," he said. "Come on, Carla."

"I would like to be sure of your feelings for me," Carla said slowly. "I would like to share with you my love for you. I would like you to tell me you love me."

"I don't know how I can make you sure of my feelings for you, but I'll try to put it into words, and then I'll live it later. I love you, Carla. It would kill me if I lost you," Jake said solemnly. "Don't ever leave me, Carla. I don't think I could stand it."

Carla nodded and sniffed. "Just love me, Jake," she begged. "That's all I ask."

Jake nodded and kissed her once, long and lovingly. "I'll spend the rest of my life loving you like you need me to. How did it feel, telling me tonight what you needed?"

"Strange," Carla admitted. "But it was nice to have you tell me that you love me."

"We'll share that love in a few minutes," he promised. "But you need to go and do something about your swollen eyes, and I need to get a bite to eat. I never got any lunch today."

"Oh, I'm sorry!" Carla said, jumping up off the couch. "I'll get you something."

Jake stood up and blocked her way to the kitchen. "No, I'll feed myself." He reached out and kissed her swollen eyelids. "You go put a compress on those eyes." He turned her around and pointed toward the bathroom. "Remember the washcloth."

Carla shut the door of the bathroom and gasped at the sight of her tear-swollen eyes and her streaked mascara. He must really love me to declare his love when I look like this! she thought ruefully. Quickly she removed all her makeup, then held a wet washcloth over her eyes as she sat at her makeup table, water streaming down her face. She stayed at the vanity a long while, until Jake pushed open the bathroom door.

"All right, I think you can take off the compress now," he said.

Carla lowered the compress and stared at her image in the mirror. "Ugh, I look awful," she said, staring at her pale skin and her puffy eyes.

"A night of sleep will do wonders for those eyes, and I'll put some color in those cheeks in a few minutes," Jake promised as he kissed her lips gently, his sensual promise sending a tingle down Carla's spine. "You're a beautiful woman, Carla, and I love you very much."

"Oh, Jake, I love you too," Carla said, her eyes shining. She stretched her arms around his waist and hugged him tightly, then laughed when his stomach growled. "Come on. First things first. You better go eat before you collapse from starvation."

Jake took Carla by the hand and led her into the

living room, where he had put a plate of cheese sand-wiches on the coffee table. "Umm, this looks good," Carla said as she sat down on the carpet and reached for a sandwich, then drew her hand back.

"Go ahead," Jake urged. "I figured you'd be hungry again."

"Thanks," Carla said. "Crying's hard work. Burns a few calories."

Jake sat down beside her. "In that case, you're going to get very fat," he said as he held his sandwich up to her lips. "Because you're not going to be doing any more of that on my account."

Carla obediently took a bite of his sandwich. "Then what am I going to do about keeping my weight down?" she teased. "Don't want to get fat, you know." She held her sandwich up to Jake's lips.

Jake took a bite and swallowed it almost without chewing. "This," he said as he reached over and kissed her lips gently. "And this." He kissed her lips again. "And some of this." He kissed her a third time, grasp-ing her shoulders in his hands and caressing them gently.

"Here, eat," Carla ordered breathlessly. "I don't want you to give out halfway through."

"With you to keep me going?" Jake teased. Neverthe-less, he wolfed down three sandwiches and followed them with two cups of coffee. "At this rate I'll be awake all night," he said.

"If you are, it won't be from the coffee," Carla teased. "It's decaffeinated." She looped her arms around Jake and drew his head toward hers. "Make love to me, Jake. I've missed you so much these last six weeks."

"I've missed you too," he said as his lips met hers. He kissed her gently at first, then as the passion started to build between them, he pushed her down onto the soft

279

carpet and followed her there. "I've missed the way you smile at me when you think the girls aren't looking, the way your eyes light up when you look my way, the way your hands and your body feel on mine." He ran his tongue around the edge of her lips. "I've missed the way you sound on the phone when you call me just to say hello and the way you curl up against me after we've made love." He plundered her lips in a deep, sharing kiss that made Carla's head spin.

"I've missed you too," Carla said softly as her hands played in the hair at Jake's nape. "I've missed the way you scrub my back in the shower. I've missed the way you always touch my face after we've made love." She reached up and planted a tender kiss on his cheek. "I've missed the way you're always in such a hurry to get your clothes off." She giggled a little as she smiled up into his eyes.

"You're in just as big a hurry," Jake teased.

Carla nodded and blushed. "I've missed seeing you without your clothes on," she said. "And I've missed rushing to your house and fixing supper for you and the girls."

"You've missed that?" Jake asked. "Carla, you're such a wonderful woman. I hope someday you come to realize just how much I do love you."

"I think I do," Carla said softly as she looked up into Jake's eyes.

"No, you don't. But you will," he promised. He reached down and unbuttoned her blouse, pushing it down her shoulders, exposing her white breasts to his gaze. He kissed each one lovingly. "See there. I wasn't in all that big a hurry to get my clothes off. I got yours off first!"

"Fun-ny," Carla teased as she sat up and took off her

clothes, exposing her body to Jake's loving eyes. "So what are you waiting for?"

Jake reached out and touched one of her ribs. "You've lost weight," he said quietly.

Carla shrugged. "I wasn't all that hungry a lot of the time," she admitted. "When I'm not happy I don't want to eat."

Jake reached out and hugged her tightly to him. "Carla, you're going to be so happy from now on you're going to be eating a horse every night for supper," he promised her as he kissed her thoroughly. He quickly shed his own clothes, leaving them in a messy heap on the floor, then threw one of the sofa pillows on the floor. "I love you, Carla," he said as he pushed her head back on the pillows. "I want to make love to you."

"Here? On the floor? At our age?" Carla asked as Jake nibbled the side of her neck.

"You're as young as you feel," he said as he let his lips drift lower, finding and touching the hard nub of her nipple. "And, Carla, you make me feel like a kid again!"

"You make me feel that way too," Carla confessed. Maybe that's the secret of love, Carla thought as Jake tormented the softness of her breast. With each other, the years fell away and they felt young, unspoiled, innocent. With each other, they forgot about the past, about the pain and heartbreak they had each known. They could start fresh, new, with all the wonder of love pure for the two of them. Carla reached around and stroked the strong muscles in Jake's back, caressing and savoring the feel of his strength under her fingers. His lips caressed both breasts until they were hard and firm under his touch, then his wandering lips traveled lower.

"Oh, Jake, this is so beautiful," Carla whispered as he

caressed the tender skin of her waist with his lips. "Oh, I've missed you so much!"

"That's over, Carla," Jake assured her, raising up to capture her lips in a vow of love. "Never again will we be apart. Not even for one night. If you can't come with me, I'll wait until you can."

"I'll hold you to that, Jake." Carla laughed as she kissed and caressed his neck and shoulders. She turned on her side and pushed Jake down in the carpet, shoving the pillow under his head. "And if you should decide that you want to leave me, I'll do this to you." She reached down and kissed the tender skin of his chest, tangling her tongue in the soft dark hair there. "And this," she said as her lips found and tormented one of his flat male nipples. "And this." Her fingers caressed the tender skin of his waist.

"And what if I still think I want to go?" Jake teased, knowing what Carla would do next.

"Oh, I might try a little of this," she teased as her lips roamed the length of Jake's body, caressing the tender skin that sheltered the hard muscles of his stomach. "Or this," she said as her lips tormented the hollow of his navel. "Or I might really get wild and try something like this," she said as her lips drifted lower. Jake tensed, knowing that Carla would tease and torment him for a moment or two before she found the center of his desire. She had been a little shy of pleasuring him like that at first, but when he had told her of the joy it brought him, she had loved him shamelessly, drawing delight from the pleasure she knew she was bringing him. Jake moaned and arched when her lips touched him without inhibition or reserve. For long moments she held him in her spell, unselfishly giving pleasure and receiving it in return.

Jake let her love him until he thought he could stand

no more, then with tender strength he pulled her on top of him and guided them together. "I love you," he whispered as their bodies became one.

"I love you too, Jake," Carla said, easing herself down on him. At first she just waited, savoring the feel of being back together with him, of touching his strong body with her lips and her fingers, of seeing the strength of his arms and chest, and of smelling the musky fragrance of his body. Then, slowly at first, they moved together, with her taking the lead, as she set the rhythm of the pleasure they were sharing. He loves me, she thought as her lips grazed the side of his face. He loves *me*, Carla. Her hips thrusting, she moved faster and faster, slowly building the spires of passion as their bodies became more entwined. Jake reached out and grasped her hips, his hands quickening her motions as his fingers caressed the tender skin of her hips and her bottom. Carla could feel the passion rising in her, and she knew from the stiffening of his muscles that it was rising in him too, that sweet delicious tension that would torment them until it brought them the ultimate beauty. Faster and faster, higher and higher, they swirled together until Carla stiffened and cried out. Jake gasped and drew her hips down on his as he arched too, moaning a little as they shared their mutual delight.

Carla collapsed, spent, onto Jake's damp chest. "That was the most beautiful thing I've ever known," she said as she rested her head in the hollow of his shoulder.

Jake shuddered with the last of his release and cradled Carla's body next to his. "You're the most wonderful woman I've ever known," he said as he brushed a strand of her hair off her face and kissed her lips gently.

Carla and Jake sat curled up under a blanket on the couch, sipping the last of the coffee. She snuggled up to him and put her head on his shoulder. "I never thought I could be so happy," she said, rubbing her nose against his bare shoulder.

"I never thought I could be happy again," Jake confessed as he reached out and fingered a hammered gold earring. "Do you ever take these off?" he asked.

"Just to sleep," Carla confessed. "For a while they and the girls were all I had of you."

Jake set his coffee cup down and put his arm around Carla. "Did you mean what you said earlier about liking to fix supper for me and the girls?" he asked quietly.

"I love to," Carla corrected him. "Yes, I did mean it. As much as I love what you and I share, some of my happiest times are with your girls."

"Well, would you like to be part of our lives on a permanent basis, then?" Jake asked hestitantly. "I know that a widower with two half-grown kids isn't much of a bargain, but would you be willing to marry me? I wouldn't want you to quit your job, but I'd love to have you share my life and the girls', if you think you might like that."

"Oh, Jake, I think I'm going to cry again," Carla said as her eyes filled with tears of joy. "Of course I'll marry you." She stopped and sniffed back the tears. "I love you so much, and as far as a bargain—not only will I be getting the most wonderful man in the world, I'll be getting that family I gave up on so long ago. I love your girls, Jake, and I'll try to be a good mother to them."

"I have no doubt that you'll be wonderful," Jake said tenderly. "Now get up off this couch and get yourself to your bed! We have something to celebrate!"

"We're going to make love again?" Carla teased, her tears forgotten as she scrambled up off the couch and scurried to the bedroom.

Jake followed her, falling down beside her on the bed.

He threw his arms around her and captured her lips in a long, drugging kiss. "So how soon are you going to marry me?" he demanded, kissing her again as she tried to answer him.

"As soon as you can make a few arrangements and I get dresses for me and the girls," Carla said when he released her lips. Her fingers traveled down the length of Jake's chest.

"And how long will that take?" Jake demanded as his lips traveled down her chest and found one already-hardened nipple. He tormented it further, until Carla was writhing beneath him.

"Oh, not long at all!" she promised.

"And what about all those feminine fripperies you brides want?" Jake teased as his lips dipped further, caressing the soft skin of her waist and stomach.

"Who cares right now?" Carla asked as his tongue made a silken swirl around the edge of her stomach. "Damn it, I'll make plans tomorrow. Just make love to me, Jake!"

Jake's chest rumbled with laughter as his lips traveled farther down Carla's body. He stroked the tender skin of her inner thighs, his own passion rising at the sound of Carla's impassioned whimpers, then his lips found the center of her femininity and caressed it lovingly, until he could tell that Carla was almost over the edge. Swiftly he completed their union, claiming the woman who meant so much to him and who would soon become his wife.

Jake lay down beside Carla and cuddled her to him. "Is it always going to be like that?" she asked.

"Well, most of the time I hope it goes a little slower," he said dryly. "I got a little carried away."

"I'm not complaining," Carla said. "Hey, where are you going?" she asked as Jake rolled out of the bed.

285

In reply he reached over and slapped her bare bottom softly. "Come on, get some clothes on. I'm not going anywhere without you. We're going to my place to tell the girls."

Carla looked over at the alarm clock. "Jake, it's after midnight! They'll be asleep!"

"So? They're big girls. They can miss a little sleep. Come on, Carla, we can take them out to an all-night coffee shop and buy them a milkshake to celebrate. I want the girls to share our joy."

"Jake, you're impossible," Carla said as she got out of bed and reached in her drawer for some underwear. They dressed quickly and in just a few minutes they headed out the door together, their faces shining with joy. And an hour later, as four beaming faces shared a late-night feast of strawberry sundaes, Carla looked around at Jake and his girls and knew the joy of her autumn love would be with her forever.

CANDLELIGHT Ecstasy Supreme